INDEFINITE

THE INFINITE SERIES: BOOK 3

NICOLE
CORINE DYER

ISBN-10: 0-9970212-4-1
ISBN-13: 978-0-9970212-4-0

First Edition First Printing
Editing by Jennifer Tovar at Gypsy Heart Editing
Cover Design by Michelle Preast
Symbol Design by David Mendoza
Formatting by Stacey Blake at Champagne Book Design

DEDICATION

To myself.
Because why not?

Chapter I

Ryan

ARISTOTLE ONCE TOLD HIM, "We make war that we may live in peace." On many occasions Ryan had believed this to be true. No truer than now when the world was crumpling right under his very feet.

War was inevitable when human nature clashed among itself. This war truly was the first World War that would trump all wars. Every mortal was in danger of losing their life no matter their race or homeland. The Risen had no mercy for those who defied them.

Those who remained loyal to the gods were one step closer to stopping the Risen's forces. Two pieces of the Staff of Brahma had already been recovered and the third was within their grasp. Yet Ryan was forced into a detour to save Grace and Colette who were captured by the enemy. The burden of recovering the last piece of the staff now rested on his friend's shoulders.

Ryan had no idea how bad things had gotten in the mortal world while he was on the island until they were transported to Arlington Cemetery.

"Why are we here?" Ryan asked.

Julia looked around the area. "This is the closest we can get without being detected."

He felt the sadness of the surrounding area creep inside his very being. "Where exactly are we trying to go?"

"The Smithsonian."

"That's an odd place," Zee said.

"The Risen have transformed into a fortress of sorts. I'm not sure how they did it but they built a massive wall around the entire grounds of the museum." Julia had a look of loathing stuck on her face. It'd been plastered there since Zee showed up for the mission.

Julia started to walk down a stone pathway when Ryan caught sight of tanks and military jeeps patrolling the surrounding area. The three of them were too deep into the trees and surrounded by too many headstones for the patrols to see their trio clearly, but it made Ryan uneasy.

He could see spotlights on top of the jeeps loaded with heavily armed men ready to shoot. "What the hell?" he asked.

Julia rolled her eyes. "The world has gone to shit, Ryan. How did you not know this? The military has been taken over by the Risen and they've set up camps for non-converters."

"What do they do with the people who don't convert?" Zee asked.

"Pretty much what they did to Ryan and Damian when they caught them. If you don't convert you're tortured until you do. If you still don't convert then you die." Ryan felt a

2

stab in his heart from how indifferent Julia seemed about that information.

As they continued down the stone path he looked out at all the graves. "Why haven't they touched this place?"

"It's sacred ground, Ryan. Fallen soldiers will always get the respect they deserve." Her snappy attitude took him off guard. She was so unlike herself that he couldn't help but concentrate on her instead of the task at hand.

"You know an awful lot about this," Zee said raising an eyebrow.

"Is the entire world like this?" Ryan asked.

Julia nodded. "Pretty much. Most countries have converted. The Risen are brainwashing the leaders and the militaries have no control over their actions. They do as they are told without question or they are put to death."

"It's like Hitler's reign all over again." Zee squinted her eyes at Ryan. If she was trying to hint at something he wasn't picking it up. "Pure evil. Don't you think?" she asked Julia.

"Fear can cause people to do unspeakable things," Julia agreed. "Though their intentions aren't entirely unjust."

"What?" Ryan whipped his head to stare at her so fast he almost got whiplash.

"Nothing," she muttered and crouched down as they came closer to the patrol. "It's about a fifty-minute walk without incident, but I highly doubt we will get to the museum without running into trouble."

"At least its still dark," Ryan muttered. "We got this."

Ryan was having a hard time not dwelling on Julia's empathy towards the Risen's ideals, but now was not the time. If she were the enemy, would she be trying to break out Grace and Colette? The fact that even part of the Risen's ideals where acceptable to her were mind-boggling.

They shuffled along the inner edge of the cemetery, partially hidden by bushes when a large searchlight pointed in their direction from on top of a passing jeep. Ryan ducked behind the red brick wall separating the cemetery from the road. Sneaking a look over the wall and the hedge covering the other side, he took in the surroundings of the street. It was almost barren.

"We need to head down the highway towards Arlington Bridge," Julia whispered as she crouched beside him. He was fully aware of how close she was. Part of him desperately wanted to brush her loose blonde hair behind her ear.

Zee came up on the other side of him and he found himself being sandwiched between both women. There was plenty of wall to hide behind, but for some reason both Zee and Julia pressed their bodies against him. He closed his eyes and took deep breaths trying not to have a panic attack. The two women in his life were either trying to mark some sort of territory or cause him internal torment... maybe it was a bit of both.

He opened his eyes and saw a two-lane road. "Which way?"

"Go right." Julia touched his thigh. The heat of her hand radiated through his skin.

"There's a patrol." His voice almost broke.

"Be thankful there aren't any dogs." Zee gripped his arm.

Have mercy on me.

Ryan looked over the wall again after the patrol whisked by. He took advantage of their absence and jumped the wall.

Soft thuds in the grass let him know Julia and Zee had made it over as well before they took off in a sprint alongside the road. Headlights warned him another patrol was closing in. Ryan quickly looked around for cover.

There was a bypass up ahead with a large group of trees and bushes along the side of the road. He jumped the road barricades and ran towards the bushes. The three of them dropped into the cover of the shrubs just before a searchlight swung in their direction. Three jeeps approached with men dressed not in military camouflage, but in black gear like his own. The only difference being they wore armbands with the Risen's symbol in white.

"What the hell?" Ryan said mainly to himself.

"There are Immortals down here too," Julia answered. "They are the commanding officers of the mortals to ensure their loyalty doesn't waiver."

The familiar feeling of anger built up inside at how treacherous his own people were. It wasn't until Zee put her hand on his back that he begun to calm. He closed his eyes and took a deep breath.

When he opened them he saw Julia glaring into his eyes with more hatred in those beautiful blues than he thought possible. He opened his mouth to say something, but nothing came out. Julia had made her choice and moved on. End of story. He'd never had to explain himself to anyone before and he didn't need to now.

Once the jeeps rolled by, Ryan managed to escape further glares from the angry woman and press forward. They departed from the cover of the bushes and started to make their way under the overpass when Julia grabbed him by the vest.

"We have to go down that road." She pointed to the road passing above.

They climbed the steep grassy hill to the top of the overpass and headed down the long road. There was nowhere to hide on the overpass just a short, column-wall lined the edges. Luckily they managed to reach the end without a problem.

A mile long list of profanity came to mind when Ryan saw their next obstacle up ahead. It was a roundabout circular intersection with grass in the middle and no cover in sight.

He scanned the site, relived that they were alone in this hellish circle. They were halfway across the field of grass when he saw another jeep convoy coming their way across Arlington Bridge. "How many damn people are there?" he grumbled.

"A lot," Julia answered. "There really aren't any civilians anymore except young children and their mothers. Everyone that has converted are used as foot soldiers."

"Balls," said Zee.

"Shit, what do we do?" Julia looked around as the jeeps got closer.

"Run," Ryan grunted. He sprinted across the field towards the trees that lined the entrance to the bridge, which crossed the Potomac River. The jeeps and searchlights were closing in. Sweat rolled down his face as he kicked himself into gear and ran as fast as his legs could take him.

"Ryan!" Julia's voice rose. He looked behind him and saw Zee had fallen down, grasping her ankle. "Pick the damn girl up or we are screwed."

Ryan ran back to Zee, tossed her over his shoulder and made a run for it again. Thankfully she was light because the jeeps were closing in on them. He was growing tired but his pace didn't diminish. They were nearly to the trees and the jeeps hadn't made it completely over the bridge yet.

"Hurry," he half-yelled half-whispered. Julia glanced over her shoulder shooting him a dirty look.

Making it to the trees Ryan dove with Zee still propped on his shoulder. He tried to be careful not to hit her head on anything as they hid behind one of the large square columns that marked the entrance of the bridge.

It was not a good hiding spot but there were no other options. He set Zee down and the three pressed against the columns. The trees offered some protection but he prepared himself for a fight just in case they were caught.

Zee bit her lip as Ryan asked, "Are you alright?"

Her eyes watered as she nodded. "Good. Just rolled it." The stubborn woman was in pain and he knew it, but like most Warriors they brushed off their pain as nothing.

"Idiot," Julia muttered to herself but Ryan heard it.

The patrol drove by without incident. Ryan thought they just might get through this mission undetected.

He turned his attention back to Zee to see she was gritting her teeth. Julia was automatically on lookout as Ryan grabbed her ankle to examine it. She winced but said nothing.

"Yeah, just rolled it," he agreed. "I think we should take a break and let it rest."

"We just got here like fifteen minutes ago." Julia shot both of them daggers. "Suck it up and let's get moving."

"It won't do any good to cross that big ass bridge while her ankle is messed up. There is no place to hide on it and we will have to run across before anyone sees us," Ryan hissed. "It will be hard enough as it is with six good ankles, let alone five."

Julia looked on the verge of slapping him. "This is ridiculous. You should have brought Cato or Damian."

"It's getting light out anyways." Ryan felt his blood boiling. It was becoming common when Julia was around. "Let's just hideout here and get some rest. We will head out when it gets dark again."

"Fine," Julia snapped. "If we get caught I'm blaming you."

Ryan was relieved. His body felt heavy from lack of rest and now was his chance to recharge. First, he had to tend to Zee. He rolled up her pant leg and slipped her boot off as gently as he could. She tried to hide a sharp intake of breath as he did so. She must really be hurting.

"What did you do buttercup?" He smirked, trying to lighten the mood.

Zee winced. "Oh you know, just felt like busting my ankle. It isn't a good time till someone breaks a bone."

Julia scoffed, drifted down to the edge of the water, and stared out at the bridge. Everything in his body told him to go to comfort her but he stopped himself. He tried to ignore his feelings for her with Zee around but it was difficult. On some level he would always be in love with Julia.

Resigned, he looked back down at Zee's ankle. It wasn't swollen or red so that was a good sign. "I think you will be able to keep it. Although, I order you not to walk on it until tonight or you will suffer my consequences."

She gave him a salute. "Yes, sir."

He couldn't help but give her a small grin, which faded when he looked back towards Julia. She was now sitting down on the edge of the water with her helmet off. He missed her terribly. Well, he missed the person she used to be.

"Go talk to her." Zee interrupted his train of thought.

"Why?"

"Because you look like someone shot your dog when you look at her and I can tell you still have feelings for her." Her expression was unreadable. This could be some sort of female trap.

"I'm pretty sure she hates me." He did his best to act indifferent as he wrapped her ankle up with a bandage from his pack. "I'm good. Really."

Zee leaned back on her elbows as he worked. "You are a terrible liar, but I get it. Believe me, I get it. Just sucks on my end I suppose. I don't know if I should even consider trying anything with you because you're stuck on her."

"Zee, I love that woman down there but nothing will ever change between us. She had a choice and she didn't choose me. I won't be second to anyone, not even for her. All I know is that I care about you a lot and I would really like to see where things go." He finished wrapping her ankle. "If you're willing?"

This woman was much more different than any others; calm, collected and very strong. Her humor was almost like a man's yet she still maintained her womanly aura. Zee was a hard woman to figure out.

To his surprise she smiled. "Eh, I guess since you're begging."

Ryan couldn't help the smile that crept on his face. He tilted her chin up and kissed her gently on the lips. "Good," he breathed out. His mouth hovered over hers, trying to decide if he should dive in once again.

She knocked him on the helmet. "Go talk to her. She needs a friend."

"'Friend' being the key word?" He grinned against her lips.

Zee pushed him away from her, causing him to land on his ass in the grass. He laughed then said, "You are a complicated creature. Do you know that?"

"It is what it is."

Chapter II

Anna

ANNA WOKE UP NEXT to Damian and a sleepy grin crept on her lips. He was awfully cute when he slept. His hair was disheveled in his face and his mouth hung slightly open. The only thing she didn't care for were the snores coming from him.

Not just baby snores either. Huge, manly snores that woke her up. She was surprised he didn't wake himself up. It was like a snorting pig with a microphone lived in his mouth.

They were in his room. Hers still didn't feel like home and they decided to get a good amount of sleep before they left to Shambhala. She looked out the window and it looked like they slept the entire day and then some. It was worth it though. She'd felt permanently exhausted from their adventure to the island full of monsters and now she felt refreshed.

Sitting up on the edge of the bed she stretched her arms into the air, a small groan escaping her lips from how great it felt. Getting up she made her way to Damian's mirror and gasped in horror.

She looked terrible. Her hair was a rat's nest and her clothes were beyond winkled. She wasn't much of a makeup person so thankfully smudged eyeliner wasn't included in her morning-after ensemble.

She hurriedly brushed her hair with her fingers then slapped her cheeks to bring some color to her face. Her work-out clothes doubled as pajamas and she tried to smooth her tank top down. Damian never cared what she looked like, but she was too self-conscious to look like a homeless person in Under Armor clothing.

"Good morning beautiful." She heard behind her.

Damian was propped up on his elbow looking at her with such an amused gaze she felt her cheeks blush. "Morning."

"How did you sleep?" he asked.

She shrugged, falling onto the bed with him. "Not as well as you Sir Snores-a Lot."

Not easily affected, he ran his hand through his hair and yawned. It wasn't fair how his hair went from messy to in-stantly perfect with just one swipe of his hand. Being a guy was so much easier.

"Would you like to wander around Urbs today?" he asked. "We can leave tomorrow for Shambhala."

"Do you think we should wait another day?" It was getting closer to the New Year and she didn't like his procrastination.

"It'll be fine." Damian was not convincing, but she took his word for it. "I just want to see what's going on with Urbs before we leave. Make sure the people are doing fine and not suffering."

She doubted things were okay. She'd gotten used to the sounds of a bustling city below at this time of day. Right now there was silence. No sounds of children playing or of deals being made in the market drifted on the air.

The scents of freshly cooked food were not coming through her window making her hungry and it broke her heart. She could only imagine how Damian must feel since this had been his home for quite a bit longer than hers.

"I'll go get dressed and meet you out front." She kissed his cheek and ran off to her room.

She changed quickly into jeans and a fresh tank top. After feeding Calypso she pulled her dark hair up in to a ponytail and made her way to the entrance of the Domus.

Damian was leaning against one of the large columns at the top of the steps with his back to her. She paused and watched him stare out at Urbs for a minute. Just by his body language she could tell he was upset and for good reason. There was no movement down below and no one in the streets from what she could see.

"Ready?" she asked interrupting his thoughts.

Damian turned around with a forced smile. She could see through it though. "Come." He held out his hand to her. She took it and felt his warmth radiate through her body. With just a simple touch this man made her feel safe.

They made their way down the steps and into the streets. Windows were closed and businesses were empty. Not even pets seemed to be out and about in the world. Urbs had turned into a ghost town.

"Are you okay?" he asked as he put his arm around her waist and pressed her against his body.

Truthfully, it made her nervous to be here. "Yeah."

They turned a corner into what she called 'China Town' and saw movement down the street near multiple closed vendors. They both stopped in their tracks. Damian pushed her behind him like the gentleman he was, which made her both thankful and annoyed at his constant protective nature.

"This is bad isn't it?" she asked. They didn't have weapons. At least she didn't.

He nodded. "The city is a no man's land. I think we should go back. Anyone out here is probably trouble."

Anna realized she was holding her breath when they turned to leave. No one was around and she released a sigh of relief until she noticed a small red dot on Damian's back. Breathlessly she said, "Stop."

Damian did as she said, turning around to face her. He looked down at the dot on his chest. "Shit."

They both scanned the rooftops of the buildings. Anna caught sight of the man pointing a gun at them. Damian held up his hands in surrender. "What is this about?"

The man said nothing as he continued to point the gun at Damian's chest. A raspy voice from below called, "What are you doing out here?"

Anna watched as three men came into view from an alley with various weapons gripped in their hands. The one that spoke was in the middle carrying a hammer. She would have thought it was funny to use a hammer as a weapon until she saw the makeshift knife tied to the end.

He had long blond hair pulled back in a ponytail and a circular burn mark on his face. Despite everything she'd been through this past week, her nerves got the best of her and she was thankful when Damian pushed her back behind him once again.

These weren't some mythological creatures or zombies to kill; these were people, Damian's people. Her people. She didn't want to fight them.

"We just came from the Domus and were checking the city out. That's it." He took a step towards them and the men held up their weapons ready for a fight. Damian paused in his attempt to go any further. "We got back from the mortal world and noticed things have obviously changed."

"No. You think?" The man laughed but there was nothing friendly about it. "The city is now run by anarchy. Anyone on the streets is far game."

"What does that mean?" Damian asked.

"It means I can kill you if I please and take whatever you have." The man grinned wickedly. "The rules are gone. We have to fend for ourselves and our own families now."

Damian's shoulders tensed. "You're kidding right? Why would you do that?"

"The Risen gave us permission to do as we please with those who don't convert. Seeing as you're from the Domus, I bet you two aren't part of the club yet." He held up his hammer and laughed. "This is where you run."

"You can't treat Warriors like this." Damian's voice grew hard, filled with aggravation.

"On the contrary, Warriors have a lovely bounty on their heads." All three men grinned like crazy clowns. They were crazy. This was crazy. From the little time she'd spent here, Warriors were the utmost respected and looked up to. Now their own people were hunting them.

"This is not right." Damian backed away pushing Anna with him. "Surely you realize this is wrong?"

The three men took steps towards them. "Actually, it feels pretty damn right. We've always lived in your shadow. Some of us were born into this world only to realize we are not worthy enough to become Warriors. Who are you to decide who's worthy?"

"The council decides," Damian interjected. "They are the only ones capable of deciding besides the Gods. The Warriors have no say in the matter."

The blond man laughed menacingly. "The council decides nothing anymore. They were the first to meet their demise when we were given our freedom."

"Anna get out of here," Damian whispered over his shoulder.

"Not without you."

"I am not going to argue with you about this. Go. Now."

"Oh don't worry, we like to make a sport of it. Besides, you are worth more alive." Blondie grinned. "The General likes to get information out of your kind."

Damian took off running, yanking her hand to follow him. She was glad she decided to wear sneakers instead of sandals. As soon as Damian let go of her hand Anna tripped and fell to the ground. Her knee shouted out in pain, and her jeans now sported a hole in the knee. Anna looked behind her and saw a thin cable stretched from one side of the street to the other.

"Dammit," Damian scrambled to pull her up to standing. "Bastards set traps."

They started running again and turned a corner. More

men were running down the street towards them. "What the hell?" Her heart raced with adrenaline and the pain in her knee throbbed.

"This is insane," Damian huffed. "Come on."

They ran down a nearby alley in the German district of town and as they turned a corner they collided into another group of three men. Anna bumped into the brick wall of a man so hard she fell to the ground. She landed on her back and one of the men jumped on top of her.

She twisted her body around and locked their arm in an arm bar like Damian had taught her. The man screamed and smacked the ground with his free hand trying to escape. Normally she would have been amused at the pain she was causing a man much larger than her, but this was definitely not the time.

She glanced up to see Damian elbow one of the guys in the nose and kick the other man in the chest hard enough that the man fell back against the wall. Damian produced a knife from who knows where and threw it at the man, hitting him right in the heart.

The guy with the bloody nose swung a knife at him. Damian dodged the swing, grabbed the man by the wrist, and twisted it around until the guy stabbed himself in the chest.

He then brought his foot down extremely hard on Anna's captor's face that she heard a sickening crunch come from under his foot. She looked away before she saw anything but the man's body went limp instantly.

"Are you alright?" he asked.

Anna was no longer looking into the loving, soft gaze of Damian's brown eyes. Instead, they were filled with an angry, deadly tension. It was so intense it made her want to hide from him.

"Yeah, are you?" She knew he was deadly, but holy hell the man was a beast.

Damian ignored the question, pulling her up and into a sprint once more. She had no idea where they were but Damian seemed fully aware of their location. All she could do was be dragged around like a dog on a leash.

He stopped when they heard men up ahead. "Shit." He methodically looked around for an escape.

"You two!" a woman's voice came from behind them. "Get in here."

A petite woman with long brown hair waved them inside her home. Damian looked wary but they didn't seem to have another option. Anna could hear men shouting in the distance, Damian really needed to make a decision and fast or she was going to make one for him.

Damian pulled Anna through the doorway and the woman quickly closed it. She immediately locked the door with a multitude of locks and turned to face them.

Without meaning to, Anna stared at the scars that decorated the other woman's body. Even though she was youthful in looks, Anna could tell she was from an older generation.

"Enemy or friend?" Damian asked. The woman playfully smacked him in the shoulder and was rewarded with a big hug from Damian. "Sorry, can't tell these days it seems."

"Are you dense?" the woman asked Damian as he set her back down. "What are you two doing out there?"

Damian smirked and gave her a pat on the back. Anna would have been jealous if the two people in front of her didn't radiate pure friendship. "I had no idea we were being hunted by our own people, Brianna. Excuse me for walking around my home city."

"Well, you are, so how about you do yourself a favor and get your ass back to the Domus?" Her arms crossed over her body. Anna had a hard time finding such a petite short woman intimidating; even with the scars, but this lady was a little ball of fire.

"Bri? Who's here?"

A man poked his head down from the top of the stairway on the second floor. He had brown hair with dodgy eyes. Once he made his way down the stairs, he grabbed Brianna's elbow and yanked her into the kitchen. His tall, portly frame didn't seem to bother the woman one bit as they discussed an obviously heated subject.

The house was small and empty. There was only a sofa and a few pictures on the wall. The stairs leading to the second level harbored god knew what, but she had a feeling it was just as bare. Were they squatters or something?

Brianna and the man came back into the living room with him looking defeated. She was small but feisty and apparently intimidating to those who knew her. Anna liked her.

"Damian, your remember my brother Drake?" She rolled her eyes.

Damian grudgingly held out his hand to Drake, who refused to take it. The two men glared at one another. Damian dropped his hand with a small laugh escaping. "Still mad?"

"I passed it and you know it," Drake growled.

"Get over it Drake. It was fifty years ago." Brianna wondered over to Anna.

"Forty-seven actually," Drake scoffed.

"Again, get over it." Brianna shoved him in the chest. "Anyways, you two really need to get back to the Domus. They will be searching for you everywhere. There's a big bounty on Warrior's heads."

"I don't understand how Immortals are doing this." Damian looked worn out. "This is beyond betrayal. How could things have gotten so bad in such a little time?"

"They moved quickly in a matter of days," Brianna answered. "Were you not here when they raided the city and strung up the council on the Great Temple? It was horrible. They were all murdered."

Damian looked as if someone had punched him in the face. Anna couldn't blame him. The men and women that'd created their laws were brutally murdered and put on display for the amusement of the Risen. The leaders of their own world were dead.

"Where are their bodies?" he asked in a low tone.

Brianna and Drake exchanged looks. "They're still there."

Damian leaned against the wall and hung his head low. It was terrible to see him this sad. She didn't know any of the council but Damian must have been close to them. He'd worked right along side them. Hell he was probably older than all of them.

"When did this happen?" he asked.

"Two days ago," Drake answered. "It seems you all were too busy in your enormous castle to pay attention to any of us down here."

"Shut up, Drake," Brianna said.

"No," he snapped. "They are there for a reason and they

abandoned their reason to lounge about in comfort while the rest of us suffer. You all are a disgrace. No wonder the Risen is trying to rid the world of you all."

Damian kept his mouth shut, as did Anna. In a way Drake was right. They weren't here when Urbs went to hell, but they were away on the island of hell trying to complete their mission. What were the rest of the Warriors doing? Could they not see the raids? Or did they just choose not to help?

"Are you alright?" Brianna asked her. "You look a little pale."

"I don't even know what to say right now," Anna answered. She felt sick to her stomach.

"I'm surprised they haven't come for you, Bri." Damian finally managed to form some words.

"Oh, they have. That's why we found an empty apartment. We're hiding out in here until they track me down again. Then it's off to the next house."

"Why would they come for you?" Anna asked.

Drake huffed and trudged back upstairs. Whatever Anna said, it seemed to piss him off or perhaps he was just a cranky guy.

"I was a Warrior once upon a time and used to be a member of the Council of Command. I retired some time ago," Brianna answered. "Got sick of being surrounded by death I suppose."

Anna was shocked and she was sure she looked the part. This tiny little woman with big, brown, doe eyes was a Warrior? *No freaking way.*

"Not to be all nosey, but why haven't you all helped the city?" Brianna asked. "It seems very out of character for you and Ryan."

"We've actually been on a mission in order to save the city. Go figure, right?" Damian laughed halfheartedly. "There is just one more piece to the puzzle in order to do that but those jackasses pose a problem. We need to leave Urbs as soon as possible."

Brianna sighed. "Sit down and wait for them to give up. They are bound to at some point. If you're going to save Urbs it won't do any of us any good if you're dead."

Defeated, Damian sat down on the floral couch that looked like it was from the seventies. Despite his unhappy face he looked cute in his jeans, black T-shirt and his prohibition era haircut. His face was getting scruffy with a beard and she sort of liked it. He looked pretty damn manly, especially with blood on him from those jerks in the alley.

God save me I think a man in blood is sexy. Ryan would be proud.

She sat next to him and was immediately wrapped up in his arms like he was her own personal blanket. Damian kissed her forehead and regardless of the circumstances she couldn't help but smile. He was by far, the sweetest guy alive and he was all hers.

"So how long have you two been together?" Brianna asked as she poured tea into chipped teacups.

Damian gladly took the drink and sighed with relief after the first sip. "Awhile now. Took me a bit to convince her though." He winked.

Anna hated talking about relationships. Why couldn't people just be satisfied knowing they were together instead of prying for private information? Did they even really care how they met? *Probably not.* Maybe she was just cynical.

"Brianna come here, I need to talk to you," Drake called down from upstairs.

Brianna rolled her eyes once again. It was her habit when dealing with her brother Anna noticed. "I'll be right back. I swear, if he wasn't my brother I'd have throat punched him by now."

"You should hit him anyways." Damian smirked. Brianna gave him a wink before she ran up the stairs, her long brown hair flowing behind her.

Drake was a weird one for sure but Brianna seemed very sweet. After what Anna just experienced she didn't feel safe anywhere though. Not even the one place Immortals were supposed to feel safe. Being in a home with a guy that hated Warrior's guts didn't seem like a very smart place to be.

They sat in silence for not even a minute when they heard rustling upstairs. Damian got up from the couch and made his way over to the banister. "Everything okay?" he called up. A large thud hit the floor above them and Damian started up the stairs.

Brianna stopped him on her way down. "Get out of here. Now!"

"What's going on?" Damian reached out to her.

Brianna smacked his hand away from her bleeding forehead. "Go. They are coming. You have to leave now, Damian."

Drake came running down the stairs and pointed a gun at Damian. "You aren't going anywhere. Brianna is the only one that is leaving."

"I am not, you damn idiot!" her petite voice roared. "I cannot believe you called the Risen."

"The bounty on their heads could make us rich. Get out

of here so they don't catch you!" Drake yelled at her. His hand holding the gun shook and his cheeks were flushed. Whatever pity Anna had felt for the guy, no matter how small it was, turned into pure hatred for him.

"Just let us go, Drake." Damian stayed calm, holding his hands out in surrender but as soon as Drake pointed his gun at Anna, Damian went into offensive mode.

In a flash, Damien ran up to Drake and twisted the gun out of his grasp before the other man could even realize what happened. Damian tossed the weapon to the side and grabbed each side of Drake's shocked face. "This is a prime example as to why you could never be someone like me, you traitorous bastard."

With one swift motion Damian twisted Drake's head and a loud snap filled the room. Brianna and Anna both covered their mouths in horror.

"Damian!" Brianna yelled at him. "What in the ever living fuck?"

Drake's lifeless body fell down to the floor, his eyes still wide in shock. Brianna ran to him but he was without a doubt dead. Anna knew this side of Damian existed, but today she was beyond shocked at what her boyfriend was capable of.

"He is a traitor," Damian said simply. "You know the law."

Tears filled Brianna's eyes but to Anna's surprise she didn't seem angry with Damian. Her brother was a traitor and Brianna was fully aware of the consequences. All Anna saw in the woman's eyes were sadness and disappointment.

"Go," she croaked.

"Come with us," Damian urged. "You will be safe in the Domus."

They heard glass shatter upstairs and Brianna picked up the gun Damian had tossed to the side. "No, you need to leave. I will hold them back. Complete your mission, save us and don't make me regret it."

"I can't leave you here to die."

"We are all going to die if you guys don't complete your mission."

"Bri-"

"Get the fuck out you stubborn bastard!" Bri kissed him on the cheek and shoved him away from her.

Anna watched the scene unfold as if it were slow motion. Bullets whizzed by their heads and pieces of the wall seemed to explode around them. Brianna ducked behind a wall and shot at men that were trying to come down the stairs. It was chaos.

Damian grabbed her hand, pulling her out of her frozen shock before they ran out of the front door. Instantly they encountered men outside the door holding knives and make-shift weapons.

Anna instinctively punched one in the groin and took his knife when he bent over in pain, making it easy enough to slit his throat. She stood there watching the blood drain from his neck and onto her shoes when Damian grabbed the knife from her hand and stabbed the other man in the heart.

They ran down dozens of streets before the Domus was finally in their view.

"Come on!" Damian yelled and she picked up the pace. They managed to make their way up the steps and closed the large doors behind them without further conflict. "Dammit Bri," Damian's mumbled to himself.

He leaned his head against the large white doors and Anna had no idea what to do. He was losing everyone he held dear. What could you say to someone after that?

"Get your stuff together we're leaving," Damian told Anna a little more forcefully than he intended. "No more putting it off."

Anna gave him an apprehensive look then ran off to get ready. He pushed off the large doors and made his way to Cato's room. His fist pounded on the wood until Cato finally opened it.

"What's up crazy?" Cato wiped away sleep from his eyes.

"We're leaving," Damian answered.

"Now?" Cato groaned.

"Now."

Damian made his way to his room and started to put his gear on. He had no idea what to pack for the trip, but he figured food would be scarce on top of a mountain and water even more so. As he finished getting ready, he saw Anna and Cato waiting for him in the doorway. Anna wouldn't look at him.

Cato yawned and lazily stuck his helmet on his head. "Why the rush?"

"Urbs is in turmoil. We need to get this done now. The sooner we get back the sooner we can help the city." Damian sauntered past them and made his way to the parlor.

Cato and Anna jogged to catch up. "What? Why?"

"Urbs has gone to shit. Let's go," Damian answered. He didn't want to talk about it. Brianna was more than likely dead and he'd just killed some of his fellow Immortals. It was not a good day.

"Where is it at?" Anna asked.

They reached the parlor and Damian tossed a crystal in front of him. "Himalayas," he said.

As they stepped through the portal they were greeted with a snowstorm on the top of a mountain. He put his arm around Anna. Her teeth were already chattering. All he could see was white all around him. Snow swirled like an angry tornado before it hit his face.

"I d-d-didn't know it was g-g-going to be freaking f-f-freezing!" she chattered.

"It's just the mortal world," Damian explained. "Once we reach between the mortal and the spiritual realm, crazy things are going to happen. Be prepared."

"How do you know?" Cato asked.

"No one really knows. It's more of a theory I've read up on." Damian shrugged.

"Great, so how do we get to La La Land?" Cato groaned.

"Meditation," Damian sighed. "Just concentrate on it and we will find the land before Shambhala. Only those with the appropriate karma are allowed there. I am pretty sure ours is good to go."

"What the fuck does that even mean?" Cato asked.

"Just concentrate on going to Shambhala and then after we reach the other realm there will be many plights we must survive," Damian said. "We are going to go through hell before we actually get to Shambhala."

"It's not just a straight shot?" Cato sighed. "Mother cracker."

Damian put his arms around Anna and Cato's shoulders and they formed a circle with their bodies facing each other. They stood on top of the snowy mountain, the raging storm filling their ears.

Damian did all he could to concentrate on a place he had never seen. From what he read in the library it would be easier to enter the realm given they were Immortals but nothing had happened yet.

The cold wind whipped around his body painfully making it almost impossible to concentrate. He forced his mind to stay on the task at hand. They needed to find the spiritual realm and reach Shambhala regardless of the horrors that lay before them.

His strength was weakening from the cold. He could feel Anna and Cato shivering beside him and his own body gave into the harsh temperature.

Concentrate.

His mind felt freed as he concentrated on the realm. The pain in his body ceased to be a concern. The altered state of being consumed him down to his very soul, to the point where his surroundings and senses were absent. His mind was consumed with only the thought of Shambhala.

It was profoundly peaceful here lost in his mind. It was all uprooted by a smack to the head that sucked him back to reality. Damian looked around to find Anna and Cato fixated on him.

"Dude, you were so out of it." Cato laughed when he backed away from Damian. "You were in some weird trance for like ten minutes."

"What?" His body felt warmer now. It was a wonderful

feeling given he'd been certain he was about to freeze to death on the snowy mountaintop. "What happened?"

"All I know is that I couldn't concentrate on a damn thing with it being cold and I was pretty sure neither could Anna." Anna nodded in agreement. "I think we were only transported here because you were clinging on to us for dear life."

The heat increased further until he felt his brow begin to sweat. Damian looked around to find himself in a baron desert with nothing as far as he could see. The cracked earth beneath his feet thirsted for water that was nowhere in sight. Every step he took was rewarded with the crunching of dried dirt below his boots.

Cato groaned. "A damn desert? I don't see anything, Damian. I think you brought us literally to Hell."

"I told you it was going to be." Damian felt the heat seeping into his lungs making it uncomfortable to breathe. "Getting there is going to be really difficult and dangerous. It's only going to get more treacherous."

"Of course it is." Cato sighed. "Well, at least we just have to worry about the heat for now."

A rumble traveled through the ground causing the small rocks that littered the ground to bounce up and down like popcorn. Something was under them. Whatever was under them was beating against the ground below them so savagely Damian felt as if he was going to fall over.

"What the hell?" Anna looked around worriedly. "You just had to jinx it didn't you, Cato?"

"My bad."

The ground begun to crack open under their feet when Damian yelled, "Run!"

CHAPTER III

Julia

JULIA TURNED AROUND BEFORE they could see the fury that built inside her. She couldn't explain how furious it was to see Ryan kiss another woman. Her head started to hurt badly.

Julia took out the flask Aden demanded she keep with her to subdue her headaches. Her hands were shaking as she brought the flask to her lips and swallowed. Instantly her head felt better. She hated Zee. Killing her sounded good.

She propped her elbows on her knees and looked out at the water. Ryan was right; passing the bridge would be very difficult. There was nowhere to hide and crossing at night would be easier.

The sun had begun to rise and melt away the darkness. She was a sitting duck right now and she didn't care. This world was disgustingly difficult to live in and her ability to cope was wavering.

"Are you okay?"

She jumped. The last person she wanted to be around right now was standing behind her. Yet here Ryan was, bothering her and asking stupid questions.

"Why wouldn't I be?" she spat.

Ryan sat down beside her and she wanted to backhand him desperately. "I don't like this new you."

"Well, get over it."

"Why are you being this way, Julia?"

"I am not being any way but what I am. If you don't like it than that is your problem not mine." *Would he just get away from me already?*

Ryan wouldn't go away though. Her hands shook very slightly. Just being around him made her mad and he noticed.

"Why are you shaking all the time?"

"I have anxiety and have to take a tonic for it." Thankfully Aden helped out with that, but it seemed to stop working as well as it used to. Her body must be getting used to it or something.

"You've never had it before." His tone was uncertain. What was he getting at?

"So?"

"I'm just saying," he started. "Before you were with Aden you were fine."

She laughed. "Fine?"

He shrugged. "It seemed like it anyways."

"Oh yeah, being in love with someone that treated you like crap was perfect. Especially when he scurried off doing gods know what when I was kidnapped. That's great too." Her habit of saying 'gods' was starting to make her mad. Even the slightest reminder of them annoyed her.

Ryan studied her for a moment and then looked to the ground. "I really am sorry for everything I did. I did it to help save us. I thought it was what you would want."

"Right."

"I thought we were fine, Julia." He looked miserable and it tugged at her heartstrings. "At least, I'd hoped we were fine. I thought when I got you back we would be together, finally, without any complications."

"Ryan, you are incapable of loving someone. Do Zee a favor and leave her alone. You will always disappoint anyone you are with. You left me to die but Aden was there and he saved me, not you. I will never forgive you for that."

"I led a search party Julia," he protested. "People died trying to save you. I couldn't let you suffer like I had in their hands. It may have been wrong to put other people in danger, but I had to. I had to get you back."

Her hands shook almost violently and she forced another swig of the tonic down her throat. Her feelings for him were painfully rising up within her. Her heart hurt. She had to get away from him. She couldn't breathe. This was a bi-polar nightmare.

"Just go back to Zee," she muttered. "She can be your new little pet."

"What happened to you?" He grabbed her hand and she froze. "You were beyond loving and kind to everyone you met. You would never speak badly about anyone. Now you are just irate with life. I hate it, Julia. You need to come back. You were the most amazing woman I've ever known in my lifetime."

She pulled her hand out of his grasp. "I grew up and

realized the world is shit. Get over it and get over me because this is who I am now."

"I can't believe this is you."

"Leave me alone and go back to your new play toy over there. You seem to care more for her now anyways." Why was she jealous?

"You moved on, Julia. What was I supposed to do?" He sighed. "I mean really, you slept with me one day and then Aden the next. Your virginity was something you took pride in and now you are just throwing yourself around as if it never mattered to you."

"I suppose I learned from the best." She laughed. "I hope Zee knows what she is getting herself into. Once you're done using her you'll just throw her away like everyone else. A couple more romps in the sack and off to the ex pile she goes."

Ryan hung his head low and she barely noticed how tired he looked. "For your information we haven't slept together. Not that it is your business."

That was definitely a surprise to her. It was a rarity in Ryan she'd never seen before. He always got what he wanted from women, her included. "Well, I am glad she is so special to you that you're willing to wait."

"Gods dammit Julia, you have no idea how much I still love you and it kills me to see you with him." He rubbed his face in frustration and she felt a butterfly flutter in her stomach. "I would do anything for you. I would die for you, but I can't live my life pining for someone that's chosen another person."

"Didn't take you long to move on, did it?"

"I had to rip off the Band-Aid."

"Good," she muttered.

"Julia please try and underst-"

She tackled him to the ground, pressing her knife against his neck. Blood started to drip from under the blade and he looked up at her in utter shock.

This felt good. She liked him like this. Part of her wanted to push the blade down harder but words of caution seized her hand from doing so.

Stop. Don't stop. Stop.

He gulped and she watched in fascination as his Adam's apple moved up and down. His life was in her hands and she enjoyed the power of it. In the corner of her eye she saw him reach towards her waist to flip her off his body but she dug the knife down harder.

"You will stop with this conversation. I am done with it. I am who I am and I don't want you. You've moved on. Good for you but leave me alone. I want nothing to do with you. The only reason you are alive is because I need your help. We are nothing to each other now."

Ryan tilted up his throat in defiance and she watched with amusement as blood dripped down his neck to the ground. "Fine then. We are nothing." He glared up at her with such animosity it almost frightened her.

She had no doubt that he could escape her clutches with ease but he chose not to. He chose to let his blood slowly drip from his neck from the small cut she carved in his skin.

Julia removed the knife and sat back down in the grass to stare out towards the water. She was glad they'd had this conversation. Now they could move on from this damn drama and get to work.

She needed to try and be nicer though. The more aggravated she seemed, the less likely he was to trust her. She could already see the doubt in his eyes. The look of hatred he had just given her was only a look Ryan had for the enemy.

Just a little more time to play the good girl until she could come clean and be her true self. Subdue the new Julia and bring back the old. Faking it was going to suck.

Ryan

He slept. It was wonderful and he didn't want to wake up. Hell, he could sleep for a week and be content after the year he'd been having.

Zee lightly shook him awake and kissed him on the cheek. "Wake up lazy." She grinned.

Night had begun to fall and he was not in the mood to do anything but relax. When all of this was over he was going to take a very long vacation.

Ryan stretched his arms out and sighed in relief. To his astonishment his body wasn't sore. Probably had something to do with the mojo Apollo did on him. He felt pretty good actually.

"Five more minutes, Mom."

"There's no rest for the wicked."

"I'm not wicked. I'm a good boy."

She smirked. "Fine, there's no rest for good boys."

"Just kidding. I'm a bad, bad boy. I need to be punished."

She punched him in the arm. "Hey, not nice," he laughed.

Zee grinned. "You're dumb, you nasty little man."

"Trust me, I'm not little." That earned him another punch to the arm. "Okay, my bad. This is abuse you know. I might turn you in."

"Yeah, you do that." She rubbed his head like he was a dog.

Julia ran up to them from the bridge and ducked down within the tree line they'd hidden in. "They seem to have bumped up security. Trucks are driving by more frequently, but instead of a group its only one at a time."

"How are we going to get past the bridge?" Ryan groaned. It was the last thing he wanted to hear after a damn good nap. It was bad enough with larger groups, but with patrols split up and more driving by more frequently this was going to be near impossible.

"Wing it?" Julia smirked.

"Wing it?" he laughed. "That's your solution?"

"It's what you do best, right?" Julia gave him an amused expression that gave him a glimmer of hope she was coming back to him. She turned to Zee. "Are you good or do you need to rest more?"

With an apprehensive look Zee nodded. "It feels better. I'm fine."

"Good." Julia held out her hand for Ryan to take and helped him up.

Zee was glaring at Julia, looking her up and down measuring her up. Ryan had to admit it was a drastic change from when she'd had her dagger digging into his neck. Right now she seemed like the woman he once knew.

They ran over to the column at the bridge and waited

for the next truck to come. It didn't take long for a Humvee to drive up with only three people in it. As soon as it passed they took off running across the bridge.

It was longer than he thought and he looked around for any possible place to hide if they needed to, but there wasn't one. It was a straight shot towards the other side with nothing but a column-lined guardrail that prevented people from plunging into the waters below.

Headlights turned down the dark bridge and Ryan stopped running as did the other two. Where the hell were they going to hide?

"Shit," Zee grumbled.

"Any ideas?" Julia bit her lip, another indication that this was his old Julia.

Ryan ran his hand over his still short hair and shrugged. "Well, we could hang off the edge."

"Are you freaking nuts?" Zee hissed.

"Some of the time," he admitted, but it was the only option he saw. "Come on."

They ran to the edge of the bridge and looked down. The water looked like a black abyss below and he had no desire to fall into it.

Zee blinked lazily at him as if he were completely dim-witted. "If I fall and get wet I will hurt you."

Ryan opened his mouth to remark but Julia beat him to it. "Probably shouldn't say stuff like that if you don't want him making a perverted remark." Julia hopped right over the guardrail.

"Thanks for the advice." Zee's eyes narrowed.

"No problem." Julia winked at Ryan and he felt his cheeks

get warm with embarrassment even though he didn't do a damn thing. Yeah he was thinking something dirty, but still... He never blushed.

The jeep got closer and Ryan couldn't wait any longer. He jumped over the guardrail, lowered himself down off the edge of the bridge and held on for dear life. All of their feet dangled in the air as they held on to the edge.

Zee had her eyes closed for some reason and Julia's arms began to shake. She looked like she was losing her grip. The jeep was taking too long to cross the bridge.

"Hold on," he whispered.

"No shit." Julia struggled to get her words out.

The jeep slowed down near them. Ryan groaned when he heard the jeep doors open and shut. They were searching.

"I thought I saw something," a man said.

"I still think you are seeing crap," a woman's squeaky voice dripped with annoyance. Ryan felt her pain. "Let's just go."

"Shut up," the man said. "I know I saw something."

"Well obviously not," the woman argued.

The two continued to argue and the conversation began to get heated. Ryan was growing more concerned with Julia by the second. Both hands were slipping from the edge before her right arm finally gave out. Her eyes darted over to Ryan with a look of utter fear as she dangled above the water by one hand.

"Ryan," she begged in a wordless whisper. "Help."

Her arms shook trying to hang on until her grip gave way. She began to fall until he caught her wrist and found himself in the same predicament she was in. He was holding up two people with one arm and his muscles felt the strain.

A painful pop came from his shoulder and he bit his lip to prevent a scream that would give away their location. With deep breaths he managed to mouth, "Climb… up." The pain in his arm felt like a red-hot poker that turned into a numb tingling sensation.

Julia did as she was told and grabbed onto his vest. She was able to hoist her small frame up and then put her arms around his neck. He winced as she touched the small cut she'd put there.

"I'm sorry," she whispered in his ear and finally managed to dangle from the edge by herself again.

He still hung from one arm; his other was totally useless now. To his relief he heard the jeep doors slam closed. Julia and Zee were the first back up on the bridge once the patrol passed and both of them helped drag him up by his good arm.

He held onto his shoulder and groaned, "It's dislocated. Pop it back in."

Zee said, "I can't."

After rotating his arm at certain angles and with a hard push on his bicep Julia had thrust his shoulder back in place with her small delicate hands. He stomped his foot as if it would get rid of the pain. "Mother fu-"

"Shhh." Julia smacked him upside the helmet. "We need to move."

They continued to run down the bridge until they saw more headlights coming their way. "Another patrol is coming," Zee whispered.

"Shit!" Julia exclaimed. "Can you hang on the edge again?"

Ryan sighed and as he rotated his shoulder and asked, "Do I have a choice?"

"We could kill them," Julia suggested.

"I vote yes," Zee agreed

He was actually amused the two women agreed on something. "Okay, I think I have a plan. One of you needs to cut my arm."

Ryan lay face down in the middle of the sidewalk wearing only his black shirt and pants. His breathing was becoming gradually slower as time went on and he felt the warmth of his blood drip down his arm.

The oncoming patrol stopped. "Who is it?" a man asked.

He felt the barrel of a shotgun prod him between the shoulder blades. "Looks like a drunk that passed out."

"No way," another man voiced. Ryan heard a door slam. "Look how much he is bleeding. Bastard probably got in a fight and lost."

"What should we do with him?"

"Bag 'em up or just leave 'em?"

"We can't leave him here, you idiots," one said. "The General will not allow bodies to be lying out in public. It sends a bad image."

"Let the mortals deal with it," another one groaned. "Its probably just another stupid mortal trying to get away I bet."

"All the more reason to bring him in." They argued for a few minutes causing Ryan to grow increasingly impatient. *Did these guys ever shut up?*

INDEFINITE

He managed to look over at the edge of the bridge at Zee and Julia. They waited for his signal to move in. Ryan's arm still ached from being pulled out of its socket but he could at least use it.

His hand squeezed the handle of the blade he hid under his stomach. One of these guys needed to hurry up and turn him over before the next patrol came.

Julia and Zee bantered silently back and forth and he tried very hard to suppress a laugh.

"The fucker moved," one man said.

Shit.

"Turn him over," another said.

Thank the Gods.

One of the men grabbed his shoulder and as he turned him over, Ryan thrust his dagger deep into the man's heart. Their eyes met briefly before the man died almost instantly. Ryan recognized him from Urbs.

The other men panicked and pointed their guns at Ryan. "Drop it," the shorter one yelled.

They were both dressed in gear with the Risen's symbol around their arms. The men had their backs to Julia and Zee. Ryan dropped the knife and held up his hands as he stood. "You goddamn traitors." Furry built inside of him when he realized who they were.

They hesitantly lowered their weapons an inch. "Shit, is that Ryan?"

"Shit! It is Ryan," the other said.

"Shit, it is me," Ryan said. The men before him worked in the Domus. They were treated with as much respect as any Warrior and he was shocked they had changed sides.

41

"Look Ryan, you are the last person we want to go up against."

"Oh I don't doubt that." Ryan smirked. "Carlos, Muhammad, and poor Ricky lying on the ground over there. You two will join him soon, believe me."

"We are the ones with the guns, Ryan," Carlos chided. "Not you."

Julia and Zee silently hoped up over the edge of the bridge and stalked up behind the two men.

Ryan smirked. "Alright, what's your point?"

The two men exchanged glances. "There's no way you can get out of this alive," said Muhammad.

"After all you've heard about me," Ryan said keeping them busy. "Do you really think that's true?"

Their false bravado began to falter and Carlos held up his gun. "It's not possible. I could kill you right now. It would be easy."

"Are you sure?" Ryan grinned wickedly.

Carlos squeezed the trigger and struck the ground at Ryan's feet. It was either an accidental shot or he was a lousy aim. Regardless it was embarrassing for the man.

"Pathetic," Ryan said. "In about five seconds both of you are going to be lying in a puddle of your own blood."

Carlos shook his head. "No, that would be you." He raised his gun again. "I'm sorry, Ryan. I really am."

At that moment, Zee jumped on Muhammad's back and brought her dagger down on his chest. At the same time Julia swiped her knife quickly across Carlos' neck. He fell to his knees before he collapsed to the ground in a bloody mess.

Zee brushed her hair behind her ear. "Do you really

think that much of yourself?" Zee asked as she pulled on Muhammad's arm and dragged him over to the edge of the bridge. "I mean I knew you were full of yourself but damn."

"What can I say?" He shrugged. "The truth is what it is."

"Enough, you cocky bastard," Julia groaned as she dragged Carlos' body to the edge, leaving a trail of blood along the way. "Help us dump the bodies."

Ryan did as he was told and helped toss their bodies over the edge of the bridge but not before removing their armbands with the Risen's symbol on it. Another patrol was coming and if they were going to pull this off they had to work quick.

After two splashes below, Zee jumped in and started the Jeep. Ryan tossed Ricky's body into the backseat and propped him up before getting in the passenger side. With everyone in the jeep, they drove towards the oncoming vehicle.

Ryan gave each woman an armband before putting on his own. "Zee does the talking. She is less likely to be known by the Risen. We need to act as if we are on their side."

"Gee thanks."

Julia nodded. "Okay."

"Julia and I will keep our heads down as much as possible. Ricky is going to be someone we caught trying to escape. Got it?"

"Yep." Zee nodded.

As the two vehicles got closer, the approaching jeep slowed down until they both came to a stop next to each other. The driver in the other vehicle leaned out of his window to peer into the jeep at Ricky's body.

"Found one." Zee smirked.

"Good. One less problem on our hands."

"Keep watch," Zee added. "I doubt he was alone."

"Will do." The man winked at Zee. That annoyed Ryan. Who knew he got jealous so easily?

Zee put the jeep in drive and they made it across the bridge without further delay. "See. Easy peasy."

Chapter IV

Damian

T HE JOURNEY TO SHAMBHALA was not going to be easy, he knew that but this was insanity. It was scorching hot and difficult to breathe here. Yet, they had to run for their lives to escape the grasp of a dragon the size of a skyscraper. Thankfully the beast was slow, but they couldn't keep running forever.

Anna was starting to fall behind and Damian was half tempted to throw her over his shoulder. The land was completely barren of any life or objects expect rocks and the cracks in the dry earth. It was endless.

With every step the massive dragon took, the earth shook underneath it. This was becoming unbearably exhausting.

"Damian," Cato heaved out with heavy breaths. "What… the fuck… are we… supposed… to do?"

"I don't… know," he heaved back.

"I can't go… much further," Anna groaned. She held onto her stomach with a grimace of pain on her lips.

Damian had to think. This was Ryan's area of expertise not his. He tried to look around for a way out. There was nothing but heat waves rising up from the flat ground.

This was an Indian creature if memory served him right and he was definitely not an expert in that area. He studied it from time to time, and he had an idea as to what this creature was, but it was just a guess. If he was right, only a god had ever killed this beast.

Damian looked over his shoulder. The multicolored creature was trudging along behind them without a problem. The thing's body was long and massive and its teeth were the size of a truck. He had no intention of being impaled by one of them.

Anna stumbled. "I have… to stop."

"Keep going… babe," he grunted.

"We've been… running… for almost… an hour," she breathed.

He looked over at her and her cheeks were deep red. Sweat fell down her face and he knew she was exhausted. He had seen her run for longer than this but the heat must be getting to her. He had to think of something to get away from this beast.

Their prayer seemed to be answered when he saw a hole in the earth up ahead. They ran up to it but to his dismay it was just a giant hole that could be easily accessed by the beast. His heart sank. There was no escaping this creature.

"What… the… fuck… Damian!" Cato yelled.

"What exactly… do you… suggest?" Damian yelled back.

He felt his temper rise. The first time ever Ryan put him in charge and he failed within the hour. No wonder Ryan was moody all the time. The pressure weighed down on him like a ton of bricks or in this case, a giant serpent-like dragon.

No one said a word and all he could hear was their heavy breathing followed by the loud stomps of the dragon behind them. His exhaustion was overpowering his body and they needed a plan.

They continued to run until the ground collapsed underneath their feet. He fell down a long open shaft with dirt swirling around his body like a tornado. He didn't dare breathe, there was a vast amount of dirt falling with them to gods knew where.

He landed roughly on a large pile of dirt and rolled over on his back. The dirt sprinkled around him from up above peppering his gear with even more dirt if that were possible.

Anna and Cato landed near him and both were trying to help him stand up. They were filthy. He looked up saw a large gaping hole in the cavern they fell through. The dragon looked down at them, possibly deciding if it should jump or not.

"Sort of looks like… a dog looking for a treat… doesn't it?" Anna asked. The dragon tilted its head from side to side trying to determine if they were worth the effort.

"Yeah… a big dog… that wants to… bite our faces off," Cato said. "I think I'm going to… pass out right here." Cato jumped down off the large dirt pile and the other two followed. He let out a low whistle. "Wow."

The cavern they found themselves in was massive and quite frankly impressive. Dirt continued to fall down in the chasm and topple over itself to reach the bottom. He couldn't believe his eyes but once the dirt reached the bottom it begun to melt into a river of golden water.

Large white lotus flowers floated in the air with a luminescent center that lit up their surroundings like lanterns. It was the only source of light in the darkness they'd fallen into besides the gaping hole that contained the dragon.

He caught glimpses of jewels as well as statues that were meticulously placed around the cavern depicting mythical creatures from almost every religion. There were sphinxes, Nanaue, and even a Kirin.

One of the lotus flowers hovered over a large statue and Damian heard Anna gasp. The large statue was that of a realistic woman's head cut off and a red liquid flowed out of her neck and down into multiple golden cups below.

"I don't like this, let's get out of here," Anna whispered.

Damian felt oddly drawn into the cavern. He wanted to go to the decapitated statue. There was no rhyme or reason, but he notice Cato was already beating him to the punch. He had to get to it first.

Cato gave him a dirty look as he bolted off towards the statue. The two of them sprinted towards the beheaded and naked woman as if their lives depended on it. He had to get there first. He had to.

Cato surprised him when he jumped on his back bringing him to the ground. They wrestled with one another, neither of them giving up or allowing the other to get closer to the statue. He had to get to one of the filled golden cups first. He wanted to drink from it. He needed to.

They were so close he could almost smell the liquid pouring into the cups. It was a sweet jasmine mixed with honeysuckle and he craved it. Cato was in his way. Cato needed to go.

A gas mask was slapped down on his face. Anna tightened it on his head before she tackled Cato from behind, slamming his chest onto the ground. She proceeded to put a mask on him. As he continued to struggle free, her knee dug between his shoulder blades.

After a few seconds Cato and himself had calmed down enough to notice Anna was wearing a gas mask as well. What the hell just happened to him?

"You stupid boys." He could see her rolling her eyes behind the mask. "Did you not see the blue smoke swirling around this damn room?"

He glanced around seeing that she was right. Swirling blue smoke coiled around the room just like the smoke from a blown out candle. "How did you know it was cursed or whatever?"

Anna was uncharacteristically annoyed with him. "I didn't. It didn't look very healthy to be breathing in. Then you and Cato started acting like a couple of nut jobs and hey, wouldn't you know it? It clicked that the smoke was crazy gas."

Cato brushed off his pants. "You ma'am should play football. That was a hell of a tackle."

"So what were you two fighting over?" Anna ignored him.

"I wanted to drink what the statue has coming out of it." Damian ran his hand along the stubble on his jaw. "It was ridiculously intoxicating."

Cato nodded. "Smelled pretty damn good."

"Well, it's probably poison but let's not find out, okay?" Anna crossed her arms over her chest.

"Now what?" Cato stared into the golden river. He was about to touch the water but thought better of it. Who knew what the hell would happen if he touched it.

"Look around for any tunnels that may lead out of here." Preferably before the dragon decided to jump down and eat them.

Cato groaned, "Can't we take a break?"

"In the gas-filled and cursed flower room? I don't think so," Anna answered for him.

Damian smirked under his mask. He was glad she didn't seem as afraid anymore. Before the catacombs, he would have thought her incapable of handling this type of world mentally. Now, she seemed just as strong as any of them.

Cato put his hands on his hips. "Well than, lead on boss woman."

Julia

Her heart broke for Ricky. He'd always been such a good friend to her in the Domus and she'd been the one to convince him to join the Risen. His heart was really never into it though. *Poor Ricky.*

She had to push his death from her mind even though his lifeless body sat right beside her. All the while Ryan and Zee rode in the front of the jeep. She found herself starring at Ryan.

He looked content with death. So much so that it annoyed her. Those three people were close to everyone in the Domus and he acted as if they were nothing. As if their lives meant nothing. It was the way of a Warrior. Heartless to the core.

She pried her mind away from the deaths of her friends and focused on Ryan and Zee once more. They were close. But how close were they really? Ryan never seemed very infatuated with women, except for herself, but who is to say he isn't that way with Zee?

Did she really care what he thought? Part of her did. Part of her would always love Ryan but she'd moved on to bigger and better people. Aden was the right hand man to the General and you couldn't get much higher than that in ranking.

"Should we dump the body?" Zee asked. Julia wanted to slap her for being so callous.

"No, we may need it again."

Julia cleared her throat. "Turn down Independence Ave."

They were on a road with a line of trees to her left and a softball field to her right. A light blanket of snow began to form on the ground as they continued down the street.

"Oh great, another bridge," Ryan groaned.

"It's just a tiny one." Zee winked and Julia quietly made a gagging face. "Oh cool, the Washington Monument."

Julia thought her eyes would roll out of her head by the end of this mission from the idiocy that came out of Zee's mouth on a continuous basis. She acted as if she had never seen things like this before and it was annoying to say the least. This girl needed to go.

Another patrol started its way down the next bridge and tension filled the jeep. She made quick work trying to sit Ricky's body upright and even buckled him in to keep him from falling. It didn't work entirely well but it was better than nothing.

"What are you doing?" Ryan looked over his shoulder at her. "It's not like he needs to worry about car safety anymore."

"His body keeps falling over," Julia hissed.

The two jeeps pulled up side by side. "Whatever you do, don't treat them like equals," Julia whispered. "Be ruthless."

"Where are you guys off to?" the mortal driver asked.

The look on his face gave away his nervousness and the guy better be nervous. The Risen demanded respect and him even speaking to them without permission was irritable.

"We found a runner and are bringing him to headquarters," Zee responded. Her tone was surprisingly forceful and intimidating.

Good, she took Julia's words to heart.

"Oh." The man looked hesitant with a hint of sadness in his eyes. He was not a true convert, she could tell. He mourned his fellow mortal. "Good job."

Ryan nodded. "Those bastards come out at night so keep an eye out. Not one person is allowed to go free."

"We know. Sir," the man quickly added.

Ryan sat back, acting as if everyone was beneath him, which was not a stretch for him. Julia remained silent. She didn't want to bring attention to herself. There was no telling who knew her and who didn't.

They continued down the bridge and Independence Avenue. Large stone buildings came into view and she inhaled deeply. This was it. Her family was trapped somewhere in these buildings.

They drove past the Washington Monument. "That thing is really tall." Zee took her eyes off of the road while she took in the tall marble obelisk tower.

"No shit," Julia grunted.

"You know, you're kind of a bitch, Julia," Zee stated.

"Your ass must be jealous from all the shit that comes out of your mouth." Julia smiled sweetly at her in the rear view mirror.

"Thanks for proving my point."

"Would you two shut up?" Ryan rubbed his jaw, obviously frustrated with their bickering.

Julia laughed and decided to listen to Ryan. She was sick of this crap already. She really wished her brother were with them instead of Zee. At least he stood up for her.

Playing nice was proving to be more difficult than she thought.

Stone buildings towered over them on both sides of the road now and it made her uneasy. There were probably snipers in these buildings and the jeep provided limited protection. They were officially in the lion's den.

"May I speak, sir?" Zee looked at Ryan, fluttering her eyelashes to act playful with him. He soaked it up with a smile creeping on his lips. "Where am I going now?"

"Take a left down the Twelfth Street tunnel." Julia was sick of their flirting. "I think we need to ditch the jeep down there."

"Why?" Zee protested.

"I don't know which part of the Smithsonian they are in and we have to search by foot," said Julia. "We can't very well be going through the buildings undetected in a large vehicle."

She wished she knew where they were being held, but she hadn't been allowed that information. Aden had told her Grace and Colette clouded her judgment and she needed to cut ties with them in case they didn't convert. It was one of the many arguments they'd had.

Zee drove down the tunnel with dimly lit light fixtures above their head. Most of the lights were broken but thankfully there was enough light for them to see.

Zee put the jeep in park and the three of them jumped out. She still felt an alarming amount of guilt for leaving Ricky down here but his body would be collected eventually. She would see to it that he received a proper funeral. Carlos and Muhammad weren't as lucky.

"So where do we start searching?" Ryan checked the clip of his pistol before holstering it.

"I think in the Natural History Museum but we have to backtrack a bit and head down Madison Drive," Julia said. "I'm really not sure where they are. All I know is that they are here somewhere."

"Should we split up?" Zee asked.

"No," Ryan answered quickly. "This is dangerous enough as it is without splitting up. We are literally in the lion's den. We need to watch each other's backs."

They ran up the ramp that led to the streets above after ditching Ricky's corpse and the jeep in the empty tunnel. The night provided good cover but Ryan stuck out like a sore thumb. All Immortals knew him and all the Immortal Risen knew her. Concealing themselves would be difficult.

They made it up the ramp, running along the bushes lining the sidewalk for additional cover. As they rounded the side of a tall stone building, Zee roughly tugged her back by her vest. Julia almost hit her until Zee hand signaled that there was trouble up ahead.

Julia peeked around the corner as saw multiple patrols walking down Madison Drive. They were armed and keeping watch. Her heart sank. They were all members of the Risen and they would recognize her instantly.

She looked up at the National Museum of Natural History and realized just how big it was. It was built somewhat like the Domus with stonewalls with long glass windows between the columns.

"Kill them or break a window?" Ryan asked.

"Can't break a window, there are alarms," Zee added.

Julia found herself agreeing with Zee. There was no other option and she hated it. "We kill them."

Ryan gave her a disbelieving look that made her feel uncomfortable. He seemed to do that a lot lately with her. What was going on in that mind of his?

"Fine, but we have to be quick." He peaked around the corner and looked back. "There are five of them patrolling. We will take three closest to us out at once and drag their bodies out of sight. Zee, use the patches we stole to your advantage and get the other two to come to you. Julia and I will jump them while they are distracted. Got it?"

Julia found herself hating this plan. She wished they could just knock them out or something but she knew better. Once they woke up, alarms would sound and the mission would increase in its difficulty. Killing was the only answer. It was always the answer.

Ryan and Zee low crawled among the bushes on the ground towards their targets. They waited until each target had their back to them before Ryan signaled to attack. Julia watched as Ryan grabbed his target and choked him with his arm while his other hand covered the man's mouth. He dragged the man still kicking to get free, out of the sight of the other targets.

Zee then took her target out with a swift snap of the neck. It was Julia's turn. Her target had his back to her and was right in front of the bushes she'd hidden behind. Now was the time.

She pulled the man over the bushes, slamming his back against the ground and out of sight. Her dagger went straight to the man's throat as he stared up at her with wide eyes.

"Julia?" The surprise and hurt in his eyes made her heart sink.

She realized this was someone she'd personally recruited. A friend from the Domus that always brought her flowers for her room. There was no other option she had to kill him.

"I'm so sorry," she whispered in his ear as she covered his mouth with her hand. She quickly swiped her dagger across his neck and could feel his blood gurgle within his mouth.

She forced down the tears that threatened to fall and made her way over to Ryan and Zee who were watching her impatiently.

"Took you long enough," Ryan hissed.

"Okay, I'm up," Zee interrupted before Julia could retort. She jumped over the bushes into the street. Zee yelled over to the men, "Guys, come here. I think I found something."

"Who are you?" a woman asked.

"New recruit. Was just sent here by the General. He told me to relieve one of you from patrol tonight. I think I found something though." Zee was quite the little actress.

As they made their way over to them, Ryan looked like a lion ready to pounce on his prey. He squatted down like a linebacker and she couldn't help but watch the way his jaw clenched when they got nearer.

"Over here." Zee pointed at her and Ryan through the bushes. As the soldiers came closer, they both leaped out from their hiding spots.

Ryan snapped his man's neck while she severed the woman's spinal cord with her dagger. Quick and disappointingly easy. This was not a good sign for the Risen if these soldiers were that easy to take out. She made a mental note to speak to Aden about this.

They dragged the bodies out of sight and covered them with any scrap or trash they could find lying around. It was a sad sight indeed. Completely disrespectful but Ryan acted perfectly at ease.

"Alright, let's get in and look around." Ryan clapped his hands together.

Julia noticed a look of pride in Zee's face. Damn, Zee was enthralled with him and it annoyed her more than it should. She probably was never with anyone as prominent in the Immortal world as Ryan was. Zee was nothing but a gold-digging, slut trying to sleep her way up the ladder. *Wow, where did that come from?*

With no guards in sight, they ran up the steps and past the large stone columns. Ryan peaked through the door then waved them inside. It was alarming how easy this was. Surly their security was better than this?

"Holy crap," Zee exclaimed as they entered the large entryway. "That's a freaking elephant."

She wasn't mistaken. There was indeed a 'freaking elephant' in the middle of the room. Dead of course, but it was still a sight to see. Julia was somewhat confused as to why it was still there given most of the Smithsonian was cleared out to make space for their headquarters.

The three levels of the museum; ground, first and second floor were visible here with open walkways looking down into the rotunda. The walls were coated in yellow but the light radiating off of the paint made it look like gold shining in the night against the white stone frame of the building.

She heard noise up ahead. Ryan pulled her and Zee down a dark, hallway to their right with different types of rocks on display. According to the sign, this section was the earliest traces of life.

Exiting the small hallway Ryan stopped in his tracks. "Dinosaurs," he said under his breath. A cheesy smile hung on his lips as he looked between the two women.

Yes, he was all male. Boys and dinosaurs went together like peanut butter and jelly. Julia couldn't help but smile at his obvious excitement.

"Have you never been to a museum?" Zee asked.

Ryan shook his head. "Never had any time. This is cool." He ran up the steps to the dinosaur area and looked as giddy as could be. "There's a T-Rex and a Triceratops skeleton up here!"

"I see that." Julia smirked. They were huge and she could see them from were she stood, but she wouldn't ruin his mood. It was odd to see Ryan like this. Like a young man excited for life. Despite her dislike for him, it was heartwarming to see.

He ran around taking in all the sights while Julia and Zee stood by one another awkwardly. She didn't have the heart to get him back on track quite yet. He was genuinely happy.

"So," Zee said breaking the silence. "I realize this is awkward and I would like it not to be."

Julia crossed her arms. "Good luck with that."

"Why are you being so rude?" Zee asked. "I mean I realize things are weird with your Aden and Ryan dilemma, but I always remembered you to be really sweet and level-headed."

She was right. Julia used to be those things and it was something she'd prided herself in. It used to be very important for her to be seen as a likeable person. She hated drama and avoided it within the Domus, but now she was miserable with everything around her. What was the point in being sweet?

"Things change. I keep telling you guys that, but it doesn't seem to get through your thick skulls."

"See, right there you were full on bitch, Julia." Zee laughed. "I gotta tell you though, old Julia was pretty damn awesome. You should bring her back."

"Then you would have competition for Ryan's affection and you would lose horribly." Julia smirked. "No offense, I am sure you are good in the sack but that man is blind when it comes to me."

"Trust me, I am fully aware of what I have to lose. But if that meant getting Julia back then so be it. Ryan and his team weren't the only highly respected people in the Domus. You, Grace, and Colette have made a name for yourselves in everyone's hearts as well."

Why did she have to be such a good person? Julia wanted to hate her but she was making it rather difficult to succeed in that mission.

Ryan came running up to them breathless with a

massive goofy grin on his face. "Guys, there are so many badass things in here. You have to see it."

Julia grinned. "Alight you little boy, we have to get
going."

Ryan literally pouted and looked back over his shoulder
at all the different dinosaur bones on display. With a defeated
look he made his way over to an area that described the ancient seas and how they changed in formation over time.

His giddiness knew no bounds. There were still skel-
etons of ancient creatures all around the room except these
looked much creepier than the dinosaurs. The water itself
never bothered her but the creatures that dwelled within it
had always reminded her of a freak show. This little display
just heightened that fear.

"Whoever painted this room had a fetish for teal," Zee
said as she looked around. "It's everywhere."

"Looks turquoise to me." Julia shrugged.

"Is there really a difference?" Ryan added as he continued to look around and read the plaques under the different
creatures. "It's supposed to be about the sea, makes sense to
me anyways."

Julia watched Zee roll her eyes. "I'm just saying it's a bit
much." Ryan one-armed hugged Zee but released her as soon
as he saw Julia watching them.

Julia heard voices coming from behind them. There was
nowhere to hide in this section of the museum and it was either run or kill. They had already wasted eight of the Risen's
lives so far and she didn't want to risk anymore.

She took off running and was thankful when the other
two followed. As she turned the corner a silent screamed

filled in her lungs and her heart seemed to leap out of her chest. Instinctively she slapped her hand over her mouth out of fear.

Ryan came up behind her laughing, his hand pat her back as if she were a child. "Did the big, mean mammoth scare you?" his singsong voice chided her.

She punched his arm. "It's not funny."

"I heard something over there," a man's voice came from behind them.

They ran again.

They made their way straight through the African history section and into the children's discovery room. She heard a commotion and a curse coming from behind her and found Ryan had tripped over one of the many tiny stools within the room. He set it back up carefully while cradling his shin.

"Dammit," he said as he hoped up and down.

"Grow a pair and let's go," Julia hissed as Ryan half-wobbled half-ran after her and Zee.

They ran into the next part of the museum and the three of them came to a halt. It was a massive blue room full of oceanic objects and one huge figure.

"Whoa," he muttered. "There's a big ass whale floating in the middle of the room."

"It's on wires," Zee pointed out.

"Shh. You're ruining the moment," Ryan whispered.

Despite whatever random moment Ryan was having, she knew they needed to keep moving. "We need to hide," Julia said. "Grace and Colette aren't down here."

"There's an elevator over there," Ryan said.

They ran as quickly and quietly as they could to the

elevator. Ryan pushed the button repeatedly as if it would help the door open faster. They made it inside before the people following them came into sight and Julia let out a breath she didn't realize she was holding in.

Ryan started to whistle as he pushed the button to the second floor and casually leaned against the wall. Zee's eyebrow rose at his nonchalant attitude. Julia was equal parts annoyed and entertained.

He nodded towards Zee. "Sup?"

She shook her head at him, but Julia saw the amusement in her eyes. Jealousy began to find its way back into her heart. What was going on with her?

Chapter V

Anna

"WHAT THE HELL?" ANNA groaned.

They went from being in a scorching hot desert during the day, to a gas filled cave and now found themselves venturing into a thickly vegetated and creepy jungle at night. She could hear all sorts of sounds in this place. Owls were doing their thing and various screeches and cries were coming from all around. There were even a few noises that sounded unnatural and unknown to her.

Cato grunted. "I blame Damian."

"What? Why?"

"Because I can." Cato shrugged.

They trudged through the trees in a single file line. It reminded her of elementary school. Cato was in the lead with Anna following behind and Damian pulling up the rear. It was difficult to maneuver around the place with broken branches and fallen trees strewn all over the path. She'd tripped over a stump not long ago and had fallen backwards onto a giant rock. Now her back hurt and she was cranky.

"How long do you think this is going to take to get through?" Anna asked. Part of her didn't want an answer. At least with the desert she could see when something bad was coming, but with a place like this jungle danger could be anywhere.

Hell, it could even be here now and none of them would have any idea that their heads were going to get sliced off. When did thoughts of head slicing become a normal possibility to her?

She tried to concentrate on anything besides death right now and the only thing she could study besides the thick debris on the ground was the back of Cato's head. Every once in a while when he moved a certain way she swore she saw a tattoo sticking out from under his vest and shirt.

She cocked her head to the side and tried to think of what it looked like. Tribal? Doubtful that Cato would mark is body with something so impersonal. Maybe it was a dragon but then again that was totally out of his realm. This dude was a Jupiter loving, Apollo worshiping kind of guy.

After awhile it started to annoy her. What the hell was it?

She was deep in thought about it being a girl's name when he abruptly stopped and she bumped her helmet into his back. The guy was tall.

"What the hell Anna?" He laughed and looked over his shoulder at her.

She couldn't take it anymore. "What the hell is your tattoo?" Manners be damned, she was curious.

His smile vanished and his eyes were directed at Damian behind her now. "It's sort of personal, Anna."

"Oh sorry," she said and looked down at her feet, ashamed of her curious nature. She didn't mean to pry. Cato was one of the only people she really liked in her new world besides Damian. The last thing she wanted was to be on his bad side. "I was just trying to distract myself from the sounds of things killing other things in here."

Cato smirked. "I'm just messing, sort of. It's not that big of a deal but it's from a time in my life I really don't care for. I could remove it but I don't see it anyways so it has stayed."

"You don't have to tell me."

"It's fine, Anna." Cato forced a grin.

"I don't want to make you uncomfortable."

"Well, too late for that so deal with it." He unstrapped his vest and pulled up his shirt so quickly that her cheeks grew hot seeing his bare skin. These men were far too accustomed to getting naked. Or maybe she was just a prude. Either way, Cato was not bad to look at, like at all.

He revealed a massive eagle with its wings spread wide across the top of his back. Under it looked like the letters, SPQR.

"Holy balls," Anna muttered. The thing covered a good portion of his back.

Cato laughed out loud this time and put his shirt and vest back on. "Thanks?"

"Sorry, it's just freaking huge!" she exclaimed. "What does it mean?"

"You're a smart girl, I think you can figure it out." Cato winked and started trudging forward through the trees once again.

"It looks like a quality tattoo. When did you get it?"

"About fifty years ago. I was drunk. I hate what it represents and I have no idea why I got it because I woke up with it."

"Oh, sorry."

"Don't be." He patted her on the shoulder.

"Why did you stop anyways?" she asked. "Oh god, did you see something?" If she made it easier for a Hell monster to eat them she was going to be upset.

"You know when you can feel someone's eyes on you? Well, that happened and it turned out to just be you. So stop." He stopped abruptly again making her run into him.

"Dammit, Cato." She shoved him forward as he laughed. "I don't talk to you a lot but sometimes I think you are an ass."

Cato continued to laugh, it was contagious and the three of them finally were able to crack a smile since coming here. She really did like him. He was like a brother to her. Unlike Ryan, who was now in her mind as one of her unfortunate hookups.

"So I have a question," Anna said as they trudged on through the endless vegetation. "If all religions are real, than how does that coincide with creation?"

"What do you mean?" Damian asked.

"Like, how did humans come to be? I mean, the whole Adam and Eve thing can't be true for everyone."

"I hate to break it to you sugar, but the big bang isn't just a theory," Cato sighed. "Humans created their religion and made it real. Now Gods exist and take care of us because that is what we need. My father told me that the gods took charge of our creation by guiding us safely into life. How they do that is a mystery to me."

"The big bang theory? I love that show, but I'm not a fan of the actual concept," Anna mumbled. "So we came from monkeys?"

Damian was about to answer but was cut off as a large branch fell from above and into their path. Cato jumped back and knocked Anna off her feet, but Damian was there to catch her.

"Shit," Cato huffed. "Damn thing almost landed on me."

Looking up into the branches she could have sworn she saw a ghostly figure dash through the tops of the trees. The moonlight was the only thing giving them any light and it could have been a trick her mind was playing on her.

A blur of a creature dashed by her on her right leaving the rustling of leaves in its wake. No, there was definitely something in here with them. *What the hell is it?*

She released her gun out of its holster. From what she caught a glimpse of the thing it was too creepy not to shoot.

Damian and Cato must have seen it too because they already had their pistols in their hands too. The three of them searched the trees for the little annoyance.

"What is it?" Cato whispered.

"If I had to guess?" Damian asked.

"Yep." Cato kept his eyes in the trees.

"A vetala."

"Need a little more information than that," Cato hissed.

"It's sort of like a vampire that can possess the dead. I read about it when I was studying Shambhala."

"Lovely," Cato said.

Anna didn't realize she was backing up until the felt something hard hit her back. Slowly she turned to face nothing more than a tree trunk but as soon as she faced back around her relief dropped. She was face to face with a humanlike creature hanging upside from a branch.

It was a disgusting thing. What skin it did have was deathly pale and dirty, hanging off its body as if it were shredded. It's bones protruded throughout its entire unnaturally long and thin frame, looking as if it hadn't had a meal in its life.

She clung on to Damian's arm until he faced her but once she turned back around the thing was gone. "What?" Concern was all over his face. "Anna, are you okay?"

"I saw it. The velveeta thing," she whispered. "It's super ugly."

"Vetala." A high-pitched screech came from the tops of the trees.

"I think it heard you," Cato said leaning towards them.

Once the creature began to screech it seemed as if dozens of creatures decided to join in. It was painful to hear. She was certain her ears would start to bleed if she didn't clap her hands over them.

Several of the boney vetala creatures could be seen hanging down from their trees like monkeys and their eyes shone brightly through the darkness. They looked curious, but what really terrified her was the drool that dripped from their ridiculously sharp teeth.

"What's the plan, boss?" Anna whispered to Damian. He looked as awestruck as she did. "Shoot them?"

"They are spirits. It wouldn't do any good," Damian said. The thin monkey people continued to stare at them. "I think we should keep moving."

They backed away from the creatures but it didn't help calm her nerves as they seemingly disappeared out of sight. Those things were straight out of a horror movie. Her brain told her to run but her body seemed glued to Damian's. He didn't say a word about it though. Anna had a feeling he could sense how afraid she was.

They continued in the direction they were going and she became aware how close not only Damian was to her, but Cato as well. She was sandwiched between them and they were obviously playing protect the damsel. For once, she didn't mind.

Just when she thought they'd lost the creatures, she heard the rusting of leave in the branches above them. Occasionally she would catch a glimpse of their eyes reflecting in the moonlight. Her heart wanted to jump out of her chest but the nasty things would probably just eat it.

"So what did you call the skinny monkey human things?" Anna asked.

"Vetalas," Damian whispered in her ear.

"How do you kill it?"

"I have no idea."

"Well, freaking fantastic," she groaned.

"Let's just hope we don't have to," Damian said.

"Oh yeah, because that's how things seem to go for us isn't it?" Her words dripped with sarcasm. Annoyance seemed to be gripping her lately.

"I want you both to concentrate on one word here," Cato whispered behind them. "Spirit. You can't kill a spirit anymore than it can harm us. Now, if it got into a body then I would be worried."

Anna breathed easy after that but she still kept her guard up. "How are the branches moving then?" She grasped Damian's arm.

"Do I look like a vetala expert?" Damian laughed.

"This place isn't exactly normal," Cato added as he looked into the trees. "Maybe they can hurt us here after all."

"You just had to ruin my calm didn't you?" Anna pushed him lightly from behind.

The vetalas kept following them but never made a move to attack. What they were doing, she didn't know, but Anna's worry was reaching new heights. There was no way they could outrun them. They were quick in the trees.

The forest was as never ending as the dessert had been. Her patience was wearing thin and she started to direct her anger towards Cato and Damian. "Are we just going to keep trudging along while those creepy-ass monkeys follow us?"

Damian put his hand on her shoulder causing her to jump. "Are you alright?" His worried voice annoyed her.

"No," she hissed, "I want them gone." Damian's grip tightened on her shoulder and she smacked his hand off. "What the hell?"

"What?" Damian's voice was farther away. She looked behind her and he was standing ten feet away.

"How did you get over there?"

"Just giving you some space."

"You were just touching my shoulder," Anna nearly yelled.

Damian looked utterly confused and approached her slowly. "No, I didn't. Are you okay?"

"Why do you keep asking me that?" she growled.

"That's the first time I asked you that!" His eyebrows furred. "Are you PMS-ing or something?"

"Oh shit," she heard Cato say under his breath.

Her face felt hot. "What did you say?"

Damian tried to pull her body to his. "I'm sorry. It just slipped out. That was uncalled for."

She pushed him off her. "Just get these damn monkey men away from us and I will be fine."

Damian's face was a mixture of hurt and confusion. She saw his eyes dart to Cato behind her. "Quit silently telling each other shit. I am sick of it. Say whatever it is you have to say out loud."

Damian came near her again but her body told her to retreat from him. "Anna, let's just talk for a second, okay? You are unnaturally hostile and I think these things are getting to you mentally."

"They are following us and it is freaking me out. That's it."

"From what I read they can possess corpses and control the bodies."

"You've said that already, smarty pants." She crossed her arms and glared at him from head to toe. "Are there any other demeaning remarks you feel the need to spout from that shit eating mouth of yours?"

Damian looked apprehensively at her. "They like to drive people mad as well."

"I sure as hell am mad." She smacked him in the chest. "I'm sick you not doing anything about them."

"I mean crazy."

Cato clicked his tongue. "Man, you never call a woman crazy. It makes them even more crazy."

"Shut up Cato," Damian and Anna chimed together. She needed to get her shit together because she knew she was overreacting. She just couldn't stop herself.

Damian tilted up her chin and kissed her softly on the lips. "Calm down, love."

Her anger began to melt away until she saw a vetala hanging down from a tree. Its long bony fingers with shards of skin ripped off reached out to her causing her scream. A long sharp fanged smile appeared on its lips that stifled her scream into silent horror. Pure evil.

A hand grasped her shoulder and she turned around seeing nothing behind her. Another hand grasped her ankle and she shuffled away from whatever was there. Her mind shook with confusion, anger, and fear as she felt her reality slipping away.

"Anna!" Damian grabbed her by the shoulders and shook her gently. "Anna they are messing with you. Whatever they are doing to you is just a trick. It's fine."

She shook her head. "It's not." Tears came to her eyes once she realized she was going insane.

"I can't even see them around her." Cato moved towards them through the thick trees. She had no idea he'd left in the first place. "Why are they targeting her?"

"I don't know, but we need to get out of here. They are messing with her mind too much," Damian said hurriedly as he briskly guided her along in one direction.

She looked out into the trees and one of the vetalas waved his gruesome hand at her with its bright smile. Blood dripped from its sharp teeth. Anna twirled around trying to look at her own body, touching her arms and legs trying to find out if it bit her.

"Anna calm down." Damian tried to hold her body against his but she was not having it.

It bit her. It had to of and she was going to turn into a creepy vetala thing like a vampire and be stuck here forever. She would never see earth again or Urbs and the world was going to end. They were all going to die here or live here forever like slaves to Shambhala.

"Anna, stop." Damian grabbed the back of her neck.

His grip was tight. It hurt. Why was he hurting her? Tears rolled down her cheeks as the vetalas circled around her in the trees. Their screeching laugh filled her ears.

Her head spun. They made her dizzy. She felt herself falling down into darkness completely numb. The last thing she could see was a vetala behind Damian, it's claw raised above his head ready to strike.

CHAPTER VI

Ryan

AS THE ELEVATOR DOORS opened Ryan could quite literally feel the heat rise up throughout his entire body in anger. They'd found themselves in the pit of the enemy's lair. The second floor of the Natural Museum had been gutted of everything that was once there. There were no artifacts of any kind up here and destruction of the preservation of historical relics struck a cord with him.

Bunk beds were lined up in rows all along the second floor. There was just enough room to pass through the aisles but nothing more. It was packed full. Ryan looked to Julia, who seemed just as shocked as he was.

"Who are they?" Zee asked quietly.

Ryan said, "The Risen maybe?"

Zee shook her head. "Those people are dirty and bruised. I highly doubt they are part of the kill club."

Ryan took a second look. The people sitting on the bunk

beds were indeed covered in filth. The entire room reminded him of a prison of sorts. The only people in here were men and not a single one of them had shoes.

"What the hell?" Ryan muttered.

"It's a prison." Julia grimaced. "They must be the non-converters. Kept here until they join the patrolling forces outside."

The three of them finally made their way out of the elevator and Ryan felt an instantaneous hatred from all the men in this room. He caught them sneaking glances in their direction but never making eye contact. These people hated the Risen and Ryan realized they must look like the enemy.

He wanted to reassure them they were going to help. To keep strong and never give in to the evils of these people that enslaved them but he couldn't. Actual members of the Risen patrolled around the floor with guns in hand and he watched as each man flinch when they passed by.

His instinct to help was in overdrive but there was nothing they could do. They had to keep on track and complete their mission.

"I don't like this," Zee whispered. "I want to leave."

"They may be held here," Julia hissed back.

"With a bunch of men? Very unlikely." Zee had a point, but if Julia was anything it was thorough.

Ryan looked down at one of the prisoners and bile ran up his throat. The man's face was bruised and discolored from an obvious beating and the only thing in his possession was a thin mattress to rest on.

Ryan was about to reach out and comfort him but Julia swatted his hand away.

"Keep it in your head. We are not here for them. We are here for Grace and Colette." The look in her eyes dared him to defy her.

"These people are hurting, Julia."

"It's better than what most people have," she countered. "These ones are actually indoors. Most are in outside camps with little to no shelter."

"Why?" Zee asked.

"To break them. These men must be on the verge of converting," Julia said.

Ryan couldn't contain his glare at Julia. She knew too much about all of this. Part of him knew she had to be a traitor but the other part knew who Julia really was. She wasn't capable of betraying their people.

The behavior she was showing and her knowledge of the enemy baffled him to the point of confusion. This person before him wasn't the woman he grew to love. Even if she were a traitor, would he be able to do anything about it?

"Hey," a man yelled at them. Ryan looked towards the voice of an Immortal making his way over to them.

Ryan turned his back to the man. "Shit."

Julia clung to his wrist. "It's an Immortal."

"Duh," Ryan whispered. "He's from the city."

"What do we do?" Julia squeezed his wrist tighter. Ryan pulled up a black bandana from around his neck, covering his nose and mouth with it. "That's the best you've got?"

"Hey, it's either this or we run for it," Ryan's muffled voice came from behind the cloth.

Julia and Zee barely covered their faces when the Immortal man came up to them. His gun was pointing a little to close to Ryan's privates for comfort and he consciously clasped his hands together over them.

"Yes?" Julia asked authoritatively.

The man looked her up and down suspiciously. "What are you doing in here? Shouldn't you be patrolling outside?"

"We were relieved," she said simply.

The man checked his watch. "The next shift isn't for two hours."

"Hey, when someone says my shift is up it's up. You don't have to tell me twice." Ryan shrugged.

The man eyed him. Ryan prayed to Zeus that this man wouldn't recognize him. Instead, his attention turned to Zee with what Ryan could only describe as a look of sexual interest. If Ryan didn't want to stab him before, he definitely did right now.

"Well then." The man cleared his throat, keeping his eyes on Zee. "Don't mix with this group too much. They are in the last stages and sensitive."

Ryan winced. "Last stage?"

"Conform or firing squad," the man whispered. "I take it you guys aren't from this section."

"No, we were in Kansas first and transferred here," Julia answered.

"Yikes. I heard there are a lot of problems there," the man laughed. "Bible belt. Hard to beat the God out of them."

Yep. I am going to kill him.

The insensitivity to these people's beliefs was baffling, especially from an Immortal.

"Are you guys still cold or what?" the man asked. Ryan raised an eyebrow in confusion and then he added, "Your bandanas."

"Oh," Julia laughed. "Yeah, it's getting pretty nippy out there. Is this whole floor just men?"

"Yeah," he answered cautiously. They needed to get away from him. The man's suspicion was starting to grow.

"Have you heard anything about the two Warriors that were captured? Have they converted yet?" Julia pressed on with her questions and Ryan grabbed her wrist giving it a squeeze. She was pushing her luck by the look on the man's face.

"No, but I know the General wants to keep them close by him. He is personally trying to break them." He looked out over the men in the bunks and sighed. "I better get back to it. Enjoy your break."

Julia pulled her wrist out of Ryan's grasp when the man walked away. "What?"

"You were pressing too hard." Ryan grimaced. "He was on to you."

She huffed. "He is just a patrol Immortal. Hardly any use out of him except to keep the peace with suffering men that probably can't even wipe their own asses."

Ryan was utterly and completely disgusted with her remark. Warriors existed purely to protect the mortals and here she was without even an ounce of sympathy towards them. "I am on to you Julia. I want you to know that." He didn't realize he said the words until they left his mouth.

She looked baffled. "What do you mean?"

He leaned down so only she could hear him. His lips barely brushed against her ear as he said, "I know you are a traitor to the Immortals. You are becoming an evil bitch and I would love nothing more than to turn you in. But we have two very honorable Warriors that need our help, therefore I will ignore it for now. Don't ever think you and Aden are tricking me. When the time comes you both will get what's coming to you."

Julia pushed him into the elevator when the doors opened. Ryan turned to face a very pissed off woman as Zee warily followed them inside.

"We are going to talk in private," she snarled at him.

The elevator doors closed and the suffering men disappeared out of his sight. His mind screamed to go back up there and release them but he couldn't. Or could he? Were two Warriors lives worth more than an entire floor of mortals?

Once the doors opened to the first floor she dragged him by his vest into the human origins section, specifically the Neanderthals area. Zee was close behind until Julia shoved her in the chest. "I need to speak with him alone."

Zee held up her hands in surrender and backed away.

Once she was out of sight, Julia's eyes seemed to fire up but he was just as angry as she was. He'd lost all respect for her and for the first time he couldn't stand to be in her presence. This wasn't his Julia.

He found his body being slammed into the glass case behind him with her forearm pressing firmly against his upper chest. He looked over his shoulder at what artifacts they almost shattered and saw a bunch of different skulls staring back.

Deciding to face the little demon in front of him he said, "What?"

"You are the dumbest man I have ever met in my life, Ryan," she snapped.

"How so?"

She pressed her body against his and the anger he felt wavered only slightly. A lump seemed to form in his throat. This was close. Too close. There was no space between them and he really hoped Zee wouldn't see this.

"I am just trying to push you away the best way I know how," she purred. Her hands ran up his arms as she bit her lip and her eyes were seductively pulling him in. "I love you, Ryan. I've always loved you. But I'm with Aden now so I've had to push my feelings aside for you and push you away the only way I know how. I am rude. I am the opposite of me. I be a terrible person so you won't love me anymore."

Ryan inhaled. Was he falling for this? Could she be telling the truth? That last little hope of doubt was growing in his mind once again and he couldn't push it away even if he tried. No matter what this woman did, he could never completely fall out of love with her.

"I know I am being terrible and I hate it," she went on. Her hands slid up to the back of his neck and he bit his lip in a vain attempt to control his urges. "I want to be myself but I have to make you hate me. It's the only way we both can move on."

"Ugh," he stammered. His fists were clenched tightly at his sides.

"I'm doing exactly what you did to me." She rubbed the back of his neck. "Make you hate me so I can protect us both from the pain. Isn't that right?"

"Why are you telling me this?"

"I can't pretend anymore," she sighed. "I want you so badly and it kills me to see you with Zee. It breaks my heart."

"I'm not sure I believe you." He gently grabbed her arms and tried to pull her off of him but she was not having it. She stood her ground and pressed herself even closer to his body.

"Please believe me," she whispered in his ear. "I love you."

Ryan's eyes closed as soon as the words left her lips. This was not happening. How was she undoing all the anger he had built for her thus far in just a few simple minutes?

"Please stop this." His voice sounded weak even to his own ears.

"I'm sorry." She dragged her teeth along his earlobe.

An urge deep inside him was bubbling up. It threatened to take over but he had to keep it at bay. Just keep thinking about Zee.

"Stop," he halfheartedly said as she massaged his neck.

She kissed him along his jaw line and his hands somehow found their way around her waist. He missed this feeling with her. Every bit of him screamed that she was lying but could he really believe it?

This was the Julia he remembered.

Julia brushed her lips against his ever so gently. Her breath was hot upon his lips just teasing him for a taste until he had enough of her torture. Ryan pulled her roughly into him by her hips. The familiar taste of her lips was a welcomed relief. He turned their bodies around, slamming her back against the glass now with her hands pinned above her head.

Their mouths thirsted for one another. Just having her entire body entwined with his once would never be enough. He couldn't shake the feelings he had anymore than Caesar and Cleo could for one another. She groaned against his mouth and it set him on edge. He needed her now.

Zee.

"Shit." Ryan pulled away from an exasperated Julia. They both breathed heavily but Ryan couldn't do this to Zee. She'd been nothing but good to him and didn't deserve this.

"What's wrong?" Julia panted.

Squeezing his eyes shut he said, "I can't do this." As he rubbed the back of his neck he mentally kicked himself for being so stupid.

She laughed and reached out to him, but he took a step back.

"No," he said more forcefully. "This is not okay."

Something in her eyes looked deceitful. "Fine."

Ryan gathered his composure and left her standing alone as he went to collect Zee. Once he found her he felt the guilt build again. She seemed at ease looking around at all the artifacts that still remained and had no idea of what'd just happened. He put his hand on her shoulder and quickly found her gun barrel pushed into his neck.

"Easy killer." He held his hands up.

"Oh crap." She lowered her gun. "My bad."

Should he tell her? "Just don't shoot me."

"No problem." She grinned. "What did drama queen want? She seemed pretty pissed off from whatever you whispered to her." She held his hand in hers.

He couldn't tell her. Time to put on his acting skills. "I told her she should sleep with the guard for information because she was pushing him too hard. She didn't think it was a good idea. Nor did she find it as amusing as I did."

Zee shook her head. "Ryan, you're such an ass sometimes. You're funny, but an ass."

"Just a donkey with a red nose at your service." Ryan bowed.

Zee rolled her eyes at him. "And apparently you're a bit brain damaged."

"Not nice." He pretended to pout and realized his lips still felt swollen from kissing Julia. Guilt was a terrible feeling. For gods sake he'd had multiple wives at the same time once upon a time. Why was this bothering him?

"Are you okay?"

He had to tell her. "Perfectly fine. Let's get going."

Julia

She sighed in relief. It was utterly exhausting lying all the time and she relished in the thought of no longer faking her emotions. Her little act seemed to work on Ryan, for now. There was one thing that annoyed her the most though, just how damn good he was at kissing and touching her.

Aden was a tolerable kisser but nothing compared to how Ryan was. She hated him but she hated herself more for getting sexually frustrated by him. It had to be done though. He was on to her and she panicked.

They were walking through the large park area towards the castle building across the way from the Natural History Museum. Trees were planted all around giving them some cover. Making it easy for them to be mistaken for shadows.

Ryan stayed close to Zee, which admittedly bothered her.

However, she kept her distance from the two. She had to play the wounded ex for just a bit longer and perhaps Ryan's accusation of her treachery would subside.

They were about halfway to the castle building when she heard a commotion up ahead. Women were screaming and gunfire went off. She heard movement behind her and saw multiple members of the Risen run towards a gathering of people outside of the castle looking building ahead. Mortal women were being led outside of the castle and herded together by the Risen.

It shouldn't have surprised her to see Ryan running along with the other members towards the women. His morals were taking over his brain. "You idiot! Get back here."

Ryan didn't stop. He kept running towards the group of women as if he could actually save them by himself.

She took off after him and managed to yank him back by his vest. Breathing heavily she said, "What are you doing? We need to get away from them, not go where they are."

Ryan scowled. "I cannot let them treat anymore people this way. I can't stand by and let them do it."

He tried to take off again but Julia tackled him to the ground. They were twenty feet away from the scene and members of the Risen ran by giving them dirty looks.

"Tripped," Zee told them as they ran by. "Hurt his ankle."

"Get off me," Ryan ordered. "We have to help them."

"By doing what?" She pulled him close to her face by his vest as she straddled him in the middle of the park. Large searchlights were scanning the area, keeping a close eye on the women that fought for their lives just ahead. "So we kill a couple of the Risen and then what? There are too many of them for the three of us. Get your head out of the clouds and use your brain. You used to be good at that."

Ryan glared but she could tell that his common sense was taking over instead of his heart. It pained him, she could see that and part of her felt sorry for him. These people were doomed and there was no helping them. The castle was the last chance for conversion and these women obviously didn't give in.

"There's at least thirty women up there," he muttered.

"I know." She looked deep into his eyes.

His eyes were haunted by the realization. This was killing him inside and her straddling him probably didn't help the situation whatsoever. So they both stood up and watched the scene unfold before them.

Men in black gear had their guns aimed at the dirty, weak women whose cheeks were stained with tears. Julia had to admit this was terrible to witness. Wasting life was a depressing but necessary sacrifice in war.

A man pointed his pistol in the middle of a dark skinned woman's head. Defiance could be seen from where they stood in her proud eyes until the man pulled the trigger. Julia heard Zee gasp behind her. This felt wrong.

"We need to get away from here until it is cleared out. Most of the Risen seems to be concentrating on them so we can make an easy escape," she said gently.

Ryan stared at all the women. His expression was stoic. She knew from past experience that his heart was broken. Totally and completely obliterated in just a few minutes bearing witness to the horrors of the Risen's power.

Necessary horrors, she had to tell herself.

"Let's find somewhere to hide in the meantime okay?" She pulled on his hand, but Zee took over guiding him along as she wrapped on arm around his waist. Julia couldn't take her eyes off them as they made their way towards the tall circular building. Jealousy was setting in.

Chapter VII

Damian

ANNA WAS A SMALL woman, but carrying her took most of his energy. Especially with her body weighed down by various guns and other weapons. He had no idea what had happened to her when she fainted but he desperately wanted to get out of this place.

Cato ran ahead of him. The density of the trees lessened and he hoped that was a sign they were reaching an end to this dark hell. So far the journey had been exhausting but not entirely dangerous and he knew it would only get worse.

"Are you alright back there?" Cato called back to him. Damian adjusted Anna's limp body on his shoulder. Her arms hung down and kept hitting his ass every time he took a big step. Normally that would amuse him but right now he was just concerned with her well-being.

"Yeah," he heaved between deep breaths. Hours must have gone by, maybe even a day. They needed rest terribly. "What about a break?"

Cato slowed down. "I don't think so. I've been seeing some odd looking tracks around here and don't want to find out who they belong to."

"The vetalas?"

"No, something else."

Cato stopped in his tracks. "Okay, maybe a little break."

"Marvelous," Damian grumbled and he heard Anna whimper. "Is she awake?"

Cato looked behind him and popped back around. "Nope. What the hell did they do to her?"

"Made her lose her mind," Damian speculated. "They didn't bother me much. I guess they were just targeting her."

Cato leaned up against a tree. "They were pretty freaky."

A rabbit hopped by and Damian watched it sniff around in the dirt. "She's going to be one hell of an experienced Warrior after all this."

"Maybe the gods brought her to us because they knew this was going to happen," Cato said absentmindedly. "I don't think they would have chosen her unless they saw the potential. They must have known we would need her."

"Maybe," Damian sighed. "All I know is that when this is over with I am going to marry her. Or at least I hope."

Cato's eyes jump up to his. "Are you serious?"

"Deadly serious."

"You haven't ever shown interest in matrimony. Not even with Aja." Cato looked immediately guilty at the mention of Aja but Damian smiled to assure him it was fine. "Well, congratulations. She's one hell of a woman."

"Don't congratulate me just yet. She might say no." *I hope not.*

"Hello? Is anyone there?" It was a woman's voice.

Cato and Damian looked around in confusion. Anna was still passed out on his shoulder and as far as they knew, they were the only humans here. He looked in the tree line and saw no one.

"Where are you?" Cato called out.

A petite woman with long black hair walked barefoot out of the darkness and into view. She was breathtaking. Obviously a woman of Indian decent, she had a luscious caramel colored skin and big, brown doe eyes you could get lost in.

He glanced at Cato who seemed transfixed with her. "Hello," he grunted.

She smiled sheepishly at him and tossed her hair over one shoulder. "Greetings."

"What are you doing here?" Damian blurted out and Cato gave him an agitated look. "I mean can we help you?"

The woman walked further out into the clearing revealing her completely naked body. Damian looked away respectfully. Cato on the other hand seemed to have dropped his jaw in the dirt.

"I am lost," her voice whimpered.

"How can I help you?" Cato started towards her but Damian pulled him back. "What?"

"Don't you think it is a little odd that there is another person out here?" Damian whispered.

Cato seemed to understand but at least this woman, or whatever she was, didn't have her claws in him like every other creature they have met thus far. "Right-o."

"Please help me," she begged. Damian almost felt bad for her but he had to look at all the circumstances. She was alone, naked and far too clean to be lost in a jungle with murderous creatures.

"Sorry ma'am, but we must get going." He adjusted Anna once more.

He tried to leave but the woman seemed to glide over to Cato. She pressed her hand gently on his cheek, looking at him like a lover and Cato melted like butter. He started to follow her.

"Damian!" Cato's eyes begged. "Help me. I'm not in control."

The woman grinned but the once pearly white teeth she had turned into a row of sharp fangs. Long tusks grew rapidly out of her mouth like a bore and her hand thrust itself roughly around Cato's neck. Slamming Cato's back into the dirt she climbed on top of him.

Damian quickly but gently laid down Anna and ran to help his friend. The small bunny he saw before decided to hop in his way. He tried to go around the poor creature until it's body started to convulse, stopping him in his tracks. It's tiny bones cracked loudly and its skin begun to peel off into a mess of blood and fur below its feet. Then it grew.

The tiny body grew bigger and bigger until it's bones were done manifesting into a large hideous beast before him.

Just like the woman, it had sharp tusks sticking out of its jaw, but this creature was most certainly not beautiful. It's massive furry eyebrows curled upwards like horns and its eyes were wild and bulging. The small cute bunny had just transformed into a massive goblin-like demon in full armor ready to crush him.

The once beautiful woman on top of Cato had disappeared

and instead was replaced by a copied image of its companion. He much preferred the gorgeous lady as opposed to these guys.

Just as Damian reached for his dagger the monster pinned his arms against his sides and screeched loudly into his face. Its breath was undeniably grotesque but that was nothing compared to its hideous appearance. He tried to free his arms but the beast overpowered him significantly.

Cato was not having anymore luck and to his horror, Damian could see the beast licking his neck. Cato was squirming to get away but like him, he was overpowered. The beast grinned, or at least he thought it was a grin and turned to its companion.

"Tasty." Its voice was a deep growl.

Damian's beast decided to lick his neck as well and he felt the urge to throw up. Its tongue was bumpy and slimy. He could only imagine what disgusting residue was left in its wake.

"Salty," his said. "Aged."

"Mine too," Cato's beast said.

Damian and Cato's eyes met. He looked as terrified as Damian felt. These things were monsters. No doubt that they were demons from hell and they had no way of knowing how to kill them.

They needed Ryan desperately. He would know how to get out of this situation. Damian was doing a half-ass job compared to Ryan this entire mission. The fact they were still alive was pure luck.

Cato's monster leaned down towards his neck again but instead of another lick it bit him. Cato screamed out in pain as the creature clung onto his neck with its teeth like a vampire drinking his blood.

Damian used all his strength to get out of his monster's grasp but nothing he did mattered. Cato's eyes started to grow heavy and his breathing was weakening. The damn thing was killing him and all Damian could do was scream out in frustration.

Cato's beast brought its eyes up to stare at Damian. "You're next." Its grinning mouth dripped with Cato's blood.

"Don't kill it," Damian's monster grumbled. "We share."

"One bite?"

"They are weak creatures. It will die."

Damian couldn't keep his eyes off of Cato's. He looked tired, drained of energy but nowhere near death thank the gods. In the corner of his eye he saw Anna move. *Please no, baby. Stay still.*

"The female," his monster pointed at Anna. "Get it."

Cato's beast let go of him but he made no movement to attack. He was a little weaker than Damian thought.

"Stop!" Damian yelled.

"Silence," his monster growled.

The beast reached Anna who was lying face down in the dirt. He didn't remember laying her that way.

The beast grinned its bloody mouth in excitement. "She looks much fresher!" it exclaimed.

The beast turned Anna's body over and to Damian's surprise she stabbed it in the neck with a large jagged stick. It clutched its wound letting out a roar like a lion. He would have congratulated her if his monster didn't throw him into the top branches of a nearby tree like a plaything.

He fell down, hitting multiple branches along the way before landing on the ground knocking the breath out of him. He rolled over onto his stomach and spit out blood.

"Son of a bitch," he groaned and with much difficultly, pushed himself up to stand.

His monster was making its way over to a blue covered Anna while she repeatedly stabbed Cato's monster in the chest as she straddled it. Damian released a pistol from his side, shooting at the beast in hopes of doing some damage to it.

The bullets struck its back and Damian almost jumped with joy as blue blood oozed from its wounds down its gold armor. His beast thankfully changed course, coming at Damian once again rather than Anna. He emptied a clip into it but it kept coming.

As he reached for another gun he heard shots going off from behind the beast. Cato was propped up on his elbow; weakly aiming his gun at its back. His shots did the trick. The beast fell to its knees and started to crawl towards Damian. His persistence was commendable, but the thing was going to die.

He tossed his pistol aside and made his way towards the crawling beast. It had a large sword strapped to its back that Damian pulled free and with one quick motion chopped off its head. The separated cranium landed on his feet and he kicked it away like a soccer ball.

"That was gross," Cato croaked. He was holding onto his bleeding neck as he lay down in the dirt. Damian ran to him and started to take out a first aid kit from his pack but Cato paused his hands from working. "Go check on your girl real quick. I'll be fine."

Damian looked back over at Anna. She was still stabbing the dead monster with a stick and showed no signs of stopping.

"I'll be right back," he said to Cato who gave him a thumb up.

As soon as his hand touched her shoulder she swung the stick at him. He managed to catch her wrist before she dug it deep into his chest. His hand became sticky with blue blood.

She looked him up and down as if trying to figure out who he was until she broke down in tears and fell into his arms. The stick dropped out of her hand, collecting leaves around it until it rolled to a stop.

He cradled her as she cried. "It's okay babe, I promise." He kissed her hair and brushed the loose strands out of her face. "Just breathe, love."

"I'm going insane. I feel it," she cried. "I want to go back to my old life. I can't do this anymore."

"Yes, you can," he soothed her as he held her close to him. "You are one of the strongest women I have ever met, Anna. You are amazing in every sense of the word. I know you can do this."

"I can't. I'm not Julia. I'm not Aja. I will never live up to them. All of this is becoming too much. Less than a year ago none of this existed in my world and now I'm in some jacked up wonderland killing god knows what, and the end of the world is on our hands. I can't handle it anymore."

Damian closed his eyes and tried not to mentally beat himself up over the pressure she was feeling. It was his fault she was involved with all of this. Stress was obviously becoming too much for her but there was no turning back from this place.

"My love, please breathe." She was hysterically crying at this point. "I promise you, after all this is done we will go on vacation for a few years and get away."

"There is no way to escape this, Damian. This world you people have brought me into is messed up. How have you live like this for so long?" she asked.

Damian sighed. "Because we make a difference, Anna. We put others above our own lives. We protect those who cannot protect themselves as much as we possibly can. We can't do everything, but at least we make a small contribution to this messed up world."

Her breathing slowed down and she looked up at him. "You are a better person than I am then."

He shook his head. "You are new to it, Anna, my love. But your heart is so pure that the gods chose you for a reason. We are here to help save the mortals to the best of our ability and I know you believe in that too. We just have to push through all this insanity and I promise you, we will bring a semblance of peace back to everyone, including ourselves."

CHAPTER VIII

Julia

"WHAT THE HELL IS this?" Ryan asked.

They walked between two of the wide leg structures that held up the large coliseum shaped building. It had three levels, not included the ground floor outside, with a large fountain occupying the center of it.

The building itself wasn't what shocked them. The fountain was empty of water but instead was filled with various works of art that must have been inside the building. They were completely and utterly ruined.

It hurt her heart.

Art was something she cherished and here it was, lying in a heap with firewood stacked on top, ready to be destroyed. Zee walked up to the heap and pulled out a painting. It was an abstract piece.

This was from the human mind. It should all be cherished and not thrown away like garbage. What were the Risen thinking when they discarded these things? It was not religious in any sense. It was art, plain and simple.

She heard movement behind her and turned to face a few members of the Risen. The three of them instantly pulled up their bandanas over their mouths and the group of people stopped when they came into view. It was mostly men and a few women that Julia barely recognized. They held more firewood in their arms and dropped them on the art in the fountain.

"What are you guys doing here?" one of them asked.

"On break. Just walking around," Ryan answered. "What are you guys doing?"

"Burning stuff." The woman grinned and held up a gas can.

Julia felt sick to her stomach as she watched them work. The woman poured gas all over the paintings with excitement. Her lack of remorse baffled her. Even if Julia stopped them the damaged had already been done.

Her hands began to shake with anger.

She couldn't help it, she grabbed Ryan's hand and he thankfully didn't pull back. Once they lit the fire in front of her, tears threatened to spill down her cheeks and she faced Ryan to block out the view.

"Take me away from here," she begged. His eyes were a mixture of pity and sadness. "Please."

"Okay," he mumbled through his bandana and grabbed Zee's hand.

They walked away from the fire-dancing idiots who were gleeful cheering in their destruction of humanity. She had no idea the Risen were doing this and the next time she saw the

General he would get a piece of her mind. This was uncalled for and completely unforgivable.

They made it a block away when Ryan pulled both Zee and her along quicker. "Come on."

They found apartments that looked abandoned. More than likely the people that once resided in them were either dead or in the converting process.

Ryan broke a window to get in and they made their way through the empty building to the top floor. He picked the lock of an apartment and the three of them made their way into the dark room.

It was cozy and obviously belonged to a young woman who hadn't been in here in a while. There were vegetables rotting on the kitchen counter. It was a small space but she was glad to see there were at least two rooms.

"The sun is coming," Zee pointed out. "Maybe we should stay here for the day and sleep."

"The castle will be empty though and we need to search it," Ryan argued.

As much as she wanted to go search for Grace and Colette, they needed their rest. "Let's get some sleep."

"Are you sure?" The look of confusion on his face was apparent.

Her hands began to shake uncontrollably behind her back and she nodded. "Yes." She had to get away from them and take her tonic before her headache came back.

"I'll take this room," Julia mumbled heading the first door on the left. "You guys have a good night or day or whatever."

She closed the room door behind her and leaned up against it. Her body started to spasm as her mind raced about

Ryan. She missed him. Seeing him with Zee killed her inside. Most of all, she was beginning to regret joining the Risen. They were evil. She was becoming evil.

Her head hurt so badly she almost doubled over in pain. It was difficult to get out the flask with her shaking hands but she managed. She drank all of the liquid in her haste to feel better and sat down on the floor, learning against the door. She would have to deal with the headaches if they came up again until the got back to the Domus.

Relief flushed her body. Her headache subsided and her body began to relax as the tonic took over. She looked around the room in disgust. Stupid mortal was messy when she lived here. The sooner she got out of this stupid place and away from Ryan and Zee the better.

She stood up and begun to take her gear off. Thoughts of Aden flooded her mind and she smiled thinking of when she would return to him and the Risen, and away from the Warrior scum.

Ryan

Once Julia shut the door, Ryan and Zee exchanged awkward glances. Standing there in silence seemed ridiculous, however he was unsure how to act around Zee with Julia in the other room.

"Are you okay?"

Ryan nodded. "Yep."

"You seem tense."

Avoiding the mention of Julia he said, "I imagine it is because a large group of innocent women are being murdered as we speak and I am doing nothing about it." He finally decided to sit down on the little blue couch in the middle of the apartment.

"There is nothing you could have done, Ryan." Zee sat down next to him, slowly rubbing his back making his tension lessen. "If we tried to save them we would have gotten killed. There were too many of them. You are our best Warrior and now the leader of us all. The world would be doomed without you."

Ryan rubbed his jaw. He didn't want to lead the Warriors into a battle he didn't foresee them winning. They had to try at all costs, but with the Risen recruiting mortals, he had no idea how they could beat those odds. The only hope they had would be to recruit their own mortals but that would only be once they defeat the Brahmastra.

He stretched his arms up in the air looking sideways at Zee. Her dark hair shone in the fading moonlight that crept into the apartment. Green eyes sparkled back at him with a mischievous look in them. She was absolutely gorgeous right now.

"What?" She raised an eyebrow.

"Nothing."

"Liar."

"So." He grinned sheepishly.

Zee put her hand on his knee, rubbing up and down his leg making his body tense up at her touch. He had no idea as to why she made him feel nervous. Usually he portrayed the jerk that acted uninterested. Most women seemed to be attracted to that type of male. Or he would be funny to make them laugh. Girls loved to laugh, but Zee was different. She saw through it all.

"Whatcha thinking about?" She moved her hand up his thigh towards his hips.

"Nothing." He tried his best to act unaffected by her touch. He was not used to going this long without being with a woman and Julia had been his last.

Zee rolled her eyes, seemed to give up on her advance and stood up. "Alright, I guess it's time for bed."

"I'll take the couch of course." He felt relieved and disappointed at the same time.

"Oh no you're not," she declared, pulling his hand to led him to the other bedroom.

Given his weakened and frustrated state he followed her. As she closed the door he took in his surroundings. It was very contemporary with its black and white décor. There were a few splashes of deep purple throughout the room. He knew this had to be a young woman's apartment. No man would have purple lilies in a blown glass vase.

Zee dropped his hand and stood on one side of the bed. Ryan made his way to the other side and they stared at each other, a bed between them along with his confused feelings. She was coming on to him, that much was obvious, but could he do this with Julia in the next room?

"Are you going to take your gear off?" Zee finally spoke. Freeing her hair from being pulled back it draped down her shoulders like two black curtains.

A lump formed in his throat, and he tried to swallow it down. This was nerve wracking and he hated it.

"Is that okay?" He managed to keep his voice calm.

Zee nodded as she unstrapped her vest and tossed it on the ground. "Your turn." He kept his eyes on her as he took his vest off but he didn't stop there. His flak jacket was next, followed by the rest of his clothes until he was in his black briefs and tank. Zee looked him up and down.

"Why are you stopping?" she mused.

"I believe it is your turn now." He crossed his arms expecting her to challenge him.

Instead, Zee tossed her flak jacket on the ground and slowly peeled off her shirt. He had to admit; a woman in combat boots, black cargo pants and a bra was pretty damn sexy. He bit his lip as he watched her undress down to just her underwear.

He couldn't help that he was comparing her and Julia physically in his mind. Both were extremely fit but Julia was pale were as Zee was tan. Julia's long blonde hair was the completely opposite of Zee's black locks. Guilt settled in even thinking of another woman when Zee was revealing herself to him.

"Your turn." Zee shook him from his thoughts.

He laughed, "This isn't enough for your viewing pleasure?"

She shook her head. "Nope."

As soon as his head was free of his shirt he saw Zee crawling on the bed over to him. She seductively moved her hands up his chest placing them on his shoulders. He started to count to one hundred in his head to calm himself down. *One. Two. Three.*

"Your scars are just thin white lines now." She examined him. "Are you going to try to get rid of them totally?"

"No," he breathed. "I barely notice them anymore." *Twenty-three. Twenty-four. Twenty-five.*

"Amazing how quickly they disappeared." Her fingers traced the faded scars along his chest.

He closed his eyes enjoying the feeling until he was roughly pulled down on the bed. Landing on his back Zee straddle him and he smirked up at her. It was adorable how pleased she looked with herself.

"You could have just asked me to lay down." He placed his hands on her thighs. *Forty-seven. Forty-eight. Forty-nine.* "You don't have to force me into bed."

"No offense, Ryan," she said as she placed her hands on top of his. "But given your reputation I expected a little more effort on your part. You just stood there like a lost puppy or something."

"I like to play hard to get sometimes. Makes you work harder for my attention." His hands moved automatically up to her waist. "You are taking advantage of me, ma'am." *Seventy. Seventy-one. Seventy-two.*

She faked offense. "Advantage? Me? What a terrible accusation."

"Well when a woman body slams me on a bed I tend to feel violated."

"I think it is impossible for you to feel violated by a woman."

"It's a sad but true accusation, I will admit."

She cocked her head to the side. "I didn't peg you to be all prudish and what not. I feel offended for having to work extra hard to get you in bed."

Eighty... five? Six? Fuck this. Ryan flipped her beneath him with ease. "Well we can't have such a gorgeous creature feeling offended. Let me change that." He placed himself between her legs.

She grinned up at him with triumph. Opening her mouth

to say something he silenced her words with his lips. She parted her mouth for him. The kiss deepened, their tongues flicking against one another.

Zee broke her lips from his, moving her mouth to nibble at his neck. Any possible self restraint he had ceased when her teeth grazed his skin, making him grow achingly frustrated below. Her hips begun to move against his in an urgent need.

"Take your underwear off," she pleaded.

Without a second thought he kicked his underwear off and sat back on his legs. Ryan pulled her up by her hands to sit up. Her chest heaved with heavy breaths. Never taking his eyes off hers, he removed her sports bra and hooked his thumbs on the waistline of her underwear.

She stared at him hungrily, making him even more excited for her. "You ma'am, are a sight to see."

Zee shrugged her slim shoulders. "You're okay I guess." She looked down at his body and then back to his eyes with an amused expression. "Just kidding. I can see what all the hype is about. You're delicious to look at."

"Delicious? That's a new one." His arm wrapped around her back and he lowered her gently back down to the bed. Propping himself over her with his elbows, she wiggled below him. "Why are you so eager ma'am?" He nuzzled her neck leaving a trail of small kisses along her collarbone.

Her body arched up against his in a desperate attempt to satisfy her needs. "Just shut up and let's do this." Her mouth crashed against his and he was much obliged to follow instruction.

As soon as their bodies were connected she let out a low moan. Quickly he covered her mouth with his hand. He didn't want Julia to hear this. Even though she gave up her claim on him, he felt guilty for being with Zee.

Zee didn't mind being silenced, actually she seemed to relish in it as her hips moved expertly with his. Her body convulsed under his in no time. He loved how he affected women so easily, but more importantly he loved having a connection to another person.

Zee was mending the wounds in his heart that Julia had reopened though he doubted they would ever fully heal.

Chapter IX

Anna

S HE HAD HAD ENOUGH of this crap. This world was stupid and evil and freaking insane. She would rather forget this whole Immortal thing and go back to being just Anna. Life was so simple before.

Damian was right when he said she wasn't ready for this mission. He knew she was too weak for this nonsense. Damian was her only savior.

She remained cradled in his arms for the next few minutes. He had the patience of a saint. He just kept brushing her hair back, soothing her just like Nathan did when she was upset. It was a welcomed feeling. Her senses gradually returned to her along with her sanity.

"Not to rush you guys," Cato croaked. "But Damian, can you patch me up?"

Anna jumped out of Damian's arms feeling selfish for her momentary meltdown while Cato was bleeding. He was pale. Blood ran down his neck past his fingers that desperately tried to stop the blood loss.

Damian ran to him, dropping down to his knees while he removed supplies from his TacMed kit strapped to the front of his vest. He went to work on bandaging him up while Anna sat alone against a fallen tree trunk. Damian was so calm with Cato, as if he had done this a hundred times. He never once showed stress or worry for his friend, even as his hands became drenched with Cato's blood.

She couldn't watch it anymore. Her nerves were rattled and she wanted to throw up. Instead, she watched a beetle making its way past her towards a hole in the ground.

Time must have gone by quickly because Damian and Cato were both leaning against a tree. Cato's eyes were closed. *Oh God, please don't be dead.*

"That thing nearly ripped through your throat," Damian grumbled.

"No shit." Cato's eyes fluttered open. He winced when he turned his head to look at Damian. "Hot monsters are my weakness it seems."

"First Oracles, now this," Damian laughed. "I know you're having problems in the woman department, but resorting to flesh eating monsters is never the solution."

"Hardy, har, har." Cato rolled his eyes as a smirk took over his forced annoyance.

Damian shoved Cato's shoulder lightly, instantly looking guilty. "Oh shit, sorry."

Cato laughed, "I'll live."

"Barely."

"Pain killers are kicking in and the stitches are fine. No

worries." Cato pat Damian on the leg in reassurance. "How are you doing over there, Anna?"

She hugged her knees to her chest. "Sorry I freaked out on you guys."

"I think you actually saved Cato's ass by freaking out so no worries." Damian winked at her. "I think we better stay here for awhile and get some rest. I'll take first watch after we eat."

No one opposed.

They sat there eating granola bars and dried fruits from their packs, which made Anna feel somewhat better. She didn't realize how hungry she was. Exhaustion was her next hurdle to face.

Cato fell asleep as soon as his head hit his pack leaving Anna and Damian to sit in silence. She slowly chewed on her dried fruit bar and took a drink out of her canteen. The color in Cato's face seemed to be returning. Damian possibly used some old ancient medicine to heal him quicker because the amount of blood Cato lost would take a normal person quite awhile to bounce back.

"How are you feeling?" Damian broke her thoughts.

"Hmm?" She realized she was starring at Cato.

"Your neck." He pointed at her vetala bite.

"Oh." She almost forgot about it and now that she remembered, it started to sting. "It's fine. I'm not going to turn into anything am I?"

Damian chuckled, "Highly doubtful." His amusement faltered as they looked in each other's eyes. His expression softened, pity lying beneath the surface of those pretty brown eyes of his.

"How do you think Ryan and Julia are doing?" She wanted to change the subject. Damian was undoubtedly beating himself up internally for bringing her here.

Their eye contact was lost when Damian looked down towards the ground. "I'm not sure. He does well in the mortal world, but he forgets that he is human. Ryan lives like he is some sort of invincible god. I would say Julia will keep him grounded, but with her attitude lately who knows."

"You suspect she's a traitor?" Anna asked.

Damian nodded. "Yes."

"Not to sound like a terrible person but don't you guys kill traitors?" The look he gave her sent chills down her spine. He was obviously thinking about this as well. "I mean, I really liked her at first, a lot actually. I thought we were becoming close. But now I pretty much hate her freaking guts."

Damian crawled over to her; draping his arm over her shoulder he pulled her close against his body. "Julia is a tough situation. We can't prove she is a traitor exactly. If she weren't, she would still be condemned to death. We have known her for her entire life and something is wrong. She isn't Julia. I don't know what it is but Aden has done something to her and it's not just a cut and dry case."

"Well, Aden is definitely a traitor and Ryan hates him. Why don't you just kill him?" She hated how casual that sounded coming from her lips. Was death becoming so normal for her? "Problem solved."

"As much as Ryan hates him I don't think he would condemn Aden to death without the proper evidence. He's not that cruel. At least not anymore. We operate with a system where the proof has to absolutely be there, otherwise people are killed without question."

"That's a stupid system," Anna huffed.

"It's not perfect, but no Immortal damns another without proof. It's an unwritten law to us."

"So I could call you one and you would die?" Anna asked raising an eyebrow. "Easy as that?"

"Basically." Damian nodded. "We can't take any chances that someone innocent could be killed."

"Stupid."

"Agreed." He kissed her forehead. "Get some sleep love."

Anna snuggled into his chest the best she could. His gear was somewhat in the way but who cared? She was tired enough she could probably sleep on a bed of nails.

"Why do you think the gods aren't intervening?" she asked.

"Best guess?"

"Yeah."

"Free will," Damian answered. "It is a terrible but beautiful thing."

"I heard they were starting to die from no one believing in them." Anna yawned. "That should be incentive enough to fight for yourself."

"That's what they hired us for." She saw him smile in the corner of her eye. "Apollo helped after all. He must care about his existence. I am sure they all do, but it really is up to us. They must have faith in us as well."

Anna would never understand these stupid rules. The gods have power, they should use it and quit letting so many people die. If anything ever happened to Damian she knew her faith would be shaken down to its core.

"I think it's stupid, but whatever. You weird old people and your traditions." Anna smirked, hoping to lighten the mood with him. She still felt uneasy in this place and wanted to leave but she had to pretend to be strong. No more going crazy and stabbing dead monsters. Damian wouldn't be able to function correctly if he was constantly worried about her.

"Can I ask you something, Anna?" Damian's voice shook.

Anna looked up at him warily. "What?"

Clearing his throat he asked, "Have you ever thought about marriage?"

Her sleepy eyes widened. "W-what kind of question is that right now?" she stammered. "Marriage? What? I mean, I don't know. It's... well... I don't know."

A little black box appeared in front of her face, sitting innocently in Damian's shaking hand. She couldn't force her eyes to his. Instead they remained locked on the little box that was about to send her into a blubbering mess.

"I'm not entirely sure what the proper customs of today's world are or what is deemed suitable when asking you this. Normally, I would go to closest male relative of yours and have it contracted with a dowry set in place." He cleared his throat. "I think I am supposed to kneel but since we are both down here I bet it works better."

"You sound dumb right now and I'm freaking out." She wanted to laugh at how pathetic he was with modern day traditions, but mostly she was panicking inside at what he was about to ask her.

Damian adjusted himself to face her. He opened the box and inside was a large diamond ring. She kept looking back and forth from the ring to his eyes until he caught her by the chin. Peering deeply into her very being, as if he could penetrate her soul with his gaze alone.

"In case I don't get to ask later..." He took her left hand and pressed it softly to his lips. "Will you marry me, Anna?"

CHAPTER X

Ryan

H E HAD MADE IT to the top of the wall of the citadel and leapt down into the chaos below. His armor shone in the sunlight making him appear as a god. Three guards flanked him almost instantly as they attacked with full force. The urgency in the battle was the same as it always was but it still brought his heart jumping out of his chest. Swords clashed against one another and sweat drenched his body as they fought.

Nothing was so intoxicating as fighting for your life. The will power and animalistic instincts. Every ounce of his being was primal as the attack continued.

His sword thrust deep into the belly of the barbarian before him, his eyes already turned glassy before the sword slipped from his insides. A smile crept to his lips. Covered in the blood of his enemy, he wanted more. Craved more.

The man to his right fell. An arrow had struck through his head killing him instantly. There was no time for pause.

A stinging pain crashed into his ribs just under his breast. He looked down as an arrow stuck out of his body. Breathing became increasingly difficult, but he had to protect himself. The barbarians gave no pity to his current state, as would be expected. His sword found one more man before he fell down to his knees unable to postpone his weakened state.

The last two men at his side covered him with a shield while the other fought to keep more attackers away. With much difficultly he stood up to exit their dire situation until he felt his neck hit hard with a heavy object from behind. The force of the blow made his body fall back into the wall and he used it for support.

The enemy was gathering quickly around him. His strength was gone. His vision grew weary and he begun to fade away losing all sense of his surroundings.

He woke inside a tent as the end of the arrow was being sawed off. A sharp and unbearable pain shot through his chest as the end of the arrow was pulled from his body. He fell again into darkness. The pain and blood loss was too much even for him.

Julia

Waking up after a long night is never easy but she managed to do it. After getting dressed back into her gear Julia made her way out into the living room. Ryan and Zee sat at the table eating dry cereal. As soon as he caught sight of Julia he let go of Zee's hand. Looking like a kid that got caught with his hand in the cookie jar, he offered her a bowl.

Julia hated the stuff but she took it without complaint and started to munch of the sugar coated flakes. Sitting in a recliner she watched as the sun started to set. She was anxious to get going. This whole experience needed to be over with so she could get back to her spot within the Risen.

Ryan glanced at her. "So did you sleep well?" He was trying to make small talk and she was nowhere near in the mood for it. "You look rested."

"Yeah," she mumbled while she glared at him.

Guilt ridden eyes darted between her and Zee. Something must have happened between the two of them because this behavior was foreign to see on Ryan. Whatever it was, his nervous ticks were agitating.

"How about you guys?" She bit the inside of her lip but her scowl managed to shine through. "Did you sleep well?" There was an obvious impolite tone to her voice.

Ryan tapped his fingers along the table, contemplation was written all over his face and his dodging eyes. Her suspicions were growing now.

"We didn't do much sleeping actually." Zee munched on her cereal starring directly at Julia. The casual indifference plastered all over her face made Julia's body flush with anger.

Ryan looked between them again and rubbed his head in exasperation. Julia felt something heavy in her chest as she watched his reaction. It didn't help that Zee seemed proud of herself in some way. Ryan was making it very obvious as to what they did while she slept. He never looked guilty.

"So do you always spread your legs so quickly for men you are attracted to or was last night a special occasion?" Julia took another bite of her cereal and stared at Zee as casually as she could muster. Inside she felt a burning sensation to punch her though.

Zee shrugged. "I just had a feeling his last sexual experience was a tad boring. Needed to spice it up a bit."

"I bet you have plenty of experience with that." Julia smiled sweetly. "Tell me Ryan, could you even feel any sensation? I only ask because things tend to loosen up down there for whores."

Ryan's eyes grew wide. "I'm just going to go in the—"

"Stay," Zee demanded, her eyes never leaving Julia's.

Ryan remained where he was and Julia laughed. "Have him trained already? I never thought someone as unimpressive as you would tame Ryan. After all, none of these Immortals even recognize you."

"I'm sure they know you perfectly well," Zee spat.

"Most Immortals do seeing as I am a top ranked Warrior." Julia crossed her legs. "Where as you, in so many ways, remain on bottom. As a last resort."

"Topped ranked Warrior or not." Zee took a bite. "It's quite obvious you're a traitor. If it weren't for us trying to save Grace and Colette I probably would have stabbed you myself by now."

"Are you accusing me?" Julia was surprised Zee actually had some sort of intelligence. She was not exactly secretive of her knowledge of this place. She obviously knew a lot but there was no way around it. Any information given to Ryan got her closer to saving her family.

Zee grabbed Ryan's hand in hers. "I am not accusing. I am one hundred percent sure you're one of the Risen's little bitches."

Julia grabbed a dagger out of her sheath and lunged towards Zee. Ryan blocked her path stopping her from getting to the little skank in front of her. Zee looked pleased with herself as she continued to eat her cereal.

"Move," Julia demanded.

Ryan blocked her way when she tried to side step around him again. "Calm down."

"Do you hear what your whore is calling me?" Julia hissed. "Do you know what the Council will do if they hear that accusation?"

Ryan sighed deeply and spoke low, "I know what they would do, Julia. You have to admit that you're different. Can you really blame us for thinking the worst?"

"So you believe her now?" Julia asked.

Ryan shrugged. "I can't think of any other explanation. When I first saw you with Aden you were sweet and sort of yourself still, but now you're just cold hearted. I don't know what is going on with you, but you're turning into a bitch."

Julia slapped him in the face. "You bastard." There was a red handprint left on his cheek.

"I would prefer it if you didn't touch my boyfriend," Zee called around Ryan.

He closed his eyes with his back to Zee. Julia saw something painful wash over his face. Regret? Perhaps he didn't want Julia to know it was something serious with Zee? She had no idea but she felt triumphant. He still had feelings for her. She needed to use that to her advantage. Zee could turn Ryan against her if couldn't control him and she couldn't have that. Not while she still needed to use him.

"Ryan, can I talk to you privately?" Julia forced her voice low.

'No, you can't." Zee smiled sweetly. "Sorry."

"Yes, you can." Ryan glared back at Zee and to Julia's surprise the girl finally shut up.

Julia pulled Ryan into her temporary room and closed the door behind her. "Do you really think that?" She leaned against the door looking timid as possible.

Ryan shrugged. "I don't know what to think, Julia."

"Ryan, you know me and you know I would never ever abandon the Immortals. Aden or no Aden." She feigned being hurt and she could see doubt in his eyes. "Please don't believe that nonsense."

"You are too different." He shook his head. He was keeping his distance from her though. "I can't ignore that fact."

"So are you," she countered. "I can't believe you would think I am capable of being a traitor."

"I'm not entirely sure it's your fault," Ryan said thoughtfully. "I don't know what it is," he finished.

"I've killed members of the Risen. I am trying to break out our fellow Warriors and above all I am working with you. The Risen's most wanted. How does that spell out traitor in your eyes?" She had no idea how else to convince him but she had to try something. "You are believing a woman you hardly know over me. How is that fair?"

"It's not her that is making me think this way about you, Julia. It's all you." Ryan finally made his way towards her. Standing directly in front of her his eyes looked into hers filled with sadness, his forehead creased in confusion. Just as she thought he was going to kiss her he grabbed the door handle. "We are done talking. The sun is down, let's go now."

Julia had to make one last attempt. "Please don't believe

this, Ryan." She put her hand on his cheek. The warmth of his skin sent a shiver down her spine and his eyes closed at her touch. "I can't live with you thinking that about me."

Ryan's voice was hoarse when he spoke, "I would never condemn you without knowing for sure."

"I don't care about being condemned. I just care about how differently you are looking at me and it breaks my heart." Julia managed to make her eyes water. "I miss you terribly, Ryan."

"I miss you too," he whispered as he opened the door, leaving her alone.

They made their way back towards the castle designed building after the sun was completely set. Julia cringed seeing the flames coming from of the center of the circular building, they must still be burning things from within the museums. No matter what her feelings were towards religion; art was innocent to her. It was odd that she valued a few strokes of paint over mortal lives.

Ryan's distance from both Zee and herself gave her confidence that her tactic had worked. Any doubt she could place in his mind would work for now. Just one more day and she was done with the charade, or at least until the General told her otherwise.

Making their way around the circular building, Ryan stopped in his tracks.

"Holy shit." He jumped back into Zee almost knocking her over in the process.

Julia covered her mouth to stop from laughing out loud. He'd almost run straight into a tall dark statue of six men in long cloaks. A few were grabbing their heads as if they were in anguish and their tattered clothes hung off their malnourished bodies.

"You okay there?" Zee chuckled as Ryan shook his hands to let his nerves escape.

"Yep," he grumbled.

"Are your people going to destroy this statue today or tomorrow?" Zee turned to Julia. "Destroying the beauty in the world seems to be your people's bread and butter."

She decided to ignore her instead of giving her the satisfaction of a response. Ryan was frustrating her with his continuous questions and Zee's accusations were completely obnoxious, even if they were right. She wanted to get away from them and concentrate on the task at hand of saving Grace and Colette.

She made her way past one of the smaller castle buildings towards the larger one. This place was utterly confusing. There were far too many buildings. Some were of modern design, some were middle ages, or Greek. The General should have picked a more connected location than this spaced out fortress.

Just as she was about to step out into the open Ryan forced her onto her backside.

"What the hell?" His hand went over her mouth, muffling the obscenities that were on her tongue.

"Did you not see the group of Risen members right in front of you?" he hissed in her ear. There were four men up ahead from what she could see around the shrubbery. "You two stay here," Ryan whispered. "I'll handle this."

"By yourself?" Zee half-whispered half-yelled. "Why?"

"They are armed with swords only. Obviously it is their strong suit and no offense, but you two are mostly gun savvy. Don't worry it'll be a walk in the park."

Ryan knew perfectly well that she was capable with a sword but Zee on the other hand was more than likely inexperienced. What a gentleman, sparing his girlfriends feelings. Julia rolled her eyes, crouching down in the grass as she watched Ryan stalk his prey.

He snuck up behind one man, pulling his sword slowly out of its scabbard and with one swift motion Ryan decapitated him. Realizing what happened, another man charged at Ryan. Her eyes went wide when Ryan punted the severed head at the charging man, who caught it out of instinct with a look of disgust on his face. With the man distracted, Ryan thrust the sword into his chest and both head and man fell to the ground in a heap of carnage.

"It's like watching a dance isn't it?" Zee stood behind her.

Julia rolled her eyes, but agreed. He was rather graceful. "Yes."

"I know you two have a past, but I won't let you hurt him." Zee sat down next to her as they watched Ryan work. "When the time comes and your treachery is fully apparent I won't hesitate to kill you."

"Is that so?" Julia asked amused.

"He won't be able to do it and I doubt he will let anyone harm you. I won't let you hurt that man. He deserves to be happy and you are nothing but a wolf in sheep's skin. I'm sorry it's come to this because I once looked up to you. Oh shit, one of them is coming over here."

Julia and Zee stood up as the man ran towards them

while Ryan parried with the remaining soldier. They hid be-hind the bushes and once the man ran through the bushes Julia jumped on his back and stabbed him in the chest. He fell to the ground with a soft thud, his hand twitched at his side as he bled to death.

"Damn." Zee looked the man up and down. "The coward never saw it coming."

"Yeah." Julia went to stand next to her. Taking a deep breath she thrust her bloodied blade into Zee's stomach. "Bet you didn't either."

Julia twisted the blade, satisfaction spread through her core when she saw the anguish in Zee's face. Once she pulled the blade out of Zee's body the woman dropped to her knees, desperately clinging to her wound. But there was no use; Julia had damaged her organs beyond repair.

Zee's eyes finally met her own, surprisingly she smiled up at her with a bloody grin. "I knew it."

"Yeah, well too bad you can't prove it." Julia kicked her in the chest.

Zee's back hit the grass and a small gasp escaped from her lips. "He will find out eventually, Julia. About everything." She coughed and blood trickled out of her mouth. "May the gods curse you, viper."

Julia squat down next to her body and watched as the life left her eyes.

"So pathetic," she sneered, wiping the bloodied blade on Zee's chest.

With her dagger she cut her own arm a few times, just enough to draw blood. She had to make it look like she was hurt in the attack. Quickly, she stuck Zee's dagger into the man Julia killed. She pried his sword from his death grip and stabbed it into Zee's stomach. Dragging the bodies closer together she hoped it looked as if they stabbed each other at the same time.

It wasn't hard covering up the crime scene. Ryan had stabbed the last man standing and was making his way over to her. With a deep breath she punched herself hard in the jaw, which should leave a nice red mark on her face. Positioning herself on the ground she pretended to be knocked out face down just before she heard footsteps crunching towards her in the grass.

"Oh… G-gods," Ryan stammered. She heard him shuffle around the grass for a moment until she felt his presence.

He flipped her over on her back but she kept her eyes closed. "Julia. Julia wake up… Please love, wake up." His voice wavered in a heartbreaking cry.

The top half of her body was lifted into his arms, leaning against his chest. He hastily took her helmet off. It felt good when he brushed her loose hair out of her face, but shock rushed throughout her body when she felt a drop of liquid hit her cheek. He was crying. Literally crying. *Ryan never cries.*

"Julia." He kissed her forehead. "Please wake up. I can't loose you too. Not you, baby… please."

He smacked her cheeks lightly to wake her and she fluttered her eyes open.

"Ryan?" she groaned.

His cheeks were streaked with tears but he smiled through them as he looked down her. "Thank the Gods." He held her tightly to him. "Are you hurt? You're bleeding. Is it serious?"

She smacked his arm lightly. "Can't breathe."

"Sorry," he said letting her go slightly. "Let me see you."

"I'm fine, Ryan. Just a few cuts on my arm and a bruised jaw." She patted him on the cheek.

"I should never have left you two." His eyes darkened with disgust.

"Why? What happened?" Julia looked around. When her eyes connected with Zee's body her hands went to her mouth in shock. "Oh no."

Ryan's tears didn't stop. He looked at Julia as if begging her to come up with a solution. He looked completely lost and it was all her fault. Did she just break the unbreakable man? Did Zee's death cause more problems than it solved? She hoped not.

"She's dead, Julia." He dropped his head against her chest. She put her arms around him, comforting him against her body. "It's all my fault."

"No, it's not." She tried to console him by stroking the bare skin on his head soothingly. "I'm so sorry. I wish I would have fought him harder."

His arms grasped her tightly pulling her against him. He was grief stricken like she had never seen. It was disturbing to watch a man who took countless lives for many years, cry over one fallen person.

"I don't know what to do," he croaked.

"It's okay." Julia grinned wickedly as his face hid against her lap. "I'm here."

Chapter XI

Anna

AFTER A NIGHT'S SLEEP, or day's sleep, who could tell in this place, Anna felt better. Her freak out over all the supernatural nonsense seemed to diminish over night and her courage came back. She felt stupid for freaking out like that. Part of her hoped is was the vetalas fault but in reality she knew she'd just lost control of herself.

She lifted her head up off of Damian's lap and immediately felt how stiff her neck was. Damian was still fast asleep. Cato however, was sitting up skipping pebbles off the ground and into a small fire they'd created before going to sleep.

It was still dark here. Did the sun ever come out?

"Hey," she said lazily to Cato. He looked up at her with an amused expression. "What?"

"You talk in your sleep, you know." He smirked, tossing another pebble in the fire.

Anna groaned, moving away from Damian as gently as

she could. He was still fast asleep and she didn't want to wake him. He looked so peaceful.

"What did I say?" she grumbled.

Cato shrugged. "That you are secretly in love with me." Anna's eyes widened while Cato stifled a laugh. "I'm kidding."

"Jerk." She looked into the flames and watched as they danced, licking around the logs like a serpents tongue. "But really?"

"But really, you said something about someone named Nathan. Also marriage." He must have seen her shocked expression and said, "Don't worry I won't say anything to Damian. That's the guy you were with when you were mortal right?"

Anna nodded. "Yeah."

"It's hard to let go of people that were taken from you. I get it." He grimaced. "When my parents died I was totally lost."

"You seemed to have turned out fine."

"Well, not many people know, but I got into a lot of trouble after they died. I was in constant fights and drank all the time. If I were mortal I bet I would have died from an overdose on multiple occasions. Not even Julia knew about it," Cato admitted.

"What changed?" Anna was intrigued. She knew so little about Cato.

Cato lay on his side, propping his head up with his arm. "The honest answer?"

"Yeah."

"Ryan." She must have looked baffled because he tried suppressing a grin. "Surprise, surprise."

"No way," she laughed. "Fighting and drinking is his cup of tea."

Cato shrugged. "He's known me since I was born and when my parents were both gone he took it upon himself to help me out. He found me in a brothel somewhere in Paris when I went missing for a few months and sort of kicked my ass."

"He beat you up? That's terrible!" she exclaimed.

"I was sort of M.I.A. off and on for a few years. I was on their team and he had been looking for me I guess. He was super mad. I felt like I was being scolded by my father again." He smiled to himself. "After he knocked me unconscious he took the drugs and alcohol away. Hell, he even paid my bill for the whores because I couldn't."

"Whores? As in plural." She looked at Cato in a new light. "I can't believe Ryan would even bother."

"Ryan is a much better person than you give him credit for," Cato said.

"He really hasn't made a positive impact on me since the day I met you three." She shrugged. "He's always been a smartass or rude to me. On occasion he seemed to give a damn but I don't know."

"The guy is a softy at heart. Believe me. I've been with those two for a long time and Ryan is just desperate for someone to make him whole again." Cato yawned. "He's been through more than anyone in this world could imagine. That asshole exterior is just a front."

"And here I had him pegged as a big ol' douche and now I feel bad for the guy. Thanks," she muttered.

Cato had a nice smile. She could see the resemblance with Julia, when she was nice, and it made her feel closer to him for some reason. "Like I said, I went off the deep end. He brought me back." He studied his hands and looked back up at her bashfully. "I don't know why I am telling you this."

"Me either but I am glad you did." She really was. "But whores? Really?"

He laughed out loud now. "Yeah. Don't tell Julia. She'll kill me. 'Treat your body like a temple' she would always say." His face grew sullen at the mention of his sister.

Anna crawled over to Cato, sitting next to him she grabbed his hand and to her surprise he let her. "I hope she will be okay," she murmured.

Cato made no attempt to pull away from her. "I can't lose her too, Anna. I've lost my entire family and I can't do it again. I won't. Something is wrong with her. I just don't know how to fix it."

"What are you two talking about?" Damian yawned, stretching his arms up in the air. Anna was slightly relieved for the interruption. Cato was so sad about Julia and she really had nothing to say to make him feel better.

Cato shrugged. "This and that." Their hands released. "Sleep good?"

"My butt cheeks are numb, but that's fine," he cracked his neck, sending chills down Anna's spine. "Should we get going?"

"I want to say no but the correct answer would be yes." Cato scooped up dirt in his hands then dumped it on the fire until the flames died out. With their gear and belongings gathered up they were on their way. "So what other hell are we going to encounter today guys? Face melting demons? Sexy ladies that turn into three headed dogs?"

Anna resisted the urge to smack him upside the head. "Thanks for jinxing it."

"I think our very presence in this place is the ultimate jinx," Cato countered.

She had to agree with that statement.

Cato took the lead again with Damian the rear. In normal circumstances she would have hated how protective they were of her, but right now she was beyond grateful. This place was a living nightmare.

Damian put his hand gently on her shoulder and she felt a sense of calm rush over her. He had that way about him that made her feel better.

"How are you doing love?" he asked.

"Better," she said honestly. "Just waiting for the next bundle of joy to pop up out of nowhere."

They stopped for a brief moment so he could squeeze the back of her body to his front in a loving hug and they continued on through the forest. She desperately wished they would end up in Shambhala and soon. The quicker they got back to the Domus the better.

She looked up towards the sky. The stars barely peaked through the tree branches. It was the one thing that grounded her, that made her feel like she was even close to the normal world and that this hell was only temporary. It made her wonder though, was this even the same sky as the mortal world?

Cato started to whistle a song that was not familiar to her, Damian groan behind them. "Not that again."

Cato whistled even louder in spite and Damian reached around Anna to smack Cato's helmet. That only seemed to make him whistle louder.

"What exactly is he whistling?" she asked. It sounded like some sort of tune a fairy would play in a cartoon on a pipe or something.

"A song he made up to impress a nymph a long time ago," Damian yelled over the whistling. "Needless to say she wasn't impressed."

"How dare her!" Anna feigned surprise while Cato whistled on as happy as could be.

Damian found a pair of earplugs to drown out the noise in his pockets. They continued on for about ten minutes before she was sick of it herself.

"Enough." She smacked him upside the head.

Cato stopped and stretched out his jaw. "Rude much?"

"No, but you are," she teased.

"I'm bored. You two aren't talking. Therefore I whistle. Get over it," he said simply. She wondered if he was partly insane or if he had a little brother syndrome with Damian and Ryan.

She gave Damian a thumb up to let him know it was okay to hear again.

"Thank the Gods," Damian said as he plucked the earplugs from his ears.

"Thank dry mouth." Cato took a drink out of his canteen. "I think I see an end."

Anna looked around Cato and her heart seemed to fly up into the heavens. She could see a treeless area that looked gorgeous as well as inviting. It was full of lush rolling grass and flowers were spread all around like some sort of Eden. The sky was bright and sunny there too. As if someone took a picture of the night and placed it right by a picture of the day with no variance separating the harsh differences.

The three of them ran towards the end of the forest. It quickly turned into a race and Anna was in the led. Cato, with his long legs, whizzed past her and just as he was about to reach the clearing Anna found herself face first on the ground.

Looking for the cause of her fall she saw vines slithering their way up her legs, preventing her from moving as their grip tightened around her body. Anna screamed, but the sound of her voice was quickly muffled when a bundle of vines wrapped around her mouth to silence her.

She strained to look for Damian and Cato but she was held down too tightly. Her entire body was wrapped in vines like a cocoon. Tears sprung to her eyes as it squeezed her tight like a hundred snakes constricting around her. Not even the word 'help' could leave her lips.

Julia

"Ryan, we have to go."

He wouldn't move away from Zee. Instead, he lay over her body and wouldn't stop praying. Ryan never prayed. She knew he believed in the Gods but he was not the type to talk to them. He always told her if they wanted to help they would. Which gave her even more incentive to despise them. They never cared.

She put her hand on his shoulder and his body tensed beneath her touch, his prayers silenced. "Please, Ryan."

"I can't leave her body here," his voice was strained. "If she doesn't receive the proper rights her soul cannot go to the heavens."

"We will come back for her, I promise," Julia urged. "We have to get going. There is nothing we can do for her."

"It's my fault." He kept repeating this same thing over and over. She was getting annoyed with this now. She died, so what? *Boohoo.* "Why didn't I let you guys come with me? Why did I insist on you staying behind?"

"Because you thought you were protecting us, Ryan. This isn't your fault. Please let's get going. Grace and Colette don't have much time."

Ryan finally sat up, grabbed Zee's limp hand and kissed her palm. He gently placed her hands over her chest and bowed his head. "I'm so sorry," he said in a whisper.

She grabbed his elbow and he reluctantly stood. They really needed to get out of this area before anyone noticed the lack of patrol. "I promise we will come back for her, Ryan."

His eyes looked into her and they were no longer filled with sadness. If anything they were full of fury right now and that meant Ryan was about to lose control. She should have waited to kill the little brat.

Ryan turned and made a beeline towards the red sandstone building walking right through the arched doors. All caution was out the window. The only thing that seemed to be on his mind was vengeance.

She caught up with him as he made his way into a large room. There were two rows of columned arches down the center of the room reaching from one end to the other. The columns were lovely. Each was colored a deep brown, grey and white. The tops of the arches were an off white color that made the brown in the columns pop splendidly.

"Will you stop," she whispered angrily. "Do you want us to get caught?"

"I don't care anymore, Julia." His eyes blazed in anger. "I want to kill them all. I don't care who they are or what reason they have joined, I want them all dead."

"With that thinking you're dooming Grace and Colette to the same fate as Zee." She wanted to scream at him but she settled for a harsh whisper. "Stop and think. Act like the man I know and calm yourself."

He closed his eyes and she was hoping that meant he was calming himself but then he punched a nearby column, breaking pieces off. That was impossible. It had to be. His hand should be broken but he showed no sign of injury.

Her eyes widened as the flakes of dust from the column settled to the ground. It wasn't often she was frightened but Ryan was a force to be reckoned with right now. Ryan clenched his fists as he faced the column he victimized.

"Umm," she started, "Ryan?"

"What?" he snapped at her.

"What can I do?" Her voice cracked from what she could only assume was fear. "I don't know what to do."

"It's funny isn't it?" he started. "The person I love doesn't want me yet survives and the one person who stood by my side is dead. I am cursed."

"You aren't cursed Ryan. I'm really sorry this is happening but we must get moving. We are in the enemy's lair and we are looking for two of our own. If they have any chance of survival we need to find them soon."

Ryan shoulders dropped. He seemed to acknowledge the truth. Looking down towards the East and West ends of the great hall he asked, "Where do we go?"

Under another set of low archways she could make out two stairways that sat side by side going up in opposite directions. "Those must go up top but we should look down here first."

"East or West?"

"East." Sad and angry Ryan was not fun to be around. She preferred the smartass version.

They made their way through the open wooden arched door and into a small hallway. It looked rather out of place given it seemed fit for a mortal's hospital waiting room. After all, they were just in a fairly Romanesque, early Gothic designed great hall. They walked through another wooden arched doorway that led into a smaller room, much like the great hall they encountered.

This room resembled a small cathedral given there were so many arches around. Arched windows ran along the ceiling and archways connected columns along the sides of the room as well. At the very East end there were even more arched wooden doors.

They walked up three steps at the other end of the room and she had another feeling of being in a place of worship or a scholarly atmosphere. Unlike the other two rooms that were extravagantly white, this one had brownish red bricks much like the exterior of the building, decorated with dark wood trimming all around. The entire room was one long arch, a vault ceiling, with rib like cross sections along the top and high ample arched windows lined down the sides of the room. It was beautiful.

This gorgeous place was plagued though. Many instruments of torture were set out on tables throughout the room;

some colored with blood. Her mind wondered to how they were used until movement caught her eye at the end of the long room.

It was Grace and Colette.

She ran to them and nearly cried at the sight before her. They were chained to two chairs facing back to back. Colette's long brown hair was chopped off to her ears. But what Julia feared the most was all the blood they were covered in.

Grace was unconscious. Colette's face had a mixture of blood and tear streaks running down her cheeks. Her mouth was covered with tape and her eyes told Julia that she was furious for her being there. She couldn't understand a word Colette was muffling so she grabbed one end of the tape and ripped it off.

"Sorry."

Colette screamed at her, "Get out! Get out the both of you, it's a trap!"

Julia turned around just in time to see Ryan plucking a dart out of his neck. He looked at her with a dazed expression and he fell to his knees. She ran towards him before his head hit the floor. Her heart pounded and she wondered why she cared about his safety.

As she cradled him against her body a furious Aden rushed towards her. "Quit touching him and get up." He yanked on her arm dragging her away from Ryan. "Out!" He pointed towards the arch room.

Julia dutifully made her way into the next room, but not before seeing Aden kick an unconscious Ryan in the stomach.

"Hang him from the ceiling," Aden barked at the other Risen members that filed inside the room.

She failed. Her friends were doomed.

Aden stalked his way towards her in the arch room. Grabbing her by the throat he slammed her back against the nearest white column. "How dare you betray us," he spat. His hand squeezed harder around her throat making it difficult to breath.

"I didn't," she managed to choke out. "Aden, I can't breathe."

He squeezed tighter. "You came with him and attempted to save those two. In what world is that not betrayal?"

"I... can't... breathe," she choked as her vision grew hazy. Her knees grew weak until she felt his hand leave her throat entirely.

Falling to her knees she grasped her neck as if that would help. Someone else was gasping for breath now and she looked up to see the General in his long black cloak gripping Aden's throat.

"I should kill you for putting a hand on her." His voice boomed throughout the room.

Aden coughed out, "Forgive me, my lord. Please."

The General dropped him to the ground and held his hand out to Julia. She took it gratefully, righting herself all the while fearing what was going to happen next. He was not known for his mercy.

"Should I?" the General's rough voice asked from under his hood.

"My lord?" she asked.

"Forgive him?" She felt his eyes on her, though to this day she had never seen his face.

"Yes," she answered and then added, "please."

"Fine. Now that that's settled, why are you here, Julia?"

"I am sorry my lord but I couldn't stand to watch Grace and Colette suffer. I know they are Warriors but my heart couldn't take it. They mean the world to me."

"I understand," he said. "However, you understand why I have been doing what I have, don't you? I want to change them. I want them on our side and with you. You see that don't you?"

Julia nodded. "Please, if you just let me try my own way I know I can make them see the light."

He seemed to ponder her statement for a moment. She had to try something, anything to stop the torture that had fallen on the closest people to family she had. Cato was her brother, but in all honesty he was becoming frustrating to deal with.

"To show a leap of faith, Julia, I will let you try. They seem utterly unresponsive to my methods. Perhaps we need another way of going about it."

"But my lord," Aden whined, "they cannot be allowed to live without conversion."

"They can and they will," the General boomed. Julia feared for Aden's safety if he didn't remain silent. He complained a lot but she was glad for the chance to do things her way. "As for Ryan, he is a lost cause. He will never succumb to our ways. Kill him, Aden. I don't care."

"No," Julia blurted out.

"Excuse me?" The General towered over her. "I offer you what you wish and you defy my commands?"

Fear rose within her. "No my lord, I just think that he is valuable. If we change Ryan then the rest of the Warriors will follow. The less Immortals that die the better, correct?"

His breathing was the only sound for a minute. The anticipation was unnerving. "I'm not convinced," he finally said.

"What if we try your way once more? Knock me out and hang me opposite of him. If he fears for my life we could force him to join. Let me try for a few days my way and if he doesn't change his mind I will kill him myself."

"Who's to say he would go for that?" Aden laughed. "He knows we are together. Do you really think he isn't suspicious of you?"

"He won't be once he see's me tied up with you hurting me," Julia countered.

"Absolutely out of the question," the General growled.

"Nothing serious," she insisted. "Just a few small cuts here or there and maybe a slap or two. I will be fine, I promise. If it helps save the lives of our people it's worth it. Please. I've been through worse."

The General grasp the hilt of his sword tightly. The leather of his gloves rubbing against the hilt made a creaking sound. "Fine. We try our way and if it doesn't work you two will make a miraculous escape." The General silenced Aden before he could speak. "Use one of your darts and render her unconscious. The more convincing the better."

"Yes, my lord," Aden answered grudgingly.

"Oh and Aden," the General voice seemed to be more pleased. "I think it is time you reveal yourself to him as to who you really are."

Aden's eyes narrowed. "Yes, sir."

CHAPTER XII

Ryan

HIS EYES SNAPPED OPEN from the cold shock of water that was splashed over his face. Water dripped off him and he shook his head like a dog removing the excess. Aden stood before him with a wicked grin and tossed the bucket to the side.

Ryan's mind was such a blur he was trying to figure out what was going on and how he had gotten here. They were looking for Grace and Colette. After they entered this room it was all a blank to him. The drowsiness wore off almost instantly when he saw Julia chained up on a cross in front of him.

When he tried to move to go to her he was stopped abruptly. His hands were chained up in the air and his feet were chained to the ground. His heart dropped. *Not again. Please not again.*

Aden grabbed Ryan's jaw with one hand and the two men

stared into each other's eyes with nothing but hatred for one another. Ryan wanted to kill him. Given the look in Aden's eyes it was a mutual feeling. Aden however, had the upper hand.

"Nice of you to join us. I was afraid you were going to miss watching me punish my future wife for choosing the wrong side."

"Did she now?" Ryan inquired. "Did she know you are a traitorous piece of shit?"

"No. I was working up to it." Aden grinned. "She will come around or I'm going to beat her until she does."

"I knew you were a little weasel." Ryan grimaced. "You and your little boyfriend over there."

Aden looked over his shoulder at his friend. "Jesse came to his senses quickly."

"Neither you nor Jesse have ever had any sense." Ryan yanked on the chains. He didn't want to be strung up like this at the mercy of Aden. This entire situation was out of his favor.

Leaving his side, Aden made his way over to Julia and caressed her cheek. "I will break her spirit and she will be anything I want. I hope you know that, Ryan. I've already made her into someone different as it is. Just a little more pushing and I will have her right where I want her."

"Quit touching her." Ryan's nostrils flared.

"She has such an amazing body doesn't she?" Aden ignored him, skimming his hand along the bottom of her stomach as he rounded the cross.

Ryan was instantly aware Julia's gear was gone, left in only her pants and undershirt. Aden took a knife out, starting from the top he cut her shirt down between her breasts.

Ryan's temper flared. "Stop."

Aden grinned. "Why?"

"You are disrespecting her. She isn't even conscious."

"You don't want to see her body again?" Aden asked. "You may have beat me to the punch with her virginity but I plan on making sure she is mine forever. Once this is all done with, she will have my child and there will be no going back."

He wanted Aden dead but mostly he wanted to get Julia away from him. This behavior was intolerable. No woman should be treated this way. "Do you really think she is the type of girl to let that happen?"

"It doesn't matter if she is or not. It will be done." Aden ran his dagger along her bare skin making Ryan grow uneasy. Having a weapon so close to her body like that was nerve-wracking. "The General is very determined for her to remain safe but little does he know I have other plans."

Ryan laughed, "It's hard to imagine him wanting anyone safe at this point."

"On the contrary," Aden began. "He wants nothing more than to save the lives of anyone he can."

"He has a funny way of showing it," Ryan said.

Aden made his way back towards Ryan with a confident walk. "Do you really think that the Gods give a damn about us anymore, Ryan? They leave us to do their work. We gave them power to help us and what do they do with that power? They squander it for their own personal existence and leave us to die in their wake. The General wants us to be the new Gods. We will take care of the mortals as they should have this entire time instead of putting the work on the Immortals."

Ryan despised how convincing that sounded. There was

no part of him that would give up his beliefs in the Gods, but Aden made valid points. No wonder it was so easy to convert the Immortals, especially the ones that didn't have much connection with the Gods as the Warriors did. "So you kill mortals in order to save them? Interesting concept."

"Utopia requires sacrifice," Aden said simply.

"Utopia? Is that what you are creating? Peace doesn't derive from chaos. Chaos flourishes in it's own personal hell. That's what you are creating. You are killing innocent people when they deserve the right to choose their beliefs. You are stripping what it is to be human away from the world and creating robots for your bidding."

"In one hundred years everyone on this planet will be dead, the Gods will be nothing but history to mankind and we will flourish. Can't you see that all war is created because of religious differences or a power conflict? We will rid the world of all that and the great time of peace will result."

"When you die I wonder where your soul goes?" Ryan decided Aden was a mad man. In theory it sounded great but in reality it was impossible. "What does your new belief think will happen? Reincarnation? Or maybe we all just don't die. Oh, I know, we all get our own planet and are the god or goddess of said planet."

Aden's jaw tensed. "You won't see reason will you?"

"By "reason" you mean turn into a brainwashed imbecile? Then no, I won't see reason," Ryan answered. "No matter what you do, I will never change my mind, Aden."

At that, Aden struck him on the cheek causing his vision to daze from the impact. "I do despise you."

Ryan ran his tongue along his teeth. "Feeling is mutual."

"I don't think it is." Aden's hand shook. Ryan had no idea what his problem was. The guy was a ticking time bomb. "Do you want to know why I hate the Gods and the whole Immortal spiel?"

"No. I really couldn't care less," Ryan mumbled.

"Well," Aden went on, "my Warrior mother had gotten pregnant with me by another Warrior who could care less about her. The Council looked down upon Immortals that are not married if they are with child. They questioned who the father was, but she wouldn't tell them for fear of my father's response. So my mother had to invent a story that she was raped at one of the bars in Urbs without any inclination as to whom the man is. Naturally she lost her status as a Warrior, shamed for her inability to fight off one man when her entire being revolved around war. Instead of living or dying with the honor of a Warrior, she lived her life out as a seamstress."

Ryan knew women had it worse when it came to being a Warrior. Everything Aden said sounded correct. Women were seen unfit to maintain the honor of being a Warrior if they became pregnant while unmarried. Depending on the mood of the Council they were even stripped of their Immortality. Thankfully, such times were in the past and they had progressed from such sexist thinking.

"Terrible circumstances, but hardly any ground to abandon our faith." Whenever Aden tore his eyes away from Ryan's glare, Ryan looked around for a way out of this predicament. No possible instrument around him looked promising to help with escape but he did notice a door that must lead outside located in the back of the room.

"My mother was terrible to me growing up, Ryan. She

despised me. Hated me for ruining her life and beat me when I would spill a drop of milk on the floor. I think it's because I look so much like my father. Anyways, she killed herself when I was a teenager. She couldn't last even fourteen years with me. Thus, I grew up with a foster family, hardly people of worth, and became a Warrior myself. Bringing me one step closer to revenge."

Aden looked on the verge of tears. Be it anger or sadness Ryan didn't know. Either way, Ryan didn't want to see another man cry or be the punching bag Aden took his anger out on.

"I am sorry that happened, Aden. I really am, but it doesn't give you the right to betray us all."

Aden picked up a rope from one of the many tables with painful devices, dragging it along the floor behind Ryan.

"Can I ask you something?"

"Do I have a choice?" Ryan grew impatient.

"When did you stop going by Alexander exactly?" Aden draped the rope loosely around Ryan's neck while he stood behind him.

"I'm not comfortable with you back there," Ryan said.

"Answer the question." The rope gradually began to rise up his chest towards his neck as Aden started to pull on it.

Ryan really couldn't remember when he stopped using his given name. During his Immortal life he had gone by many names and Ryan was just the latest.

"I really don't know." He answered honestly.

"You know what?" Aden squeezed the rope tight enough to make it uncomfortable, his mouth close to Ryan's ear. "My mother told me that when I was born I looked so much like my father that she gave me a name that started with the same letter as his. She hated him very much. I didn't understand it and she never told me why. It probably added to the hatred she had for me."

Ryan's throat tensed up, not from the rope but from the nervous pit in his stomach that grew larger as Aden continued to speak.

"Okay?"

"I know you believe I've always imitated you in every way, Alexander, but did you ever stop to think that perhaps I couldn't help the similarity. That maybe, just maybe I inherited these traits?" Aden's voice grew tense with anger while the rope grew tighter around Ryan's neck. "I never could understand what my mother saw in you."

"You're lying," Ryan croaked.

"Why would I lie to you, Father?" Aden pulled tighter on the rope causing black dots to float before Ryan's eyes. "You never wondered why I hate you? Why I competed so hard with you over everything? Why I look identical to you? Where I got my attitude from?"

Ryan's vision was leaving him. "S-stop."

"You know what's even better, Father? I took away the one woman that mattered to you and I couldn't be happier knowing how much pain it causes you."

To his relief Aden let go of the rope. He took long slow breaths and glared at the man who claimed to be his son. "I don't believe you, Aden. Everything that comes out of your mouth is a lie."

"Why would I lie about being the son of Alexander the Great?" His voice boomed throughout the room in false praise. "You really need to think hard about this. Same age, same looks, same attitude. My mother was pure until you got your hands on her and she killed herself because of you. Another woman you tossed aside for your own satisfaction."

"When were you born? What was her name?" His throat was throbbing but it was nothing compared to the beating of his heart.

Aden stood directly in front of him. His eyes murderous slits. "You don't deserve to know." His fist connected with Ryan's stomach so hard that Ryan's feet gave out from under him. His wrists rubbed painfully against their bindings. "I want it to eat at you. Never knowing the woman you damned along with the son you damaged indefinitely."

With difficulty he managed to stand up. "If I knew, I would have been there." He clenched his fists to get the blood pumping through them again. "No one ever said anything to me about being with child."

Aden clenched Ryan's jaw tightly with his hand. The pain was nothing compared to the look in Aden's eyes. "She knew how you are. Knew you would have cared less about her, just like everyone else that entered you life. You would have ruined her more than you already did. Including me."

"I still can't believe this," Ryan groaned. His hands desperately wanted to grasp his stomach for even a small amount of comfort.

"Believe it, you bastard." Aden laughed when he punched Ryan in the ribs. Pain shot through his ribs like a bullet. "I feel good about this. It was a long time coming. Do you know how hard it was not killing you all these years?"

Ryan grunted, "I have an idea. You weren't exactly my favorite person either." He spit out a small amount of blood.

"And technically you are the bastard here." Salt in the wound? Perhaps. But even if Aden was speaking the truth, Ryan could only deal with so much before his anger took over.

"Too true." Aden walked over to Julia and stroked her cheek. "I have you where I want you, Alexander. I do hope you enjoy the show."

Ryan pulled at his chains, trying desperately to escape their grasp. "You stay the hell away from her."

Aden picked up a knife, dragging it along Julia's porcelain skin. The muscles in his hand flexed as he dug the blade into her flesh; a trickle of blood ran down her lower arm. There was nothing but pleasure in Aden's eyes.

Julia was unmoving. Ryan had to wonder if she was even alive, but her chest showed signs of breathing to the slightest degree. To Ryan's disgust Aden kissed her neck as he sliced her other arm with the blade. He had seen the look of pure evil in a man before and he was witnessing it once again.

"Would you like to play now, Father?" Aden grinned.

Anna

Her head kept hitting small rocks while she was being dragged along the ground. Anna had no idea where she was going or who had her but they obviously didn't give a damn about her wellbeing. She tried to scream, but her mouth was closed shut by the vines that ensnared her body.

They stopped. Anna wriggled and rolled the best she could

but nothing worked. Her bindings were so tight around her body it was hard to breathe. The world was momentarily silent around her. Damian. She hoped he was okay, but she heard nothing. If him and Cato were caught too they were truthfully screwed.

She managed to squeal when her body was lifted into the air and tossed over someone's shoulder. Her head bobbed uncontrollably with the heavy steps her kidnapper took and she was getting dizzy. The sounds of water sloshing around her grew nearer and nearer.

Whatever had her, dropped her to the ground without care and she landed painfully on her arm. The vines offered no padding and if she could swear out loud she would have. The sound of two more heavy objects dropping gave her the realization that Cato and Damian were in the same predicament. There was no help coming for her.

The vine's hold on her began to lessen. She prayed she was being freed by something that wanted to save her and not eat her.

As her face became exposed it became glaringly obvious the creature unwrapping her was not here to help. The demons in front of her were worse than any nightmare or scary movie she had ever seen.

It's elongated bony fingers reached out to touch her face, but their long tapered nails were in the way. It's eyes slanted up so high that they reached the brim of their dead, root-like hair that swirled on top of its head like a crown of thorns. The thing that scared her the most though, was their mouth. It stretched from ear to ear in a permanent grin, displaying dangerously sharp fanged teeth. It resembled a dragon fish from the depths of Hell.

Her bindings were loose enough now that she was able

to crawl backwards away from the creatures that cocked their heads at her like they were enjoyably studying a specimen. Their grinning faces snapped at her like a crocodile as panic ran through her entire body so fiercely she began to sweat and shake uncontrollably. It was difficult to breathe with how fast her heart was racing. She was paralyzed by fear.

Anna pried her eyes away from the demons and saw what she believed to be Damian and Cato, still wrapped up by the unmoving vines. The creepy creatures were coming towards her. A few had already reached Damian and Cato and were leaning over them with weapons in hand. The fear was still there, but she snapped out of it enough to pull out a knife to protect herself from the pale dirty demons.

As she blinked, waiting for them to make a move, something hard and cold grasped her free wrist. She looked over her shoulder coming face to face with a taunting grin. Its teeth gleamed in the night, dripping with saliva that fell on her shoulder.

She screamed. She couldn't help it. She wanted to pass out her head was so dizzy.

The creatures moved quickly as they cut the bindings from Cato and Damian with primitive weapons. In no time all three of them were tied to large tree trunks that faced a circular clearing. Cato kept shouting inappropriate words at them so they gagged his mouth with an old, disgusting cloth. Anna looked at Damian for some sort of reassurance, but he looked just as fearful. Not a good sign.

Damn forest. They were almost out of this hell and now they were at the mercy of these demon things that couldn't stop looking delighted.

The five creatures gathered up wood and started a fire in the middle of the clearing. She looked at Damian once again and watched his expression turn from fear to grave.

"Damian. What are they?" she whispered.

"I don't know." His tone was grim. "But I think we're their next meal."

Anna's eyes widened as she watched the creatures work. They built the fire up in a large pit in the ground and she could feel the heat licking her skin. They worked quickly building something around the fire that started to look like a rotisserie.

"Bring the loud one," one called out. It's voice sounded like nails on a chalkboard and it hurt her ears.

Cato struggled against his bindings as a pair of the creatures moved towards him and cut him down. Cato thrashed out with his fists but the creatures were unnaturally quick. Even with their weak looking bodies they overpowered him with ease.

While one worked on finishing the rotisserie, another began to strip Cato of his gear and clothes. Cato yelled through the dirty gag that he still had in his mouth, trying to pull his arms away from their grasp but it was not good.

They had him down to his underwear when Anna had to look away. It felt wrong to see Cato like this. The man was literally being stripped of his dignity before being cooked alive. She prayed to God for help. There was no way of escape. No way of fighting their way out. They needed a miracle.

A flash of light erupted in the sky shooting down towards the ground like a meteor but landed silently in the trees ahead. The creatures stopped what they were doing and looked around curiously.

One of the creatures spoke, "You two check it out. You other two hold the animal."

Damian looked over at her. "Can you reach any weapons?" he whispered.

She couldn't help but watch Cato flailing nakedly around while the demon creatures grasped tightly at his wrists. "No. Can you?"

"No."

"Here you go," a voice from behind her whispered, as the hilt of a dagger slipped into her hand. She almost screamed out in surprise, but a gloved hand came around the tree to cover her mouth. "Silence little one," the man whispered.

She did as she was told and remained quiet once her mouth was released. There was something about his voice that made her feel calm. It was musical, beautiful almost, and she longed to hear him speak more.

The vines that held her against the trunk were cut loose. "Stay against the tree," the musical voice chimed once again. "I will free your companion."

She sneaked a look at the man who was dressed fully in gold armor as he ran swiftly and quietly towards Damian. A long sword gleamed in his hand and a gold shield rested on his back. He was a beast of a man. His huge muscles glistened as the firelight danced off his tanned skin.

He cut Damian's bindings and whispered something in his ear. Damian stood still watching after the man in astonishment as he came back over to Anna.

"You are free little one. Save your friend."

"How?" she whispered.

"I am already much too involved with the human war," the man said. "I cannot intervene further."

"Please," she begged. Trying to avoid this man's perfection was difficult. He looked like he was made of marble with flowing dark hair to his shoulders. "We can't beat them. They are too fast and strong."

One of the demons screeched catching her attention. Cato had freed an arm and managed to punch the leader's jaw. It raised its claw like hand and swept it over Cato's chest leaving five gashes down it.

Cato screamed out in pain as he clutched his chest.

"Please!" She wanted to cry.

His kind and wise eyes looked into Anna's. "This is twice you have prayed for my assistance, Adrianna." He smiled broadly flashing pearly whites. "I will help you and your companions, but be warned that our assistance is very limited. Discipline may be thrust upon me but I will take the chance."

Anna's eyebrow rose in confusion. She'd prayed to him twice? Who did this guy think he was?

"Who are you?"

The man merely winked and took off running towards the demons. He removed one of the two swords he carried from its sheath. Anna squinted as she watched him wield the weapon that shone as bright as the sun. It was unlike anything she had ever seen.

He brought his sword down swiftly on the demons and as soon as it touched their skin they fell to ashes. If possible, he was more graceful than Ryan in a fight. Twirling and thrusting his weapon so fluidly, it looked like a dance.

Anna made her way over to Damian whose mouth was wide open in shock. The fight was over in seconds, which made Anna feel inadequate at how easy it was for the man.

They couldn't even get away from these creatures let alone fight them.

"Whoa," Damian mumbled.

"Yeah." She nodded.

Cato hopped away from the man on one foot while he tried to put his underwear back on. He fell in his attempt and was helped up by the golden hunk that managed to gain Cato's trust. The four of them met by the blazing fire and the man thankfully sheathed his sword. Her eyes just couldn't take the brightness of it.

Goldie held out his hand to Damian.

"Greetings, pagan."

"I prefer polytheist." Damian shook his hand carefully. "Who are you and how did you do that?"

The man laughed. Like his voice, it was musical and Anna felt herself swooning over him. "I am Michael the Archangel. Or St. Michael, whichever you prefer. Anna asked for my assistance and I felt the obligation to assist given you three are attempting to save our entire existence."

"Oh." Damian nodded. His gaping mouth was gone and replaced with indifference. "Well, thanks."

"Thanks?" Anna elbowed him. "That's all you have to say to him? Shouldn't we bow or something?"

Michael laughed and held up his hand. "Not necessary. You three have proven far more worthy of honor than I."

Cato shrugged on the rest of his clothes but he still looked sheepish. "Thanks for saving my ass."

"Cato!" Anna couldn't imagine how they were so nonchalant around an angel.

"What?" he asked. "He did."

"With pleasure." Michael smiled brightly. "Now I must leave you to your mission. I doubt we will meet again my friends. I wish you all the luck of the world."

"Wait," Anna said. "Why can't you help us?"

Michael paused as if deciding his words carefully. "It has always been the way of us, Adrianna. We leave the predicaments of humanity to be solved by their own free will. Occasionally we send our messengers, the Immortals, to assist if the situation requires it, but we rarely intervene directly. You have opposing beliefs, as do the gods. Some believe to stay out of the conflict while others, such as myself, wish to help. It is difficult to sit back and watch the world be ruined but our superiors wish to remain neutral."

"That's odd given they could be destroyed for eternity in this particular war," Cato grumbled.

"We were created by man. It is only fitting that our destruction should come by them. In the end, good will prevail. I am sure of it," Michael said. "Alas, I must go before God realizes what I have done. Farewell and good luck."

Chapter XIII

Damian

"D IDN'T YOU TELL ME one time that Michael was an Immortal?" Anna asked.

Damian nodded. "At one point he was. Then he was elevated when the religious spike for your God came to an all time high."

"Does that happen a lot?"

Usually Damian didn't mind her constant questioning but now was not the time to figure their world out. Especially because the other two demons that captured them were still out there somewhere. Besides, it had been more than two millennia since he had seen Michael last and he still had a big head about himself that rivaled Ryan's.

They made their way towards the end of the forest once more, approaching the lush green grass and actual daylight.

"Sometimes. Certain faiths grow. If an Immortal is known, like Michael is, then they become something bigger," he answered.

"We like to work hidden from the mortals but there are some that don't work that way. It happened with demi-gods as well such as Herakles."

"Herakles?"

"Sorry, I forget most of you know the Roman version. Hercules."

"Your world is so confusing," Anna grumbled.

"Our world," Cato corrected. "There is a lot you don't know about or have even seen."

"Well, tonight I think I saw plenty. Creepy vines, skeletal monsters, an angel and your naked butt." Anna wriggled her nose.

Cato sighed. "Anna, I know what you saw was mouthwateringly tempting, but I can't do that to Damian. He's my boy."

"Your boy?" Anna laughed. "Where did you learn to talk like that?"

Cato shrugged. "I heard it when I spent a week in California not too long ago."

"When was this?" Damian asked.

"A little bit before we retrieved Anna. Not important."

"You are a secretive creature, Cato," Damian said. "I never know what's going on with you."

It wasn't surprising. Cato, like Ryan, was a free spirit and did what he wanted. Then again it wasn't like they were around one another all day everyday. Hell, Damian occasionally went to Hawaii alone for fun.

"You and Ryan are too caught up in yourselves to really pay attention to me. I get it, but it would be nice to be included in your lives once in awhile," Cato murmured.

"What are you talking about?" Damian was taken back by Cato's sudden mood swing.

"It's always the Ryan and Damian show. I'm just the third wheel."

"We've never thought of you that way."

"Well, you treat me that way."

Damian stopped walking and grabbed hold of Cato's shoulders. "You are just as important as Ryan. You always have been. You have no idea how much we have needed you and how much we care about you."

Cato looked as if he were contemplating his next words. "I get it that it has always been you two. I really do. You were children together. Don't worry, I'm fine."

"Stop." Damian's jaw clenched. "If you felt this way you should have said something. We leave you alone because you seem to want to be left alone, Cato. That's it."

"Quit making this a big deal."

"You made it a big deal."

"Dude, shut up."

"No, Cato you're our brother." Damian saw the smallest tug of a smile on Cato's face.

Cato patted Damian on the shoulder. "I get it, man. Thanks. Would you like me to buy you a dress or are you going to quit being a little girl about it?"

Damian punched him in the shoulder. The smile on his face couldn't be contained. "Quit. It's true. Don't ever think we don't see you as an equal."

"Not to break up your little chat, but can we get going? I need some sunlight in my life," Anna barged in.

"Damian decided to get all deep on me out of nowhere," Cato grumbled.

"You're the one who threw a fit," Damian argued.

"Would you two shut up?" Anna interjected. "You both love each other and care about each other. Grow a pair and move on."

Damian looked at Cato, who mirrored his weary expression. "Yes ma'am."

They finally made it to the grassed area and to Damian's relief, the end of the ceaseless night. All around them he saw nothing but beautiful land filled with well-maintained flowery vegetation. In the distance he was sure he saw a pond of water surrounded by rocks and tall palm trees. Perhaps this was a sign they were nearing Shambhala.

They were running low on water and he welcomed the thought of drinking his fill of it. As they trudged across the grass his eyes were gradually growing used to the bright light. He kept his guard up, glancing around at his surroundings. Usually when something was too good to be true, it was, and he didn't want anyone to get hurt again.

Anna slipped her hands in his and he felt the engagement ring on her finger under her glove. She had avoided the topic from the get-go but he didn't want to push it. He asked and she was too stunned to speak. He put it on her finger to give her time to answer. If something were to happen to him, he wanted her to have it no matter what her answer would be.

"Are you okay?" he asked quietly.

Anna nodded and squeezed his hand tight. "Just thinking."

"About?" He pressed lightly on her finger and she nodded. "I know we haven't said a word about it since I asked. Please don't worry about giving me a quick answer. I know this is fast but regardless I wanted to give the ring to you to show you how I feel."

"Can it be a promise ring for now?" she inquired.

Damian scrunched his eyebrows in confusion. "What's a promise ring?"

Anna looked nearly as confused as he felt. "I don't know the exact definition, but I think it means that you promise to be faithful and loving, and promise for us to have a future together sort of thing."

"Isn't that what marriage is, Anna?"

"Yeah, I guess."

"Then I don't understand the difference," he laughed.

"Me either."

"Call it what you wish. The only thing I can hope for is for you to agree to marry me, but only if you truly want to. For now it can be your promise ring if that makes you feel better."

Anna looked relieved as she stood on the balls of her feet to kiss his cheek. "I love you."

Cato cleared his throat loudly. "Don't worry about me. I'm just standing right here listening to you two talk all lovey-dovey and what not."

"I thought you were invisible, Cato?" Damian teased.

"Rude."

Damian smiled to himself and looked down at the ground as he walked. The grass was so thick that he couldn't see the earth below. They made their way to the pond surrounded by palm trees. Each of them were grateful to find that the water was fresh.

They drank as much as they could and filled their canteens for the journey ahead. Once his body was refreshed, Damian realized they were stuck in a canyon. On one end sat the forest. Opposite from that was where they were now. The canyon walls trapped them were made of sharp jagged rocks about fifty feet high. There was no way to climb it without the possibility of impalement.

From what he could tell, there was only one option and a very unpleasant one at that. They had to go back into the forest and head off into the other direction. Hopefully there was a gap they could escape through on the other side of the canyon or a possible cave.

"Well shit," he grumbled.

Cato fell to the ground in exhaustion. His arms and legs sprawled out at his sides. "I give up."

"No you don't," Damian grunted.

"No, I don't," Cato groaned. "Now what?"

"All I know is that I am not going back in there," Anna said matter-of-factly, looking at the forest in disgust.

They were all exhausted, hungry, and petulant. How could they come this far only to come to a dead end? His frustration grew after every obstacle. The day? He had no idea. For all he knew they were too late. Time might not work the same here either.

Damian glanced at Anna. She looked ill and he was just about to ask how she felt when the ground shook. Like the steady beating of a drum the earth began to tremor beneath him. The water in the small pond started to dance and splash over the edges onto the grass surrounding it.

"Damian?" Anna's voice was full of fright. She looked even paler than before.

Just as he was about to speak a roar in the distance echoed throughout the canyon. His head snapped in the direction of the forest and he could see the tops of the trees swaying from something large pushing past them. All they could hear was the cracking of wood and the sloshing of water as they were rendered silent.

"Damian, now would be a good time for a plan." Cato jumped up from his sprawled out position.

There was no time to think as the edge of the tree line exploded with large splinters of wood and leaves toppling down into the meadow. The dragon from the desert stood at the edge of the forest breathing heavily. With another ear splitting roar the beast ran towards them with its eyes blazing and the earth cracking under its weight.

"Damian!"

Anna's voice broke him out of his trance. They were like fish caught in a barrel with nowhere to go. He had to make a decision quickly as the dragon was nearing. Ryan needed to be here.

Damian's arm was yanked forcefully until he turned around to face Cato.

"What are you doing?" Cato dragged him closer to the pond.

"Submerging ourselves. Let's hope that big bastard gives up."

"We could drown with our gear on." Anna had a point.

"Got any better ideas?" Cato jumped into the pond water splashing in Damian's face. Cato was fully submerged which shocked Damian. The pond was obviously deep and not a pond at all. Things never seemed the way they appeared here, for better or for worse.

With no other options, Damian jumped into the water and kicked as hard as he could to keep himself afloat. His gear started to drag him down just as Anna had predicted.

Anna grudgingly jumped in next and they all bobbed in the water as the beast got closer. His legs kicked hard to keep afloat until the dragon stomped itself right above them. "Dive!"

The three of them gave into the weight of their gear and submerged deep into the crystal clear water. Damian opened his eyes and could she the claws of the dragon splashing in the water trying to reach them. Bubbles of air escaped his lips at a slow pace. He prayed to Zeus for the dragon to leave as his lungs strained for air.

Cato grabbed his arm, pulling him towards the wall of the pond where he faced a dark tunnel leading away from the claws that continued to dig for its prey. They risked drowning if the tunnel led to nowhere. Or they had the option of being mauled to death. Drowning seemed to be a more hopeful option so they kicked their way down the tunnel and into the darkness.

The gamble paid off as their short swim came to an end when Damian could see the top of the water was rippling. His lungs struggled as he kicked hard towards the surface and was granted relief once he broke above the water.

His quick breath slowed once his lungs were steadily filled with air. The cave was stale and humid. Stalactites hung above his head and throughout the cave, occasional drips of water landed on the slippery uneven limestone floor. The only light source was from up ahead and it twinkled against the wet ground, barely revealing the secrets of their dark domain.

Anna and Cato popped up out of the water gasping for breath, their eyes widened at the magnificence before them.

"Whoa," Anna declared.

They swam to the edge of the water. The weight of his gear was heavy so Damian had to heave himself out of the water. After he yanked Cato and Anna out onto the ground, the three silently made their way to the source of the light.

"What the hell is this?" Anna asked.

Damian looked down the bright hallway before them and whistled. The walls looked to be made out of pure gold, decorated with red and blue paintings depicting scenes of gods and goddesses. The uneven slab in the cave abruptly turned into a blood red carpet that led down a never-ending hallway. It was completely out of the element of the cave but to make sense of its belonging would be futile. Nothing made sense here.

It wasn't the seemingly random appearance of the hallway that bothered him. Instead, it was the ten-foot tall statue of a dark blue, almost black woman with four arms and her tongue protruding from her mouth. The same statue lined both sides of the hallway about ten feet apart. A necklace of human skulls hung around her neck covering her bare breasts and a skirt of human arms hung from her hips.

"Are those real?" Anna gasped behind him.

Damian came closer to examine one of the statues, a decision he regretted. To his horror, the arms that created the skirt were indeed real. Blood dripped from the seemingly fresh appendages down to the carpet.

"Real arms and heads," Cato nodded. "Looks like each one of those statues has them too."

The statues four blue arms held something in each hand. One, a dagger, the other a trident and those weren't so bad compared to the other two hands. One of the lower hands held a bowl catching the dripping blood from a dismembered head that was being held by the fourth hand. The woman's eyes burned red with rage and her disheveled black hair flowed down her back.

"Who is it?" she whimpered.

Damian got closer trying to get a better look at the severed head of a black haired man. There was nothing special about him. There were no markings of any kind on his skin except for the blood that trickled out of his mouth. All Damian could hope for was that these were not the heads of people who ventured down here.

All of a sudden the eyes of the severed head popped open revealing a glazed, lifeless stare. Damian jumped back in fright and into Cato. The head seemed to gasp for breath but only the sound of a squealing pig escaped its lips and severed trachea.

Anna clutched Damian's arm, but his eyes refused to move from the shrilling head before him. Its eyes bulged and tongue flapped around its mouth uncontrollably. Damian could just barely make out a word it was desperately trying to say. "Run."

"Screw this," Cato's voice cracked as he clung to Damian's other arm.

Hastily, Damian moved Cato and Anna further down the hallway at a brisk pace to distance themselves from the living head. As they made their way past the other identical statues that lined the hallway, each of the heads the statues held started to come to life. Each hissed one word from their lips as blood dripped from their throats, "Run."

Chapter XIV

Ryan

RYAN WATCHED WITH DISGUST as Aden touched Julia in an undignified manner. His hands grazed over her breasts down to her womanhood. Exploring her body as she hung unconscious with such malice in his eyes that it worried Ryan.

He couldn't believe this was his child. Aden's mother, whoever she was, must have been mistaken. He was always so careful and cautious when it came to his sexual prowess over the years that it was hard to imagine impregnating someone.

Every encounter with Aden replayed in his mind over and over until he became exhausted. Aden's unexplained hatred for him, his appearance, everything pointed to Aden's words being true, but it couldn't be. This had to be a ploy to get him to join the Risen or something just as terrible.

Aden, now holding a bucket full of water, stood in front of Julia facing Ryan. "I suppose I should wake her up for this." Aden's smug face needed a beating.

As soon as the water touched her skin, Julia's body noticeably tensed up from the shock of the cold. A surprised gasp escaped her lips as she shook her head free of the water running down her face. Ryan's jaw tensed as he ground his teeth together. No woman deserved to be treated like this. Not ever.

"Hello, darling." Aden's palm struck her face. "Sleep well?"

"Aden, I swear if you touch her again I will kill you," Ryan growled.

Aden's eyes lit up with delight. "I don't believe you are in any position to threaten. Keep your mouth shut. I am talking to my betrothed."

Julia's eyes burned with hatred as she looked upon Aden. Not one ounce of her physical being seemed to hold affection for the man before her.

"What are you doing?" she hissed at him, her lips set firmly in a grim line.

"You betrayed me, Julia. I will not forgive that." Aden's smile was nothing more that malicious. "I will make sure you won't do it again, regardless of what the General warns."

"So this is who you really are?" she hissed. "Killing innocents? Hurting fellow Immortals? Is this what the Risen is truly about?"

Whatever sort of betrayal he thought Julia was capable of was passing. If she were one of them, how could they be treating her this way? She seemed shocked about Aden's involvement but something wasn't adding up about this situation.

"No." Aden smirked. "The General despises killing the

Immortals. He would do anything to save us all, but not all of us have seen the light. Thankfully he doesn't know you're here. He would kill me if he knew. I'll make sure you never speak of it."

Ryan laughed. "Stop trying to make a murderer seem judicious."

"He is a visionary." Aden held his arms out wide. "Once we are declared the new gods we will do more for the mortals than ever before. The old gods have given up on us and we shall give up on them. Their time is over and done with. It's time for a new reign."

There was only so much idiocy Ryan could take in one sitting and he had reached his limit. No matter what Aden said, no matter how good he tried to make the Risen seem, betrayal of the gods was not an option.

"Whatever you are going to do to me just do it already. I am sick of the foreplay."

With long strides Aden closed the distance between them. Taking Ryan's jaw into his hand, he dug his nails painfully into Ryan's skin. Aden's mouth was inches away from Ryan's face when he whispered, "You won't reconsider, Father? Think about the power you and I would have. You once dreamed of conquering the world and here is our chance. Together as father and son."

Ryan looked deep into Aden's eyes, at first with anger but when he truly looked at Aden a feeling of remorse and shame rooted in his heart. For a fleeting moment, it was as if Ryan were looking into the eyes of Aden's mother once more. The truth shook his core. Aden was his.

"No."

"Why?" Aden's voice growled with urgency. "It was your dream once. We can do this. Make the world better with one ruling power. Helping our followers as we see fit."

"And how would we do such a thing? Kill innocent people? Julia unwillingly at your side?" Ryan inquired. "Never."

"Fine, you can have her. There are more women in the world I can place beneath my shoe." Aden shrugged. "Greatness requires sacrifice, Father. You have always known this."

Every time Aden referred to him as 'father' a sliver of pain shot through his heart.

"I will not."

Anger consumed Aden's face. His nostrils flared and eyes closed to slits. Aden's fist connected with Ryan's jaw. "Then you are a fool."

"Let us go, Aden," Julia pleaded.

"Oh no." Aden turned towards her, his sinister chuckle echoed throughout the room. "There is no way I will give up the opportunity for you to witness Ryan's demise."

"You really are a little maggot," Julia spat in Aden's direction.

Aden's back faced him as he leaned in towards Julia, whispering something Ryan couldn't hear. While they talked back and forth Ryan's thoughts raced trying to plan some sort of escape. He stared at Jesse who was silent throughout the entire encounter. He looked completely bored and on the verge of falling asleep.

The sound of skin hitting skin brought his attention back to Julia. Her cheek was bright red.

"Not going to change your mind?" Aden chided as he looked over his shoulder.

"You heard my answer." Ryan glared. Even if he were his child, his actions made Ryan want to kill him.

Aden made his way over to a table with instruments displayed neatly. He picked up a whip with spikes on the end of its tassels. "Recognize this? I used it on you before, when I asked the General if I could have the honors."

Ryan bit the inside of his cheek to stop himself from responding. He wouldn't give Aden the pleasure. Aden had caused more mental and physical pain than Ryan had ever experienced in his life. It was something he would never forget.

"You did that?" Julia's face contorted with fury.

Aden's grin widened. He looked on the brink of insanity. "Yes. It was quite fun too. Even Jesse got to have a little one on one with him and Damian."

There was something in Julia's eyes that seemed genuinely hurt. Did she have feelings for Aden even after knowing he was a traitor?

"You animal," she mumbled.

"Speaking of Damian," Aden went on, "where is he? You two are joined at the hip."

"Couldn't tell you," Ryan grumbled.

"Really? That's strange." Aden walked around Ryan, dragging the whip behind him along the ground. Its spikes haunted Ryan. The memory of their pain was fresh in his mind. "Just the two of you then?"

Ryan's eyes narrowed at him. "Yes."

"Odd." A venomous grin reached to his eyes. "Warriors never go on a mission without at least three. Unless you lost one. Did you lose someone, Ryan? You typically leave a trail of carnage in your wake."

"Screw you," Ryan sneered. Aden was playing a game. It was glaringly obvious he knew there was another with them.

Jesse came between them with a small body slung over his shoulder before he carefully laid Zee's body down. Ryan cringed but didn't look away when her face had turned lifelessly towards him. Her lovely tanned skin was paling quickly.

"We found her along with a couple of our men," Aden interjected. "I have to say, I was surprised you left her corpse there to rot without a burial. Just like every woman in your life. Tossed away to the vultures while you parade about your own business."

"You are evil, Aden. There is no redeeming quality about you. When I get the chance I will kill you."

"You've said that already." Aden stepped over Zee's body, holding the whip in his hand. "Now, on to the main event."

Julia screamed, "No!"

Aden looked over his shoulder at her. "Don't worry darling. You will get your turn and I'll be sure to avoid your pretty face."

With Aden now behind him, Ryan braced himself for the familiar feeling of his flesh being ripped off. The sound of the whip registered in his mind before the actual pain. It was as if he were plunged into a raging fire, black specks appeared before his eyes as he tried to focus on reality. He forced himself to remain aware. Julia couldn't be left alone to the mercy of Aden; he had none.

Ryan managed to lift his head to see Julia, she was screaming but he couldn't hear a word. Another hit from the whip sent his body into a shaking mess against his will. Weakness overcame him as he hung from his wrists unable to keep himself up.

A blurry Aden came into view before him with a wide smile on his face. Water was dumped over his head to awaken his senses.

"Poor, dear old dad," Aden whispered. "Would you like more now? Or should I give our lover over there a few hits?"

"Get away from me you little shit," he croaked. His eyes were clearing enough to see tears pour down Julia's cheeks. There wasn't much else he could do but pray. "Zeus, whose hand guides the path of men to a welcome place, bring us home again."

"Stop that," Aden groaned.

"I pray to you to lead me. If my life will not be spared, I beg of you, spare Julia," Ryan went on. It was getting harder to speak. "I have been resistant to you. Apologies, for I praise and honor you. Zeus, who punishes the guilty, yet rewards the honorable. Please don't let your anger against me burn for Julia as well, for you are the protector of the just and avenger of the wronged. I pray to you Zeus, grant me your favor."

Aden backhanded Ryan. "You are a fool. They won't do a damn thing for you and you know it. They have given up on us and the world they swore to protect."

Ryan looked up at Aden the best he could, a small smile managed to tug on the corner of his mouth. "Maybe so, but it's worth a shot."

From somewhere in the room Ryan heard a knock.

"Yes?" Jesse's voice wavered.

Ryan's gaze locked on Julia but her eyes were fixed upon Zee's body. Against his better judgment, he found himself looking upon Zee as well. She was so beautiful, even in death. Her demise was his fault entirely. There was no denying it. The most he could hope for was that she was with her loved ones. Even without ritual of a proper funeral.

While Jesse was otherwise engaged, Aden had made his way over to Julia with the whip in hand. Ryan's heart felt as if it had jumped out of his body.

"Stop."

Aden winked as he turned back towards him. "I am so very glad you still love her. This makes it even sweeter." He held up the whip, ready to strike her from the front.

"Aden!" Jesse roared as he ran over to him. "He's here."

"Who?"

"The General." Jesse looked at the whip. "What do you think you're doing?" his voice was low.

Aden's face paled looking down at the whip. Did he not realize what he was doing? Ryan was almost positive Aden's mind was losing its grasp on reality.

The attention of everyone in the room gravitated towards the huge man in a dark cloak that had entered. From his clenched fists to his quivering shoulders, Ryan could almost sense the fury in the man.

"I thought I told you not to harm her?" the General boomed as he strode over to a fear stricken Aden.

"I thought it was supposed to be minimal," Aden countered but the fear in his eyes gave way of the truth. He had every intention on hurting Julia as badly as he could.

The General ripped the whip from Aden's trembling hands. He gave a nod to Jesse who looked as if was about to vomit but instead forcefully slammed Aden's body to the ground. Catching him off guard, Jesse was able to quickly chain Aden's hands to a stake hammered into the floor.

"I am so sorry, brother," Ryan heard Jesse whisper to Aden as he finished securing his wrists.

"Please, my lord," Aden cried out in anguish. "I wasn't going to hurt her with it. I swear. I was just scaring him!"

"Don't take me for a fool. You will be punished, Aden. But make no mistake, not even a thousand lashes will grant you forgiveness."

"Please," Aden begged.

Without hesitation the General brought down the whip against Aden's back with a single powerful lash. Aden's screams echoed throughout the room and blood sprayed the ground when the spikes ripped his flesh. He collapsed to the ground, writhing from the pain.

Had this been Aden, the man Ryan hated, he would have been fine with his suffering. Ecstatic even. However, Aden may very well be his son and that changed things. It caused complicated emotions within. Sure, he hated the man for what he had done to Julia and for all other crimes he has committed, but at the same time, he felt guilty himself. Aden could have been a much different person had Ryan been there for him his entire life.

The General raised his arm once more but Ryan found himself unable to withstand the abuse any longer.

"No more," he croaked.

The energy in the room changed. Breaking apart the tension a laugh escaped the General's lips. "You wish to see me have mercy upon the man that has harmed not only you but Damian as well? The man that was about to torture Julia, a man that is a traitor to the Immortals?"

"Yes." Ryan knew it was baffling. Hell, he felt insane for

saying it but how could he not? If Aden were indeed his child, what sort of father would he be if he let his pain continue? "Hurting him will not change what he has done. He's had a taste of his own medicine so leave it at that."

"I never pegged you for being merciful." The General dropped the bloodied whip as he walked past Aden's trembling body towards Ryan. "I believe any chance of you joining us has been tarnished hasn't it?"

"It was tarnished from day one," Ryan spat. "You can torture everyone that I hold dear but it won't change anything. All you are doing, all you have ever done, has made me despise you and your kind even more."

"Then I suppose we have reached an impasse." His gaze seemed to wonder in Julia's direction. Her face was furious with tears of anger rolling down her cheeks. "Jesse, grab Aden. I need to speak to you both privately."

Releasing him from his bounds, Jesse draped Aden's arm around his shoulder and followed the General slowly out of the room. Aden's legs wobbled while he walked, but Jesse kept him firmly in his grasp.

Ryan's children seemed doomed from the start of their existence. A curse that stemmed from their father.

Once the door slammed shut, Julia yanked on the chains that held her to the cross. "I think I can squeeze my hand out."

Ryan laughed but the humor was lost in it. "Even if you could, then what? I can barely stand, let alone run."

Ignoring him Julia tugged on the chains. Her face contorted in pain. He heard a small pop. Biting her lip, she managed to pull her hand free but her thumb stuck out oddly. "You can and you will. We have to get out of here."

"Are you okay?" he asked.

Julia nodded. "I think my finger popped out of the joint or I broke it. I'll live." She worked on her other wrist and managed to wiggle her way out of it without popping anything.

Ryan grinned from ear to ear. "Good girl."

Julia took a bow before she hurried over to Ryan. "Shit, it's locked." She left his side for a moment and came back to him with bolt cutters. He cringed thinking about what they would use those for as a torture device.

"Grab Zee and let's get out of here."

Anna

This was stupid and terrifying and she wanted this nightmare over with. They continued down the never-ending hallway lined with blue ladies holding severed, talking heads and it was giving her whiplash. Never had she ran so much in her life. Not even in boot camp and that was saying something.

"Can we please find a way out of here?" Anna huffed.

"Sure, because we haven't been trying to do that," Cato grumbled.

"I guess since Ryan isn't here, you're the designated ass," Anna retorted.

Cato laughed but didn't make another comment. Anna was kidding with him of course but the constant running was making her agitated.

"What are we even running for?" Cato breathed out

heavily. "Nothing is happening except the freaky talking heads."

Their pace slowed until they all came to a halt. The heads continued to chatter the word 'run' but nothing seemed to happen. Looking to Damian for some sort of guidance she could see he was just as confused as her.

"Perhaps it's just a trick? It doesn't seem real," Damian said finally.

"Those look pretty real to me." Anna pointed at the heads.

"This just feels odd." Damian took in their surroundings as the heads chattered along. "I think it's some sort of illusion."

Cato poked one of the heads in the cheek with his finger, jumping back when it's eyes met his own. "Nope, it's real."

Producing a dagger, Damian sliced the hair the blue lady held in her hand and with a disgusting *thunk* it fell to the ground. Rolling over to Damian's feet, it looked up at him with it's mouth gaping. Yep, she wanted to throw up.

"What was the point of that?" She covered her mouth with her hand as if it would prevent her from vomiting.

"I don't know," Damian sighed in defeat as he replaced his dagger in his belt. "Just trying to figure something out."

The sound of stones piling up on each other came from behind her. Fearing that the walls where caving in she turned around only to find her fears heightening. The giant blue lady statue was standing up, her stone body released flurries of fragmented stone as her limbs came to life.

The ground shook as she took a heavy step towards them. Her eyes bulged wildly, full of hatred, and her hands gripped her weapons tightly.

"I think she's mad about you taking her head away," Cato whispered.

"Yeah." Damian backed away from the massive statue that came to life. "I think we should listen to the heads now and run."

"Yep," Anna said.

"Sounds good," Cato agreed as they set off down the hall.

As they ran, the blue lady made her long heavy strides slowly, sending tremors through the ground. She seemed to almost taunt them at this pace, as if they had no chance of escape.

"Now what?" Anna hissed.

"I think we should go back to the cave," Cato said.

"We've been led here for a reason. Whatever our path is, it must be done here," Damian answered.

"So what do you suggest?" Cato asked.

"Kill Kali?" Damian said.

"Kali?" Anna asked.

"These statues are of the goddess Kali," Damian answered. "When this is all over with I swear I am going to make you go to school about the gods."

"There's a school for that?" she asked.

"Of course there is," Damian huffed.

"Focus!" Cato yelled. "How do we kill her?"

It was an excellent question. It seemed impossible to kill a goddess and extremely blasphemous for an Immortal to try and do so.

"Maybe we don't?" Anna suggested.

"What?" Damian and Cato chimed together.

Anna shrugged as they ran. "She's a goddess right? Aren't

they on our side? We fight for them so they should like us, right?"

Confusion washed over Damian's face. "Yes, but how does that help us?"

"Maybe we should show her respect?" Anna suggested.

"So you want us to stop running, get down on our knees and face the black goddess of death, time, and doomsday to show her respect? Are you insane?" Cato asked.

She had to admit that it sounded ridiculous but killing a form of a goddess seemed to be the opposite of what the Immortals were about. Anna mentally kicked herself for what she was about to do. She stopped running and turned to face Kali.

The goddess stopped before Anna. Towering over her, Anna dropped to her knees and bowed to the goddess. The only thing she could think of to do was to show her respect and obedience to the multi-limbed blue lady. She could feel the presence of Damian and Cato's bodies down next to hers.

Damian dared to speak, "Goddess Kali, please forgive us for our impertinence and allow us to continue our mission. We are unworthy of your kindness, but dare to ask for your mercy on us, your subjects through time."

Anna risked a glance up from the ground and saw the goddess tilt her head from side to side, contemplating Damian's request. No matter what face this lady made, it frightened Anna down to her core.

"Immortals?" the goddess somehow asked. Her mouth didn't move but the question echoed in the hallway. "Why have you come here?" Her voice was surprisingly sweet and calm.

"We are on a mission to save the existence of the gods and wish to reach Shambhala," Damian answered.

"The Immortals wish to consult with the Worthy Ones?" Kali asked.

"If you allow us to, yes," Damian pleaded.

"Granted."

Anna barely blinked and the statue had disappeared before her very eyes. Damian grabbed her face and kissed her passionately on the lips.

"What?" she laughed.

"You are the most brilliant and beautiful woman I have ever met." He grinned.

"Yes, Anna is amazing," Cato said dryly. "Now what?"

"Welcome, Immortals," a male voice boomed through the hallways. The hallway scene before them flickered like a bad movie until it was replaced with an unimaginably beautiful spectacle before them.

Anna staggered to her feet as she looked upon the gorgeous city that appeared before them. The city was placed on an island filled with lush green vegetation. Tall buildings shimmered like gold and silver reflecting in the sunlight. Waterfalls floated in thin air, poured down into the clearest water she had ever seen.

Standing on the brink of the city, she slipped her hand in Damian's as she took in the most breathtaking sight of her life. Urb's beauty had nothing on this place.

"Whoa."

Chapter XV

Ryan

T HEY HAD MANAGED TO escape the castle and steal a jeep with little to no effort and were almost the point where they could travel back to the Domus in a portal. He couldn't bear to look back at Zee's body, so he kept his eyes forward.

Julia drove like a bat out of hell while he sat in the passenger seat. He could feel blood trickling down his back, but his main concern was that Grace and Colette were okay.

"Hey," Julia finally broke their silence.

"Hey."

"What's going on in that mind of yours?" she asked.

"That this was all a waste. We didn't even get Grace and Colette out. Zee died for nothing," Ryan sighed.

"Actually, they got out," Julia said.

"What?" He studied her face. "How?"

"When you fell to the floor after Aden knocked you out, I cut them loose. There was a back door they escaped through

before Aden knocked me out too." Julia shrugged. "They didn't want to leave without us but I made them."

"I hope they made it back then." Ryan didn't say anymore on the subject.

His heart ached for Zee. He wished he could hear her voice one more time. He only experienced her love for one night when he thought there were many nights to come. She managed to soften his heart when Julia had hardened it. It was a feat in itself but she did it.

It wouldn't do to dwell on the subject so his mind wondered to thoughts of Aden. How could he possibly be his son? Truth be told, it made sense but he couldn't accept it fully. He tried to think of who his mother could be, but no Warrior that had to give up the lifestyle due to pregnancy came to mind. When was Aden even born?

He knew absolutely nothing about the man he helped create.

"Ryan?" Julia asked.

"Yes?"

"I'm sorry about Zee. I wish I could have done something, anything, but I couldn't." She bit her lip. A nervous reaction that peaked his interest. "If I could apologize to her I would."

"Apologize?"

"For what I said in the apartment. I was jealous and it was wrong of me." Her eyes remained on the road and he could see them began to well up with tears. "I know what we had is over with because of my relationship with Aden. Zee was beyond amazing and I get it-"

"Please stop," he interrupted. "I don't want to talk about her right now."

Julia nodded and drove in silence. They made it over the bridge were they'd killed Ricky when Ryan realized there were no patrols in sight. Something was wrong about that but he didn't care. He just wanted to get home.

They went over a speed bump and Zee's body fell to the floor of the jeep. Julia glanced over at him worriedly. "Do you want me to stop?"

"No." He looked forward with his jaw tensed. He couldn't bear to touch Zee more than he had to and the sound of her body falling sickened him.

"Please talk to me," Julia begged.

Ryan rubbed his face in exhaustion. He was slightly relieved when they got closer to the portal zone. "Don't mention her again, Julia. I am warning you." She merely nodded and he felt guilty for being short with her. "I am just in pain, Julia." Both physically and mentally.

"It looked so painful." Julia's brow creased. "I could hardly bear to watch it, Ryan. Your poor body has been through way too much in such a short time. I can't even begin to understand how you are even functioning at this point."

"Because I have to," he answered flatly.

"Doesn't matter how strong your will is, Ryan. The human body can only take so much and it's a miracle you can even stand."

"Perhaps the Gods are looking out for me after all," he said. He really couldn't imagine any normal human going through what he did and coming out as well off as he was. Even after what Aden just did to him, a normal human wouldn't be unable to move.

Julia placed her hand on his thigh and he tensed from her

touch. It was not unwelcome but it was foreign somehow. It felt odd having her touch him so sweetly with Zee's body lying in the back of the jeep. He didn't deserve to be cared for.

She seemed to sense his feeling of discomfort and removed her hand. Without realizing what he was doing he stopped her and placed her hand back on his thigh. Making brief eye contact he said, "I do miss you."

The way she smiled was something he remembered from a time before Aden. "I miss you too, Ryan."

"So is it safe to say you're single now?" He tried to lighten the mood, but it was difficult given the circumstances.

Julia grinned wider. "It's safe to say. I know it's terrible but I really hope Aden is okay."

Ryan had to agree. "I imagine he is fine. In a lot of pain, but fine. The General needs him."

"We're almost there." She nodded towards her left.

Ryan could see the cemetery come into view. Never had he been so happy to see a place that memorialized death before.

They had made it safely back to the Domus without a problem, which bothered Ryan. However, it wasn't enough to deter his thoughts away from Zee, who now lay on the couch in a never-ending slumber.

Once he heard footsteps coming closer his heart pounded in his chest and Zee's team came into view. Julia had run off to get them. Their cries when they saw her body broke his heart. Both women were similar to Zee's appearance, which tightened the burden around his heart. The reminder made him realize what he lost. She was his hope for something more and that hope was forever banished to the lands of the gods.

"Cyra, Amanda." Ryan made his way to them but they pushed past him and towards Zee's body. Like everyone else, they must see this as his fault, which was nothing but the truth.

"What happened?" Amanda asked.

"We were on a mission to obtain Grace and Colette. We needed a third and I asked Zee to come along and help." Ryan focused his attention on the ground. He didn't dare to look into their eyes and see the hatred that must reside there. "She was killed right before we reached our targets."

"Look at me, Ryan," Cyra ordered in her authoritative voice.

Ryan reluctantly looked at them and he was shocked to see, not hatred, but sympathy in their eyes. He was dreadfully confused and his face must have shown that.

"I am sorry, Ryan," Amanda wept.

"What?" he asked.

"*We* are sorry," Cyra corrected. "She spoke very favorably of you and cared for you deeply. By the look on your face it was reciprocated."

"You aren't outraged by me?" he spluttered. "I got her killed."

Amanda strode over to him placing a small delicate hand against his cheek. He was forced to look into her dark brown eyes that matched the color of her long curly hair. She regarded him with such sadness he could hardly survive her gaze.

"You restored a passion to her core that she believed had

vanished long ago. She died happy and that's because of you. We all know the risk of a mission and this was no different. I want to thank you for giving her happiness once again, even brief as it was." Amanda kissed his cheek and turned back to Zee's body.

He felt like he was going to pass out from the mental and physical mistreatment on his self as of late. Zee was dead and they didn't hate him for it, but he wanted them to, needed them to. Yet here they were, thanking him? He didn't want to be thanked. He wanted to be yelled at. He wanted someone to confirm the guilt he felt so deeply.

"We will prepare her body for this evening." Cyra wouldn't look at him now but remained by Zee's side as she smoothed down her hair and adjusted her hands over her unmoving torso. "It would be much appreciated if you placed her on the pyre."

He wished he could decline but there was no way to avoid it without offending the women. He merely nodded before making his way back to his room. Ryan couldn't stomach to be around them much longer, especially not around Zee's motionless body. He missed her more than he thought imaginable for only having her around for such a brief time.

"Hey, wait up," Julia called after him, suddenly appearing by his side. "Why did you leave?"

"I can't be around her, Julia. I can't do any of this," he grumbled as they traveled down the hallway towards his room. "They thanked me for getting her killed. I shouldn't be thanked. I should be punished for what I did to her. Yelled at, screamed at, hit… something."

"You didn't do anything, Ryan. As they said, Zee knew of the risk of a mission. We all do. She died a Warrior's death and according to her team, happy." The last part appeared difficult for her to say.

Coming to his room he tried to close the door behind him but Julia shoved it open.

"What is your damn problem, Ryan?"

They stared at one another for a moment before his hand connected with the stone wall by his door. The unpleasant feeling of his bones cracking shot through his hand but it didn't stop him from hitting the wall with his other fist. He was mad, furious, and wanted someone to make him pay for what he caused.

There was no holding back his feelings any longer. Years of pent up frustration and guilt roared from his lungs as he fell to a pathetic heap on the floor. Another loved one, gone. He couldn't bear it. It was the reason he tried his hardest to stay away from Julia. Yet with Zee he gave in and his nightmare became reality.

A hesitant hand touched his back rearing up the pain from Aden's whip.

"Ryan." She was being cautious with him as a man would with a wounded animal. "It wasn't your fault."

Ryan crumpled into her lap, like a child. She stroked his head with her hand making his nerves settle down but in his moment of weakness his entire male bravado was tarnished. The humorous thing was, he didn't care. He couldn't contain thousands of years of guilt any longer.

"Please tell me she was wrong." Ryan's voice was raw.

Her touch paused. "Who?"

"Zee." He skimmed her unreadable face. "About you being the enemy."

After a moment of unbearable silence, Julia placed a kiss on his forehead. "Do you want the truth, Ryan?"

He sat up so suddenly he grew dizzy. "Yes." He almost didn't want to know the truth.

Julia remained still as she sat back on her legs. "I will be honest. At one point I had considered it."

He was stunned, his body moving slightly away from hers. "What?"

Her cheeks flushed while her attention was set on the floor. "You have to admit that our existence is practically un-needed in this new world, Ryan. I love the Gods with my heart and soul but they really seem to have abandoned humanity and left it to evolve on its own."

"So she was right." The world was crumbling around him all over again. Would this hellish nightmare of a life ever end?

"Gods no!" Julia insisted. "It was only just a thought, Ryan. It is tempting, isn't it? To save the mortals as we see fit. Providing absolute bliss to the world because they know without a doubt that we exist to protect them. But I knew I could never sacrifice the innocent for a silly dream. Even an alluring one as that."

Ryan couldn't believe what he was hearing. "The Gods are our saviors, Julia. We are but humble tools of theirs to provide balance."

"Do you truly believe I'm unaware of that fact? As I said, I love them and always will but they have shown us nothing for decades, Ryan. Nothing but a dwindling existence has been given to us. We were left with only the question of when our next loved one will die. Like Zee died. They did nothing to prevent it yet they had the power to intervene."

"Traitor."

"No," Julia insisted, "because I didn't do it. I couldn't do it. I am telling you why I considered it only briefly but the sacrifice of life was unthinkable."

"The fact you even considered it is a betrayal."

"Are you trying to tell me you haven't considered it? The ability to end war and religious conflict with one unified belief of the masses doesn't appeal to you? The mortals will kill each other over their differences until they are extinct." Julia shook her head. "I am not saying what the Risen is doing is right. All I am saying is they are on to something that is of a rising concern. I think once we eliminate their threat we can find a solution for the mortals in our own way. A peaceful way."

Ryan had to contemplate what she was telling him. His instinct was to dub her a traitor and leave it at that, but the truth in her words hit him to his core. The mortals were constantly killing themselves over their petty differences and someone needed to intervene. Yet the gods remained silent.

He shook his head as if it would remove the thoughts from his mind but the realist in him supposed she was right. However, the gods gifted humans with the ability to create their own destiny. Could he really just take that away for the prospect of peace?

He abruptly remembered the vision he saw with the Oracle of Julia standing by Aden's side in front of a tortured Ahmose. Was it false or a certainty? This woman was so imbedded into his heart that even the obvious truth remained uncertain.

While in thought Julia must have closed their small distance, taking his face into her hands, forcing him to look into her eyes. Incredibly, he could see the woman he fell in love with residing there.

"Please don't hate me, Ryan. It was just a thought and I promise you I am loyal to the Immortals."

"I don't know how to believe you." He placed his hands over hers. "How can I? Everything points to you being a traitor. Especially your relationship with Aden." He tried hard not to think about that fact.

Julia bit her lip as a tear rolled down her cheek. "I love you, Ryan. I would never betray my family. It's just hard to feel like this life means anything when we are so forgotten by everyone."

He could understand that feeling more than anyone. "I am so confused right now."

Julia giggled through her tears and to his surprise, kissed him gently on the lips. "So am I."

Pushing her gently away from himself he said, "I can't do this. Not now with Zee gone. It's not right."

She sat back on her legs folding her hands in her lap. "I understand but I need you right now, Ryan. I can hardly contain myself. I was such a fool thinking anyone would be better than you for me."

Grasping hold of her hands, they stood up together and he held her tenderly against his chest. "Give me time, Julia. That's all I ask."

She squeezed his midsection and pain shot through his back once more. Julia quickly let go of him after he gasped out air.

"Oh Gods I am sorry." She dragged him to his bed, forcing him to lie down on his stomach. He knew better than to fight her when his body was torn up. "Stay there and I will get some medicine."

Ryan couldn't help but chuckle through the pain. This was the woman he remembered.

CHAPTER XVI

Anna

"HOLY CRAP." ANNA GAPPED as they walked along the grass pathway towards the massive palace ahead. Everything was beyond beautiful and perfect here, she felt she was walking into an actual fairy tale. The tall pointed towers reached up as high as the empire state building and the city below was overgrown with flowers and plants covering its walls.

She would have thought the city was abandoned but the way the flowers grew looked artistically done. There was a vast expanse of plant life that she could barely tell the houses were made of stone instead of blossoms.

The city itself was a revelation, but the people who resided there came as a total shock. They were tall beings that went barefoot with small amounts of linen covering their perfectly sculpted bodies. The women were gorgeous model types and Anna had a hard time keeping her eyes off the men that had abnormally perfect bodies. Damian seemed to find her astonishment amusing and nudged her every time her eyes wondered.

Two very tanned, handsome, muscular men led them to the king's castle. They had their black hair pulled back in long braids that reached past the middle of their back. Anna thought about how terrible her hair must look to them.

"We stand out like crazy," Cato whispered.

"I don't know about that. You're tall enough that if you took your shoes off and ran around half naked you'd fit right in," Damian spoke lowly.

Cato replied, "Not a bad idea."

"I've seen enough of your naked butt. Still can't get it out of my head." Anna shivered.

"I know it's quite amazing isn't it?" Cato winked.

Anna almost slugged him in the arm but as they made their way throughout the city, residents stopped their daily business to look at them. Their heads cocked to the side as if looking at aliens from another planet being marched through their homes. She felt like a specimen under observation.

"How are the streets grassed over with them continuously walking on it?" Anna whispered to Damian who shrugged as his answer.

They made it to the palace that had the tallest towers in the city. Flower vines stretched up the walls of the castle in blues and whites. The already opened gates were bare of any vegetation.

Walking up the steps into the castle, they entered a large throne room where an absolutely gorgeous man sat. Long black hair was pulled back from his face and draped over one shoulder. Every muscle seemed to protrude from his body for their viewing pleasure. Her mouth dropped open at the sight of him but her attention was quickly drawn to a group of women that couldn't keep their hands off Damian and Cato.

"Umm…" Damian looked at the women in obvious discomfort. "Can I help you? Hey, don't touch that." He glanced at Anna and she couldn't decide if she was angry or amused by the women pawing at her uncomfortable boyfriend.

Cato graciously allowed them to touch every inch of him with a smirk plastered on his lips. The women appeared confused by their weapons and gear more than anything, acting as if they had never seen them in their lives. Even a two year old knows what a gun is.

The man on the throne cleared his throat loudly making the women retreat back to their spots in the room with their heads bowed down. Anna caught a man looking at her curiously and she shifted in her boots uncomfortably. He was looking at her like a piece of meat he wanted to devour.

"Welcome Warriors." The man's voice was smooth like honey and almost otherworldly. "To what do I owe the pleasure?"

"We are here to request for your permission to acquire the piece of Brahmadanda's staff in order to prevent our existence from being destroyed." Damian sounded so formal; his voice was foreign to her ears.

The king, she assumed, looked rather annoyed by the request. "Why would we grant such a request?"

"The existence of the mortals and Gods hang in the balance. Without it, we will all surely parish to the clutches of our enemies," Damian continued. "Once our mission has seen triumph, I swear by the Gods we will return the piece to you and your people for further safekeeping."

"I am in need of further explanation." The king rose from his throne.

Damian described what was going on in the world with such elegance and intellect that Anna had a hard time trying to understand what he was saying. Her vocabulary was definitely not as educated as his.

"So the Gods created Immortals only to be destroyed by them. A fitting end wouldn't you agree?" The king's eyes narrowed.

Damian's jaw clenched at the statement. "Your highness, we beg for you assistance in this matter. Pardon me for my insolence, but why do you appear so pleased about this?"

"I am not." The king smiled. "I wish to speak with you three alone." He clapped his hands and the room emptied without question. These people were certainly obedient.

The king came down from his throne and stood merely feet away from them. His smile faded when he wiggled his jaw as if it hurt. "You have no idea how difficult it is to keep pretenses such as this up with the public."

"What do you mean?" Anna finally managed a small amount of courage.

"My people have never known pain or any sort of discomfort of any kind. We have lived in a world with nothing but ease and tranquility. They cannot grasp such ideas as war or sadness as you and I do."

"Then how can you?" she asked.

The king smiled kindly at her as if she were a child. "I have been bred with the knowledge of these things. Every ruler is given information of the outside world which most of our people will never know. When our prophecy of war comes to light we will be ready with an army without fear of pain or mutilation. It seems our time may be close at hand."

"Prophecy?" Cato asked.

"I apologize but this is for our knowledge alone. Although, I believe some mortals have stumbled upon our truth." The king exhaled. "I will provide you with the piece of the Brahmadanda staff. Please stay and rest yourselves for the evening as I imagine your journey here was rather unpleasant."

"Just like that?" Cato's brows scrunched together and Anna realized she was doing the same.

The king looked puzzled with their disbelief. "How is this not understandable?"

Anna started to say something but Damian interrupted her with his head bowed. "Gratitude your highness."

The king nodded once at them and strode off back towards his throne. "My pleasure Warriors. If you would be so kind as to wait here for my servants to show you to your rooms." With that, he walked down a hallway beside his throne leaving them standing awkwardly alone in a foreign place.

Anna finally had the chance to look around the throne room. Its beauty flabbergasted her. It was decorated only in gold and different colored jewels from floor to ceiling. Tapestries hung along the walls and cushions lined either side of the room reminding her of an Indian harem.

The tall, young man that was eyeing Anna earlier came into the room and she immediately seized Damian's hand. He looked down at her with his eyebrow raised.

"What's wrong?"

"That guy keeps looking at me weird," she stood on her toes to whisper in his ear. Damian looked on the verge of laughing.

The young man ushered them towards the exit of the throne room. Colorful arches lined the hallway they entered with flowers and animals painted exquisitely on the columns. The ceiling was made of glass so clear she could see the blue sky up above as if she were outside. The floor was covered in vibrant mosaics depicting animals, farming, and what she assumed were their Gods.

The young man led them up a stairway into another hallway with a glass ceiling.

"You do know why he is starring at you right?" Damian kept his voice low.

Anna shook her head.

"They have never seen a woman like you before. He kept to himself unlike the women that flocked Cato and I," Damian answered.

"They looked like they were doing more than flocking," Anna grumbled.

"These people don't understand things like boundaries." He smirked. "They don't know suffering or age. In many ways they are like the Immortals, but we still have our basic human traits. They don't even know what it is to desire something. It's pure peace here."

"So they don't have sex?" she exclaimed. The young man looked back over his shoulder at her and she slapped her hand over her mouth.

Damian bit his lip trying not to laugh at her outburst. She was mortified. "I don't know about that, but I am sure they do."

They stopped in front of tall, double gold doors with swirling designs carved into it. The man held out his hand gesturing for them to enter.

"This is the dwelling for the companions. I will show the single man to his chamber now. The king offers an invitation to dine tonight with him. How shall I reply?"

Damian gave the man a slight nod. "We would be honored. Thank you."

"See you guys in a bit," Cato said. The young man bowed to Anna and Damian before he ushered Cato down the hallway to the room next to theirs.

Relief spread through her body in an instant after realizing they were finally safe. Damian opened the large doors revealing the most beautiful room she had ever witnessed. After living in the Domus, that was saying something.

The ceiling was made of a glass dome with tall windows across the room that looked out towards the flowery city below. The room was white with deep blue flower calligraphy decorating the walls and gold trimming. The bed was oddly placed in the center of the room with a large canopy draping over its sides. Candelabras were placed throughout the room waiting for nighttime to come so they could be brought to life. It was absolutely, without a doubt how she was going to decorate her room at the Domus.

"Impressed?" Damian grinned down at her, pressing her to his side.

She nodded. "Uhh, duh." She ambled tiredly over to the bed filled with fluffy white and blue pillows. The urge to jump into them was strong.

Damian grabbed her by the waist pulling her down on

the bed as if reading her mind. "Feel better now that we are safe?"

"I will feel better once this whole Risen mess is done and over with," Anna said.

"I think we all will." He entwined his fingers with hers. She stared at all the tiny scars on his hand. She couldn't get over how lucky she was to find such an amazing man.

She ran her hand over his chin. "You have a beard growing."

"I know," he sighed as he leaned into her hand. "Having a smooth face has been the least of my worries these past few weeks."

"I like it," she admitted. "Looks good with your hair cut. All manly and stuff."

He smirked as he kissed her nose. "You are such a wondrous creature."

"And you are such a cornball." Anna kissed his nose back.

Damian played with the ring on her finger through her glove, staring off into space. She waited for him to say what was on his mind but he never did. Her eyes started to feel heavy and she almost dozed off when a knock came at the door.

"Come in." Damian sat up looking as if he had almost fallen asleep as well.

A young woman and man shuffled inside their room with a bow. The woman said, "We are here to prepare you for the banquet this evening and clean your belongings from your journey."

Damian stood up and Anna clumsily followed. She looked down at her gear, which really was a dirty mess and she suddenly felt terrible for lying on the clean bed.

"Thank you." Damian held out his arms from his sides.

Anna scrunched her nose. "What are you doing?"

"Allowing them to do their job," Damian whispered as the man and woman approached them. Damian made a motion for her to do the same so Anna held out her arms and watched in horror as they started to undress them.

Her lady had retreated into an adjoining room for a few minutes and once she returned she held two white silk robes in her hands. Anna was thankful for the coverage. Being in her underwear in front of strangers was not exactly comfortable.

The woman gestured for Anna to enter what she believed to be the bathroom.

"This way, Miss."

Anna cautiously looked back at Damian but he nodded in reassurance. He beamed with amusement. "It's fine, Anna. She is going to bathe you." Horror washed over her face. "Let her," Damian insisted a little more firmly.

Against her personal judgment, she listened to him and marched into the bathroom. The woman had apparently started the large bathtub that looked more like a small swimming pool while she was in here gathering the robes. The only thing Anna could think about was why does one person need a bath this big and what sort of plumbing did these people have.

She was startled when the woman slipped off her robe. When she started to take off Anna's underwear she twisted her body away.

"It's fine, I can do it." Anna tried to smile sweetly but the woman looked taken back by her insistence.

Anna quickly climbed into the bubble filled tub once

she stripped down. Before she could melt into the deliciously warm tub she felt water cascade down her hair giving her chills. She realized the woman was washing her hair and she mentally kicked herself to let her. The lady obviously didn't mind doing it and it was clear Anna refusing her help confused her.

"You are tense, Miss," the woman said.

"Yeah, just a little bit." She began to scrub Anna's back and her comfort level was shot to hell.

The woman stopped. "Are you unwell?"

"I'm fine. Just not used to people undressing and washing me," Anna admitted.

The woman moved along the top of the tub to face Anna directly, she studied her intently making Anna cross her arms over her chest. Like the rest of her people, she had long black hair pulled into a braid behind her back but she had red jewels woven into it.

A white tunic barely covered her body leaving nothing to the imagination and gold bangle bracelets crawled up her arms. If Anna didn't know any better she would have thought the woman was a princess or someone important. Her skin was just as tanned as her own but her wide doe eyes were far more stunning than Anna's.

"Why?"

"We don't really... you know... like... we don't get naked unless it's in private," Anna struggled to say.

"Why?"

This woman was like a little kid asking why repeatedly. "Because it makes people uncomfortable and it's inappropriate."

"Uncomfortable?"

"Yeah, like… people get upset with it and stuff." She was having a hard time trying to explain it. Defining words wasn't exactly her job that was Damian's.

The woman started to play with her braid as she looked at Anna in curiosity. "What is upset? This word is foreign to me."

"Like, mad. Haven't you ever been mad?"

"Apologies, Miss, but I don't understand this word." The woman cocked her head to the side.

"Nothing has ever made you unhappy or you didn't like something?" Anna asked.

The woman continued to study her with those wondrous eyes. "I am not sure. Life is a gift and I enjoy it to my fullest extent. If we are not happy then what could we be?"

"Sad," Anna answered.

"Sad," the woman rolled it off her tongue. "I know of this word but have never experienced this. Sad is terrible, yes."

"It sure is," Anna agreed.

The woman started to scrub her body again but her facial expression told Anna she was thinking heavily. "You must live in a world with extreme sorrow. Why is it that way?"

"People are more concerned about themselves I guess. They want power, money, and to control everyone else."

"That is not reasonable. Your people should help one another live peacefully. Not watch others live in sorrow."

"That's life I suppose." Anna shrugged.

"It should not be."

Chapter XVII

Ryan

HE WALKED TOWARDS THE pyre with Zee's limp body resting in his arms. Her gear was immaculately clean and her hair swirled around him as the breeze came up from the ocean. Ryan despised being asked to do this.

Many Warriors had shown up for her funeral, lining the beach wearing their gear. It gave him a sense of strength from so many other pained hearts coming together as one. He was not alone in this heartbreak.

He laid her gently down on her wooden bed and placed her hands over her chest. Ryan gazed down at her trying desperately to create a permanent picture of her in his mind. How could someone so pure of beauty inside and out be slain so viciously?

Ryan pressed his forehead against hers, leaving a tender kiss on her brow for the last time. He couldn't move from her side because that would mean she was truly lost to him. It wasn't until a hand was placed on his shoulder that he rejoined the present. He turned to face Amanda and Cyra. The both of them held torches in their hands waiting to engulf Zee's body in the flames.

"It's time," Amanda said gently.

Ryan looked back to Zee, tucking a loose hair behind her ear as he held back the tears threatening to fall down his cheeks.

"Goodbye, Zyanya," he whispered.

He made his way over to where Julia stood. Her expression was unreadable but from what he could tell she was rather uncomfortable. Could he really blame her given the situation? As much as he appreciated Julia being here for him, there was no one he needed more than Damian and Cato right now.

Amanda and Cyra walked around the pyre and began to touch their torches onto the smaller pieces of wood. Within minutes the pyre became engulfed and he watched as Zee's beautiful face disappeared into a blackened corpse.

They watched and waited to see her soul welcomed by the gods and brought to the heavens but nothing was happening. Panic rose into his chest rapidly. Why were they denying her?

"Julia?" his voice wavered.

"I don't know." She must have known his meaning and looked as confused as he felt.

The Warriors started to talk among themselves, everyone wondering what was taking so long for her spirit to soar beyond. Amanda and Cyra sprinted over to Ryan with fear in their eyes.

"What is happening?" Cyra fret. "This isn't right."

The night sky started to churn forming storm clouds and the heavens rumbled above. Lightening went off in every direction as a chill wind started to blow ashes from the pyre all around them. The wind picked up so forcefully he feared the pyre would be distinguished. The pyre needed to finish the job so her ashes could drift out to sea.

Lightning struck the beach and the Warriors started to back away and onto the land. Ryan looked up into the sky observing the formation of a tornado directly above him. This was highly unusual weather in Urbs especially the materialization of a cyclone.

An impossibly wide strike of lightning crashed down against the beach leaving behind a man wearing a black suit with his white shirt unbuttoned at the top. His dark brown hair and beard were trimmed neatly. He looked as if he were a model for a suit company.

No sound remained except the crackling of the fire and Ryan looked around himself. The Warriors were all on their knees bowing down to the man except for Ryan. He held his ground because he had no idea who this man was. For all he knew it was the General in his true form. Nevertheless, the man seemed fixated on Ryan.

Casually striding over to Ryan with his hands behind his back, Ryan prepared for a fight but instead of surprising him with a blow the man held out his arms to embrace Ryan.

Ryan took a step back from his arms with his hand on the hilt of his sword.

"Who are you?"

The man chuckled. "You are losing your touch, Alexander."

His eyes widened at the sound of his first name on the man's lips. There was something familiar about this man that Ryan couldn't place.

"Pardon my fleeting memory but who are you?"

"Alexander, I am Zeus. Your father." Ryan couldn't help but laugh out loud even given the current circumstances around him. The man who claimed to be Zeus looked utterly offended. "Surely your mother conveyed that to you?"

"She did, yes." Ryan's mouth was stuck between gapping and a smirk. "My mother had told wild tales trying to nourish my legend to anyone within earshot."

Zeus embraced him whether he liked it or not giving Ryan a rather rough pat on the back as he did so.

"Your mother was not lying, Alexander."

"I fail to see how a woman can get pregnant from the wind? Which is how my mother told me you came to her." All his mortal life he was told the same thing and here he was again, listening to the same nonsense his mother fed him. The façade ended when he pretended to drink the poison his generals tried to kill him with so many years ago.

"If you must know the details, Alexander, your father was indeed Philip II of Macedon, but I am also your father. On the night you were conceived I possessed your father and lay with your mother. So you are not fully a demigod but your are also not just human," Zeus explained.

Ryan was having a hard time believing his life was even real at this point. First he had a child he never knew about that hated him with a passion. And now he finds out that half of his paternal blood was that of Zeus. Why were his life secrets starting to come out when the world was approaching an end?

"Even if what you say is true, which I completely doubt," Ryan started. "I am confused as to why you believe now was a good time to break the news."

"Your mother told you and I assumed you believed her so this wasn't meant to be a confession of shorts." Zeus put his hands in his pockets. It was rather unnerving how young he looked. Just a bit older than Ryan in his thirties perhaps. "Mainly, I have come to take Zyanya to the heavens. It seems our powers are diminishing at an alarming rate and it must be done physically."

"Physically?" Ryan asked.

Zeus nodded looking as if it were a normal occurrence. "Yes, I must reach into her and bring her up myself. Her death was quite the unfortunate event. She proved nothing but deserving of being accepted."

"She died in battle. How is that more unfortunate than the rest of us?" Ryan asked.

Zeus placed his hand on his shoulder giving it what was meant to be a reassuring squeeze. "You will find out, I promise."

"I truly am sick of all the riddles and tricks the Gods play on us."

"I am aware, but know that we are doing our part. Our powers are weakened, Alexander. We are doing what we can with what we have. Don't lose faith in us and I promise we will prevail in the end."

"It's becoming increasingly difficult," Ryan admitted.

"We don't blame you." Zeus seemed unaffected in the slightest. "Well, I better get to your companion before her soul is lost in the world." Ryan's intake of breath was fast and Zeus laughed at his concern. "Don't worry, Alexander."

Zeus made his way up onto the pyre, unaffected by the flames that danced around his form. To Ryan's horror, Zeus reached into Zee's burning body breaking open her rib cage with such a sickening crunch that he had to turn away from the scene. He focused on Julia, who was still bowing right beside him. She reached up to grasp his hand and Ryan took it willingly holding on tight.

Before he knew it, Zeus stood next to him with a shining ball of light in his hand. White and blue swirled within the globe seizing Ryan's interest. Zeus held it at eye level to give him a better look.

"She has a beautiful soul, Alexander." Zeus admired the globe, her soul's light twinkling in his eyes. "Her loved ones will be happy to see her."

The ache that was briefly gone came back full force in his chest. "Take care of her."

"I will pass it on to her god, whom was much to weak to claim her in their current state. I am merely here to offer my assistance on bringing her to the heavens. I knew how much my son cared for her."

"I hope you would do the same for all the Immortals that risk their lives for the Gods." Ryan almost had an angry tone. He wondered if Zeus was watching him close enough to know what was going on in his life.

"We will. You have my word," Zeus pledged. His attention was on Julia now. "Julia, I wish to speak with you."

She hesitantly stood up and kept her head low as she followed Zeus away from the crowded beach towards the water. Ryan focused on Zee's body feeling a weight lifted knowing her soul was no longer in there. Now it was just the vessel of the woman he knew. It still hurt to realize that not to long ago her loving embrace was entwined with his.

After just moments, Julia and Zeus returned to Ryan's side. Julia's face was flushed and her cheeks red from either anger or embarrassment. "Alright then. Until we meet again, Alexander."

"Please call me Ryan," Ryan groaned.

"I will not," Zeus insisted. "That is not your name and it's unbefitting of your stature."

"I have had many names and this just happens to be the most recent of them," Ryan argued. "I don't favor Alexander anymore."

It felt odd to say the name himself.

"Sorry to disappoint you but you will always and forever be Alexander the Great. It is not something to be ashamed of." Zeus bowed his head to Ryan and then to Julia. "Farewell. Until we meet again."

With that, lightning struck into the sand once more and he was gone. Ryan looked up to the heavens and saw a new star forming before his eyes in its bright, shinning glory. He felt at ease knowing her soul was saved and that Zeus, whom claimed to be his kin, was able to do it.

"Goodbye."

Damian was washed and dressed by the young man at his service and he couldn't help but feel a little reminiscent of the past. He realized he missed things like this. It was refreshing to be doted upon once and awhile.

He was dressed in a long ornate red and gold coat with buttons the length of the jacket reaching down below his knees. Under the jacket he wore trousers that were tight around his ankles yet extremely loose throughout the rest of the leg. Highly old fashioned yet extremely elegant.

They returned to his room and waited for Anna to come out of the bathing chamber. One thing that has never changed over time was how long it took women to get themselves ready for simple occasions. Most of the time the wait was definitely worth it.

"I want to thank you for your assistance, Jagat." Damian turned to the man as he stood with his hands behind his back. Like most of the residents in Shambhala, he was tall, fit, tan, and had long black hair. He reminded Damian a lot of the natives he encountered in Babylon with Ryan long ago.

"There is no need to express your gratitude. It was my pleasure." Jagat smiled warmly showing perfect, white teeth.

They continued to wait so Damian lounged back on the bed and instantly regretted it. If he could sleep all day long he would, but it was almost time to dine with the king and there was no way he would insult the man after the generosity they were shown.

"May I ask you something?" Damian's eyes threatened to close.

"Of course."

"Do your people have sexual relations?" Damian inquired. Anna peaked his curiosity on the matter.

"Of course," Jagat chortled and Damian couldn't help but laugh as well. "May I ask you something, sir?"

"If you stop calling me sir then yes."

"Are you and your wife with-" he begun but was interrupted when they heard the doors of the bathing chambers open.

Anna bashfully walked into sight wearing a beautiful Indian sari. The fabric was wrapped around her hips with the extra cloth draping over her left shoulder yet baring her midriff. It was made of a fine silk he had not seen in ages that was decorated with elaborate gold floral woven into the blue material. Topping off the look, her hair hung down in loose curls with blue gems woven into her dark locks.

Damian was frozen in awe at how stunning she was. Anna's beauty rivaled any princess he had ever met in the history of his existence.

"What?" she barked.

Damian's dropped jaw turned into a lopsided grin as he realized how un-ladylike her grammatical brashness really was. It felt unusual hearing it come from someone who looked like royalty yet it was an aspect about Anna he loved.

"You are stunning."

The woman that helped prepare Anna for dinner nodded in agreement. "She looks like a woman now."

"Will you stop saying that, Esha?" Anna rolled her eyes.

"I mean it purely as a compliment madam." Esha beamed while she continued to mess with Anna's hair. "I do wish you would have let me put Mehndi on you."

"If I knew what that was it might have been an option," Anna groaned. She looked exhausted from being worked on by Esha all evening but to Damian it was worth the wait.

"It's like henna tattoos," Damian explained knowing Anna would be familiar with such things. "It's not permanent, but dyes your skin with intricate designs."

"Ohhh." Anna nodded. "Yep, no thanks, Esha."

"You are a stubborn female," Esha chuckled. "Keep her well, sir."

"I intend to." Damian held out his arm for Anna to take while they were ushered out of the room by Jagat and Esha towards the banquet hall. Damian was having a hard time keeping his eyes from wondering over Anna.

"What?" Anna exhaled hastily.

"You are the most radiant woman I have ever seen in my lifetime." He couldn't help but say it. She was always gorgeous to him but tonight she reviled Aphrodite herself.

Anna didn't look convinced. "I'm sure you've seen better, Damian."

He shook his head. "Never. Not once, my love. I have something to tell you though and I hope you don't think this was my doing."

"What now?" Anna mumbled.

"You seemed to be dressed as a bride," Damian whispered.

"What!"

"Don't worry. I won't allow it, but the Mehndi comment gave it away. Typically it is applied to the bride before a wedding." Damian wanted to laugh at her expression but subdued it. "As I said, don't worry. I highly doubt they had that in mind especially because they referred to you as my wife."

Anna sighed with relief. "Here I thought I was going to have to get married to save the world." Damian tried not to feel offended but his smile faded unwillingly. Anna must have sensed she said something wrong because she added, "Not that I would mind it."

"It's fine, Anna," he tried to reassure her but the sting of her words still lingered. "When and if you are ready, I will always be here to say yes to. I didn't lie when I said you are the most radiant woman I have ever seen. I just hope you don't come to your senses and realize you deserve the best."

Jagat and Esha smiled sheepishly at one another as they entered the tall double doors leading into the banquet hall. Damian stopped walking without realizing it, having a brief flashback of his mortal life long ago. Ryan sat head at the long table wearing his military armor, beckoning him forward to sit at his wedding feast when he wed Roxanna.

Anna's grip tightened around his arm bringing him back to reality. It was rare he fell back into a memory like that but it always left his head muddled. He studied his surroundings trying to anchor himself to the present.

Meticulously draped silk, embroidered in gold, silver, beads and jewels hung elegantly from the ceiling and alongside red accented walls with copper painted pillars. Bright colorful tapestries hung attractively against sections of the wall that were made with such delicate craftsmanship it was obviously hand made. Even with so many different colors, they had managed to make the room feel warm and elegant.

A low floor table ran down the span of the dining hall sitting on top of hand-knotted rugs. Suspended pendant lanterns lit the room. Golden cutlery and dinnerware were nearly hidden by the overflowing food taking up the entire table.

Jagat and Esha ushered them to the end of the table where the king waited, calmly watching their entrance. Cato was already seated on one side of the king wearing a similar outfit as Damian's except in green.

"By Jupiter, is that Anna?" Cato wiggled his eyebrows at them with an overly disturbing grin on his face.

Anna stuck her tongue out at him but must have quickly realized she did it in the presence of the king because her cheeks flushed. It didn't seem to faze the man in the least because he said, "She is a beauty beyond compare."

"I most assuredly agree." Damian squeezed Anna's hand as they sat down across from Cato on the richly colored floor cushions in front of the table.

"Now then." The king clapped his hands together. "How do my guests feel after becoming cleansed?"

"Considerably better now, thank you." Damian offered him a curt nod.

"I do apologize but I realize we were never properly introduced." The king tipped his goblet to his lips. The thing was profusely decorated in jewels. "I am Aniruddha, the twenty-first King of Shambhala."

"I am Damian and this is Anna." Damian gestured towards Cato across the table who was eyeing the food on the table. "That is Cato. We are Immortal Warriors chosen by the gods as you know."

"Such peculiar names." Aniruddha set his cup down, folding his hands under his chin as he studied the three of them. "Cato is somewhat familiar, a Roman name?"

Cato dragged his eyes away from the plate of cooked goose to answer. "Yes, your highness. My father was native to ancient Rome and I am a Reborn Immortal."

"Damian," Aniruddha tried out his name next. "I know of Damianos, a Greek name."

Damian was astonished by his knowledge but recalled

that these were a people of high intelligence. "Yes, that is where it is derived from, but I go by Damian."

"So you are a Greek?" Aniruddha plucked a grape from its vine, popping it in his mouth as he waited for Damian to speak.

"More or less."

"Explain." Aniruddha's tone was friendly enough yet Damian felt a reluctance to answer.

He wasn't ashamed of his past, yet Ryan made it clear they were never to speak about it if possible. It was hard to break the tradition of hiding his true self from others. But Damian decided in this moment that it was his life. He could reveal whatever he wanted without Ryan's permission.

"My first name, from when I was mortal, is Hephaestion," Damian relayed the information. "I am Greek but primarily claim to be Macedonian."

King Aniruddha grew overly thrilled by what Damian divulged about himself. "You are Hephaestion?" Damian nodded but he did so cautiously. Most people didn't have that reaction when learning his name. "You were an extraordinary man."

Damian almost choked on the wine that barely reached his tongue and a strained laugh unwillingly escaped. The table was becoming full of guests and the attention was uncomfortably placed on Damian.

"I would have to respectfully disagree."

"Of course you were extraordinary! How could you believe otherwise?" King Aniruddha exclaimed. "You were the key factor to Alexander the Great's success."

"I appreciate the praise but taking false acclaim would be

an insult to Ry- I mean Alexander's legend." More guest's attention were directly on Damian and the noticeable enthusiasm radiating from the king's voice. Damian shifted uneasily on his cushion and was thankful Anna grabbed his hand under the table giving him a reassuring squeeze.

"You must realize how significant of a role you played in his success? You were his confidant and his closest supporter. In many ways it appeared he looked to you for guidance and reassurance."

"Ryan, sorry, Alexander was very firm on his vision as to what he would accomplish in his lifetime. No one could influence him one way or another, except himself. I was merely there to listen and give my best judgment to my friend even if it were ignored. However, I will always treasure your words of praise."

King Aniruddha smiled softly behind his cup before saying, "It looks as if some of his stubbornness rubbed off on his right hand man." That was one fact Damian could agree on.

Never in his life did he think of himself as a key factor in Ryan's endeavors. Perhaps he was a buffer at times, but other than that Ryan ran his own show. He did manage few minor victories in his mortal days. However, his life would never match up to Ryan's success nor would he expect it to. Exceeding the glory of Alexander the Great was a near impossible feat.

"So I gather Alexander refers to himself as Ryan currently?" Damian confirmed with a feeble nod. "This I don't understand. You are who you are and you are not who you are not. Instead of learning from your past you are concealing it, letting it overpower you instead of driving you to more fruitful ventures. Hephaestion is a name to be proud of my dear Damian, not cower from."

"Hephaestion is a little out dated and somewhat hard for people to say." Cato managed to sneak a goose leg from the plate during their conversation. His mouth was filled with meat as he talked making Damian groan with embarrassment, yet as he looked at the king there was nothing but absolute amusement there. After hundreds of years Cato had yet to learn to chew with his mouth closed.

The guest's attention slowly drifted away from Damian's origins and onto one another. He was thankful for that. Attention was Ryan's bread and butter, not his.

Throughout the evening they ate and chatted about life in the mortal world. Damian tried not to reveal all the devastating information about what was going on for the sake of King Aniruddha's people. He envied their peaceful existence but pitied them for their ignorance.

"So Anna," Aniruddha started, "is that your full name?"

She coyly shook her head, her curls bouncing against her chest drawing his undivided attention on her again. She was so damn beautiful.

"No sir, umm… highness sir." She closed her eyes and let out a heavy breath. "It's Adrianna."

"Again, your real name has much more beauty to it. Fitting the woman before me most assuredly." The King shook his head. "Silly Immortals."

"Not to rush your highness, but when can we obtain the Brahmadanda? The world of the Immortals have a time limit and if my calculations are correct we have three days before the weapon is released."

"I will never understand the thinking of you mortal beings. Killing so many souls that are a part of our entire life force. Every life is precious and should be treated as a gift." As if the other guests had heard his words, the entire table silently held their goblets up in a toast. "You will receive it tomorrow when you depart."

"Your kindness never ends, your highness. We are forever in your debt," Damian said.

King Aniruddha bellowed a hearty laugh making Damian's cheeks redden when the rest of the table joined. "Debts don't exist here, dear Damian." He was glad the king finally started to call him that. "We are ecstatic to assist in prolonging the end of the world, until the anointed time set by our prophecy."

The more Damian heard about this prophecy of theirs the more nervous he became. From the sounds of it though, they had a timeline to uphold until their prophecy came to light and the time wasn't upon them yet. He dreaded the thought of another world ending mission to fight for.

"Enough talking about business." The king clapped his hands. "Bring in the entertainment!"

Chapter XVIII

Ryan

SOME MIGHT SAY HE was going crazy. That he'd lost all sense of reality on his obsession of war. He might even partially agree, but Ryan was fully aware of himself. He knew the fine line between brilliance and insanity.

He had pushed all of the furniture in his room to one side and began to map out the world on his wood floor with red paint. The only clothing he bothered to wear were a pair of briefs. But in all honesty he could care less if someone walked in on him naked. He was in the zone.

Paintbrush in tow, he crawled on his hands and knees as he continued to map out the world with as much detail as he could possibly recall. When he was finished, Ryan tossed the paintbrush aside and climbed on top of his dresser to look down at his handy work. "South America is a little big but that's fine. Texas is safe for America. Italy is in trouble... No, no, not there... maybe there?"

He paced along the top of his long dresser running his hands through his hair. There had to be more countries opposed to the Risen than this.

Ryan jumped off his dresser and walked over to where the paint was located. Plucking the blue paintbrush from its can, he began to mark places completely run over by the Risen with X's. "Australia seems neutral thus far, but Kenya… ugh!"

He tossed away the paintbrush, replacing it with a knife hanging from his wall and twirled it around in his hand out of habit. "There must be a way."

A knock came at his door but Ryan didn't move his eyes from his work as he ignored whoever wanted his attention.

Knock, knock, knock.

"Perhaps if we overtook the UK…"

Knock, knock, knock.

"Go away!" However, the door opened slowly which Ryan tried his best to ignore. "Russia is gone. Dammit… there could be… no." He shook his head.

"Uhh, Ryan?"

"Maybe if we could take back Japan?" Ryan rattled on and threw the knife at Japan on his makeshift map. It stuck into the floor with a soft *thunk*. "Could be possible."

"Ryan?"

"Could they abandon Australia and combine our powers?" The frustration of it all was becoming clear. Their forces were too outstretched from one another. "No… Maybe…"

A sharp pain rushed through his cheek followed by a hand-sized burn and he finally snapped out of his feverish thoughts.

"Ryan, snap the hell out of it." Caleb snapped his fingers in Ryan's face. "You alright man?"

Ryan swiped Caleb's legs out from under him and jumped on top of him, his hands quickly wrapping around his throat. "Whose side?"

"What?" Caleb gasped for air, his eyes were wide with shock but it fed into Ryan's anger.

"Aden and Jesse. Both traitors. Whose to say you aren't as well?" Ryan glared.

"Ryan, please," Caleb choked. "I… can't… breathe."

"No shit." Ryan grinned as he felt his sanity begin to waver. "Answer me."

Caleb kicked out his legs from under Ryan, even tried to buck him off but nothing worked. "I'm not," was all he could muster to say through his collapsing throat.

Ryan released him but kept his eyes suspiciously on him. "I highly doubt that."

"It's true," Caleb coughed. "I've been against it from the beginning when Aden tried to recruit me. I've been trying to run the Domus alone since Cato, Damian, and you have been M.I.A."

He studied Caleb while he continued to cough. His eyes watered from the pressure Ryan had put on his throat. Could he really trust this man? His team was so deeply involved with the Risen?

"I'm keeping my eye on you," Ryan hissed as he stood up, going back to his map on the floor.

Caleb's demeanor changed. He was timid and cautious as he pushed himself up from the floor. Not that Ryan could blame the man for being fearful. Never had Ryan put hands on him. Caleb was always kind and gentle, the opposite of his other companions.

"Ryan?" Caleb tried to get his attention while he remained a safe distance away. "We need your help trying to get the mortals out of danger. They are dying at an alarming rate and I have been sending teams on stealth missions to help as much as we can, but it doesn't seem to be doing much good. We need a new strategy."

"You are wasting our resources," Ryan growled. "We need to attack in larger numbers. Recruit the mortals to join our forces with us as their leaders. This is war, the time for stealth missions are over for our kind. We need armies."

"Sorry but it just seems very unlikely that that would work. The mortals don't know anything about us, let alone enough to follow us."

"Caleb, I am working on a plan as we speak," Ryan hissed. "The mortals will have to wait until we defeat the Risen on our home front. If we don't succeed at that, we won't be any help to the mortals if we are dead. This is our priority for now."

Damian.

By the will of Zeus he wished his friends would appear any moment to provide a shred of hope for their future. He should have gone with them.

No, they can do this.

"I wonder how he got all those people to believe in him?" Caleb blurted out.

"What do you mean?"

"Well, in order to change their faith, mortals would require proof of his divinity. I mean, a big guy with a deep voice can't just show up and demand they believe in him. Their minds don't work that way." Caleb had a point.

Ryan leaned against his dresser, finally deciding to give

Caleb his attention. "Magic perhaps? I'm not sure. My best guess is that he showed them things that seemed impossible in their eyes and gathered enough followers to actually give him those powers."

"If that were the case wouldn't magicians have taken over the world?" Caleb laughed.

"Good point." Ryan smirked. "But Immortals are different. Michael was once one of us remember? Now he is a divine angel with supernatural powers. Heracles was a demigod who became an Immortal and then turned into a god himself. We are people that don't exist in a world of limitations like the mortals do. We have the capability of becoming more than just ourselves."

Caleb dropped his eyes as he asked, "Are you going to become a god as well?"

There it was. The question everyone kept asking him since Zee's funeral when Zeus showed up to tell him he was a smidgeon part god. "I'm not even a demigod, Caleb. Heracles was half god and had powers while he was mortal. I, on the other hand, have no powers at all."

"I think you do." Caleb shrugged. "You did the impossible as a mortal in a time where failure was always inevitable. You never lost a battle and you conquered countries by the age of eighteen."

"Maybe you didn't hear about my time in India," Ryan scoffed.

"I did, but I also know that you exceeded everyone's expectations. You are the individual every Warrior, mortal or Immortal, dreams to be," Caleb insisted, but Ryan merely rolled his eyes. "It's true."

"Will you all quit saying that shit? We have all proved our worth. I am no different than any of you." Ryan looked deep into Caleb's seemingly innocent brown eyes.

Caleb always reminded him of a child. He was merely eighteen when he was Chosen. Caleb would never grow the features a man deserved to have. He used his youthful appearance to his advantage though. Those boyish brown eyes looked on the verge of aggravation at what Ryan was saying.

"I wish you would became a god, Ryan."

"Why's that?" Ryan bit the inside of his cheek to prevent himself from laughing at such a ridiculous notion.

"With you as a god we could restore lost faith back to the mortals. You could open their eyes to the truth that their gods are indeed real. That their gods care about them and that the General is nothing but a showman working the right angles." Caleb was mulling over his own words. "We need to renew the Immortals belief in the Gods as well Ryan or all this fighting and risk will be for nothing."

"I can do all that, simply as a man with honor."

Julia

"How are they?" Julia brushed her fingers over Grace's bruised cheek.

"Grace is having some issues but Colette seems to be pulling through." The healer informed her. "How they got out of there in this condition is baffling."

She insisted that both women were treated in the same room with most of the healing staff there to monitor them. Julia wouldn't let anyone slack off when it came to Grace and Colette's health. They wouldn't die or so help her one of the healers would.

"What about Colette's leg?" she asked.

The healer placed the picture of her x-ray over a light for Julia to see. "It was broken in three places. We had to put a rod in her leg to keep it together."

"You couldn't just give her a healing tonic?" Julia wanted to choke the woman.

"No, it was too extensive for that. It was almost shattered. Magic and medicine can only go so far, Julia. You know that." Julia did know that. When Damian and Ryan were badly injured it was a miracle Ryan pulled through at all. "There's a possibility she may be discharged as a Warrior because of this."

Or not, given the Council of Command is dead and the Warriors will be nothing but a memory anyways.

"Keep me informed of their conditions." Julia took a step closer to the small woman, ferocity in her eyes. "And just so we are clear, if they die, you will follow."

Before she could see the healer's response, Julia was out the door heading towards her room. Once she was in her chambers she shut the door and nearly had a heart attack. Aden stood against the wall looking furious yet weak.

"So, has my little bitch been a good girl or a bad girl?"

Julia crossed her arms over her chest. "Excuse you?"

Aden's fist wrapped around her throat and slammed her into the wall. "Either you are a tremendous actress or you have switched sides again, Julia." Aden's lips hovered over hers as he pressed his body against her shaking one. "Which is it?"

"I told you already." She struggled against his body. His grip wasn't tight enough to prevent her from speaking. "I needed to make him think I was on his side. I am still with you."

Aden squeezed harder momentarily before he released her entirely. "I don't think I believe you, love."

"Believe it. Weather you like it or not, we need Ryan. He can convince the Immortals to trade sides and with that, less death on our hands and more of our kind to rule the mortals."

"Don't you ever say his name in my presence," Aden hissed. "I don't want to hurt you again my love but trust me, I will."

Her heart raced at the thought of him doing so. He hit her so often his company scared her but for some reason she believed he had every right to do with her as he pleased. Part of her hated that.

"I'm sorry." She looked down at the ground. Being submissive was new to her. "Believe me when I say I am with you."

Aden seized the back of her hair pulling it painfully down, forcing her to look up into his eyes. It hurt but she wouldn't say anything to make him even angrier with her. His moods were terrifying.

"Do what you must to convince him, Julia but when the moment comes that you realize it is impossible, you better inform me. I will take care of that disease once and for all while we stand in a pool of his blood." Aden kissed her roughly, bringing the feeling of bliss and disgust all at once. Her hands started to quiver.

Aden noticed her body's reaction and snatched her face into his grip looking angrily in her eyes.

"Have you taken your tonic?"

Julia shook her head. "I ran out."

"Damn girl." Aden backhanded her cheek. "I will have it delivered in your room within the hour. I must leave before anyone knows I am here."

Julia held onto her cheek, forcing back the tears that threatened to escape. No woman should put up with this.

"Okay."

Aden pushed her out of the way of the door. "Don't be late taking it."

"Aden, wait." Julia tenderly grasped his hand making his body stiffen. "Are you okay from the whip?"

Without an answer he yanked back his hand and left her alone. Julia dropped to her floor and held her head in her hands as the tears finally spilled over. She loved him, didn't she? Yet he was so cruel and nothing she did was ever good enough.

Could she be dreaming or was this a hell she couldn't escape from?

Her attempts to make Ryan see reason were becoming limited. It was almost time for the ultimate showdown making her urgency for him to join even more pressing. Yet, her mind was muddled with her feelings for both Ryan and Aden, not on her task for his allegiance.

On occasion she hated Ryan, but right now her hatred seemed to subside. She couldn't think straight and had no idea what she truly wanted. The Risen or the Immortals? Aden or Ryan? What the hell is going on with her?

She remembered clearly that she wanted to kill Ryan at one point, a few times actually but right now she just wanted to be around him. So here she was, on her way to his room. Just as she came to his door she could hear voices within. She peaked through the cracked door catching a glimpse of Caleb talking with Ryan. What was he doing in there?

Julia bit her lip not being able to decide if she should invade their meeting or to just leave. Her curiosity got the better of her when she heard them mention different countries and something about a coalition. They were too quiet for her to really understand so she leaned in closer to listen.

It was her bad luck that she accidently bumped into Ryan's door.

"Shit," she muttered lowly.

Caleb appeared at the entrance giving her a seething look she had never seen on his face. She always liked Caleb, so much so that he was one of her favorite Warriors yet he was giving her the death glare.

"What are you doing?" he spat.

Julia blinked at him. "What?"

"Who is it?" Ryan yelled towards them but Caleb blocked her from sight.

"Just hang on," Caleb forced cheerfulness out of his voice. "Why are you in the Domus, Julia?" His voiced was replaced with malice.

"What do you mean?"

Caleb gave her another disapproving look. "I know you are part of the Risen and the only reason I haven't said anything is because I truly care about your well being, not to mention Ryan's sanity would be compromised."

"Why do you care about Ryan?"

"He is quite possibly the only person that can get us out of this mess you traitors have started," Caleb growled. Seeing how much resentment he had towards her broke her heart. Like Damian, Caleb was an amazing and honest man.

Her head throbbed. "I just wanted to see him for a minute."

"You are walking a very thin line, Julia." Caleb's voice was full of warning. "I know Aden's affection for you yet I can see Ryan still means something. Don't think Aden will be forgiving if you betray him. I love him as a brother but he isn't someone I would cross."

"I can take care of myself."

"I hope so because Aden will kill you if he believes you are against him," Caleb cautioned.

Julia was no fool, she knew what Aden was capable of and it added to her confusion about her feelings for him.

"For god's sake, who is it?" She heard Ryan come from behind Caleb and the door was pulled further open.

Julia gasped at the sight of him in his underwear with paint marks smudged on his body. For some reason she couldn't avert her eyes from his bulging region until Caleb snapped his fingers in her face.

"Oh," she stammered and felt her cheeks redden. "I just… umm…"

Ryan was happily amused by her reaction. "What is it, Julia?"

"I just want to talk," she finally said, twirling a strand of her hair between her fingers to calm her embarrassment.

Ryan exchanged looks with Caleb she could only describe as a silent stare down. "Later?"

Caleb nodded leaving Julia with Ryan in his black briefs that left nothing to the imagination. She was having a hard time focusing on anything but his body right now. Ryan stood aside for her to enter his room and as she did so she took in her surroundings.

A massive map was painted on the floor marked with points she knew to be the Risen's stronghold and weaknesses. He was obviously doing his research.

"Can I get you anything to drink?" She tore her eyes away from the map on the floor and realized he was watching her like a hawk.

"Oh, no, thank you." She smiled softly but she could tell he was scrutinizing her now.

She was still finding it difficult not to stare at his body until he turned his back to her while drinking from a glass and she saw the wounds on his back from Aden. She had stitched him up as soon as they got back to the Domus but it needed a lot more healing.

"What do you want?" His voice held a small amount of tension within it.

Julia stared at her shoes, trying to focus on her words rather than the gorgeous man before her.

"I just wanted to see you. Is that okay?"

His bare feet were adjacent from hers, his body was so close she could feel his breath on her skin, making her heart quicken. Not again. He cannot affect her like this again, yet he did. He was a drug she couldn't quit.

"Are you uncomfortable?" he asked quietly.

Although inside she was screaming 'yes' she shook her head no. She hated him being so exposed but she wanted nothing more than to take in the sight of him. His perfectly muscular figure begged to be touched. His eyes told her of his wanting, even his clenching fists became intoxicating to watch knowing what they were capable of doing to her. This was not okay to think about.

"Colette's leg has a rod in it and Grace is not doing very well," she blurted out. Tears started to well in her eyes and she tried so hard to force them back. 'Tears are a sign of weakness' as Aden kept telling her. "They don't know if she will pull through and she looks so terrible, Ryan."

To her surprise she was pulled against his bare chest with his arms wrapped around her as if he could shield her from the pain. Giving into her weakness, she sobbed in his arms while he rubbed her back. Her hell of a reality became too powerful to hold back.

She hated but loved both Ryan and Aden. She was loyal yet disloyal to both the Risen and Immortals. Jupiter forgive her, she killed Zee and had yet to tell anyone her secret. Guilt finally grew inside her over the woman's death. At the time it was amusing, fun even, but now it was nothing more than horrifying.

Her legs trembled, threatening to collapse until she was whisked into Ryan's arms and laid gently on his bed. Ryan cradled her against him and she let him even though she was not worthy of his kindness. All she could do was cry and let him soothe her until the tears stopped and a small weight was lifted off her shoulders.

Ryan continued to smooth her hair back and hold her against him even after she calmed down.

"Are you alright?"

"I don't know."

The steady beat of his heart relaxed her. She pulled her head back to look at his face. His demeanor was calm but his eyes told a different story. He was disheartened.

"What can I do?" he asked gently.

Before she could contain them, her feelings took over and she pressed her mouth roughly against his. Lacking grace, she straddled his lap making her shorts slide up her thighs.

The hesitation in his touch was obvious. Frustratingly he wouldn't kiss her back but instead, gradually pulled himself away from her.

"Julia stop."

"Please," she begged, moving her mouth against his again, but he held her back at arms length.

"Stop," he ordered more forcefully.

She wanted to weep from his rejection. "Why?"

"I can't do this. It's too soon."

Julia frowned down at him but made no attempt to move from his lap. His hands were placed on her hips, giving her a slight indication that he did indeed want this. He just needed to be pushed.

"Because of Zee?" she asked quietly to which he nodded. "I don't understand it. It was a one time thing wasn't it?"

"Sex with her was a one time thing because that's all we could have together, but my feelings for her were far greater than you think." Ryan breathed out a short breath of angst. "After you got with Aden I never thought I would find someone I cared for again. But then Zee came along. I know it was quick and the timing was terrible, but I felt happy with her, which was surprising. I didn't think I could feel that way about two women at the same time."

"You loved her?"

"I don't know but I think I was beginning too. When I knew you were lost to me I made a promise to myself that I would give her everything I could offer. But then she was taken from me too. I can't just jump into bed with someone so easily, Julia."

"After me you jumped in with her."

"You moved on from me. She died. There is a difference."

Julia's heart felt like it was tightening in her chest. The fact he was so infatuated with another woman truly hurt. All thoughts of Aden turned to disgust as it was becoming clearer to her that she hated him as well as the Risen. The one man she wanted, that she'd ever wanted, was right in front of her.

"Please, Ryan." She wrapped her arms around his neck, feeling somewhat triumphant when he closed his eyes at her touch. "I need you."

"It's not right," he whispered with his eyes still shut. "It's disrespectful."

"It's not." Julia ran her hands up his chest, stopping to grip his shoulders. "You don't dwell on the past, Ryan. You move on to a better future, but you never forget."

She leaned down and nibbled on his earlobe. Julia heard his sharp intake of breath while his hold on her hips grew tighter with need. "Please don't do this to me."

She kissed down his collarbone, stopping briefly to ask, "Do you want me to stop?"

"Yes," his voice was weak.

"I don't believe you." She moved her hips against his, feeling just how she affected him.

"Dammit, Julia." He flipped her on her back and pushed her legs apart with his own. Crawling on top of her he pressed his body against hers. His eyes were glazed over from want and his lip quivered while he took deep breaths. "How do you do this to me?"

Before she could answer his lips silenced her own, his tongue parting her lips to deepen the kiss making her feel victorious. This is what she wanted and who she wanted. Not the Risen. Not Aden. She wanted Ryan and her old life back.

Caught up in the moment her hands gripped his back making a grumbling of pain break their kiss.

"I'm so sorry." She bit her lip when their eyes met but there was more amusement than pain on his face.

"There's my Julia." He traced his thumb along her mouth. "Always biting that lip."

As if forgetting she had clawed at his injured back, his mouth captured hers once again and she could feel he how ready to take her. He pulled her up to sitting just long enough to remove her tank top and he pushed her back down on the bed.

His mouth left hers leaving sweet kisses down her chest and stomach that was a combination of torture and bliss. It didn't last long before his lips were on hers again. She was eager for more so she took his bottom lip between her teeth making him groan against her mouth.

"Fuck, I missed you." The look in his eyes was turning animalistic.

She had to tell him about Zee before this went further. She wouldn't be able to live with herself otherwise.

"There's something I have to tell you."

"What?" His breath was heavy with wanting.

She tried to speak but the words wouldn't escape her lips. It was as if she lost the ability to talk even as her mind told her mouth what to do. Why couldn't she tell him?

"What?" he asked again but the words refused to form.

"I missed you too," was all she could say. Ryan smoothed back her hair from her face so tenderly she closed her eyes. This is what love truly felt like. Not a hit to the head.

"You really have no idea how much I've missed you."

"Don't tell me, show me," she commanded and he graciously obliged.

Chapter XIX

Anna

"So is it just me or does King What's-his-face have a hard on for you?" Anna couldn't help but giggle when his eyes went wide. "What?"

"Well don't you have a dirty mouth?"

"Sorry, but it's true. He was all about you being such a badass rather than Ryan." She felt proud about that and he should too. Damian was much more than he gave himself credit for.

After dinner they decided they needed to gather their strength and went straight to bed. However, Anna was in the mood to talk about some things that Damian was gracious enough to answer with his eyes closed.

"I still can't believe we have two days until the Risen pulls their bullshit," Anna sighed.

"My, my, my, you are on fire tonight, Anna." Damian laughed at her 'dirty mouth' but pretending to be a lady during dinner wore her out. "It is slightly terrifying to think about though."

She absentmindedly twirled a lock of Damian's hair around her finger. "What do we do once we get back?"

"Prepare for war."

"Oh goody." She rolled her eyes. That meant fighting people that really wanted to kill her who have much more experience than she had. "This is going to be dangerous isn't it?"

"Very."

His short answers seemed to be an indication he was tired of talking. So, she lay back on their bed, still wearing the little getup she was tossed into for dinner. It was pretty comfortable but just having everyone's eyes on her constantly was super unsettling.

"You were breathtaking tonight." It was like he could read her mind.

"Thank you." She kissed his lips, drawing out a smile from him. "You looked like a weirdo."

His sleepy state seemed to diminish and she quickly found herself on her back with her hands pinned above her head.

"You ma'am, are being very rude and crude tonight."

"Rude and crude? Easy with the rhyming, Mr. Poetic."

"I would hardly call that poetry, Anna." He kissed her gently and when he pulled back she only saw love in his eyes. She loved that about him.

She wrapped her arms around his neck, pulling him down to kiss her again and he willingly did so. She felt no need to push this moment further than kissing. She enjoyed the feeling of his soft lips on hers, teasing her mouth with a flick of his tongue every so often.

"I am so lucky to have you." He gave her a peck on the cheek.

"You bet your sweet ass you are." She hugged him tightly against her body. "I wonder what Cato is up to."

Damian went back to lying beside her with his eyes closed. "I have no idea. Knowing him, he probably found a woman to prey on."

"Do you really think they would go for it?" she laughed.

"Absolutely. He is someone new and different. The appeal would be too great for someone who believes in nothing but bliss," Damian laughed. "He better not get us in trouble though."

"Like Ryan would?"

"Exactly."

"He slept with a Queen of India, right?" Anna asked.

"Yeah. He had a lot of problems there as a mortal and decided to give them a little payback."

"What happened?" She propped herself up on her elbow.

"Many things." Damian's eyes were shut and his jaw was tensed. "We marched into India and many of our soldiers died along the way. We weren't prepared for the natural dangers of their land. It was all new to us and we couldn't even begin to know how to survive. Once we actually made it to a real battle it was the first time any of us saw an elephant."

Anna laughed but noticed Damian bit the inside of his cheek to contain his irritation.

"Sorry, but elephants? How is that scary?" She had read much about their past but couldn't for the life of her understand why elephants were so terrifying.

"They were massive beasts that could crush a man to

death with just one step. Our horses were scared to death of them and it took a lot of coaxing to even get near them."

"Okay." She decided to change the direction the conversation was going given he was getting upset with her. "He holds a grudge because the fight was difficult?"

"It's not really the reason he holds a grudge. The main reason was how his men started to turn on him. His ambitions grew and they hated being in India. They all wanted to go home and he blames India for his inability to conquer the known world. Also, his horse died there."

"Wasn't he Immortal then?" she asked. "Didn't you tell me that you were both Chosen when he established Alexandria in Egypt?"

Damian finally grinned. "Damn, you do listen don't you? Yeah, he was Immortal which gave him even more of a big head going into India."

Even to this day Anna couldn't wrap her head around the fact that Ryan was Alexander the Great. "How old are you guys again?"

"I believe we were around twenty-five when we were Chosen. I honestly don't remember anymore."

"Sweet. I'm still younger than you." She beamed.

He leaned over her to give her one more kiss on the lips. She could never grow tired of his affection. "Any other questions, my love?"

She had so many questions about his life but there was one above all that bothered her. "Did you love him then? Like you love me now?" Her stomach began to twist and turn as if she would be sick.

"I thought we were past that?"

"We are. I think. But that doesn't mean I can't be curious." The fact that her boyfriend and his best friend had sex with each other was still hard to get over. She knew it was in the past but the concept of it was still new to her.

"Words cannot describe how much I care for Ryan and how much I will always love him. But I am not *in love* with him, Anna. Nor have I ever been. It was different when we were mortal. I can't explain it."

"Hmm," she grinned.

"What?"

"You're cute when you're uncomfortable."

"You little…" He started to tickle her and she laughed uncontrollably. "You did that on purpose didn't you?"

She rolled on top of him and straddled his hips. "Maybe I did. Maybe I didn't." Anna kissed his nose.

"You ma'am, are pure evil." Damian looked just as amused as she felt. "Does it really even bother you?"

She shook her head. "Nope. I got over it for the most part. It's still kind of weird to think about though."

"Agreed." His hands ran up and down her thighs and she enjoyed the light massage he was giving. She enjoyed seeing him happy like this. Their conversation almost took a bad turn but he never seemed to fully get upset with her. He was Mr. Perfect.

Anna made a decision right then and there about their lives together. Catching him off guard was a favorite pastime of hers.

"So when are we getting hitched?"

Damian's hands stopped abruptly. "What?"

"That's me saying 'yes,' dumb-dumb."

"How much wine did you have at dinner?"

"Being tipsy doesn't change my answer."

Damian cocked his head to the side as a huge grin crept onto his lips. "Are you serious?"

She nodded and chewed on her fingernails nervously. The look on Damian's face was everything she could ever hope for from a man, pure unwavering love. When he didn't answer she began to get nauseous.

With one swift motion he pulled off her sari and threw it somewhere on the floor. His hands trailed up her chest, stopping to cradle her cheek. She couldn't help but say, "Taken a sari off before, I see."

Pulling her down to his lips he whispered before he kissed her, "Don't ruin the moment."

They both hastily removed each other's clothing and once they were both undressed Anna sat back on her heels eyeing the v shape leading down his waist.

"Yum."

Damian gave her a dimpled grin. "You ma'am, are incorrigible."

"Better get used to it."

Julia

Did I really just sleep with Ryan? Yes.

Without a doubt she did and her sore and tired body held testament to the fact. This time was so different than the first time with Ryan. It was new, unknown territory before. Even with Aden it was different. This time it was nothing but pure ecstasy that radiated throughout her entire body and soul. It was perfect.

Just thinking about it on the way back to her room gave her shivers down her spine and a yearning for more. Yet, there was one thing that bothered her deeply about the experience; her inability to tell Ryan what she had done. It clawed at her belly knowing the evil she created within the world. She needed to tell the truth.

The memory of Zee haunted her and the guilt was becoming too heavy to carry. How could she have killed her so easily? It was sinful and she needed to face the punishment for it, even if it meant being stripped of her life.

As she got closer to her room she stopped in her tracks. Harsh yells were coming from behind her door causing her body to unwillingly shake in fear. Daring to tip toe towards the crack in the door she soon realized she was the cause of the problem.

"If she isn't back in five minutes I am going to go look for her," Aden yelled.

"You can't waltz around the Domus anymore, Aden, and neither can I." She could tell by the strain in Jesse's voice that he was trying to calm down his friend. "Why the hell is this tonic wearing off so much anyways?"

"Her body is becoming accustomed to it. I've been strengthening the dosage almost daily to maintain the desired affect," a man she never heard before said. "This is the strongest one I can come up with without completely turning her mind into a blank slate."

"Maybe that's what she needs!" Aden yelled.

"You can't be serious?" Jesse sounded stunned. "This is Julia we are talking about, not just some random person."

"What difference does it make? We need a permanent solution even if that means erasing all of her memories," Aden insisted.

"You can't be serious," Jesse urged.

"Get your hands off of me and yes I am serious. She's a liability right now and we must maintain her loyalty to us." She heard shuffling within her room but her body remained frozen in place. "Ryan is much stronger with her on his side. She needs to be out of the picture."

"You do realize the General will not allow this?" the unknown man said. "The tonic was made to target specific behaviors and subside goodness within. Nothing more."

They were poisoning her. No wonder her mind was so messed up lately! That damn tonic was not for her headaches. It was to make her a vile creature capable of atrocious things.

"Will you just go out there and find her?" Aden hissed. "Put your hood on. We will discuss the matter later."

Julia's heart raced as she started to run down the hallway trying to get away before they found her. The footsteps pounding behind her made it clear she'd been seen and she forced her legs to move quicker.

"Julia, stop!" Jesse called after her.

"No you lying bastard!" she yelled back over her shoulder and saw Jesse gaining on her with Aden right behind him.

She rounded the corner and ran straight into Emma. "Dammit Julia, what are you doing?"

They both fell hard to the ground but Julia staggered up

and continued to run, ignoring Emma's cursing after her. She had almost made it to the parlor room when her body was tackled and she landed on her stomach. Julia kicked back at Aden's face as hard as she could but he caught her around the ankles and Jesse grabbed her arms.

"Let go of me." She struggled against their grasp and Aden covered her mouth to keep her quiet. She bit him.

"Dammit, girl." Aden's fist connected with her cheek before they began to haul her back to her room.

She kept wriggling her body trying to get loose from them but their grip was painfully tight on her. Aden looked infuriated beyond belief which made her extremely happy. Stupid little bastard made her so messed up in the head that she did unthinkable things. Her heart broke into pieces just thinking about what she had done.

Against her best efforts they managed to get her back into her room where a tall, overly skinny man stood with a vile of her tonic in his hand.

"No!" She thrust her legs forward at Aden trying to push him hard enough that he would lose his grip.

They managed to get her on her bed. "Julia, just stop," Jesse pleaded as he pinned her body down. Aden produced straps from under her bed and bound her wrists and ankles at the corners.

"That's better." Aden straightened up once she was bound tight. She couldn't move at all. "You will pay for that bite, my sweet."

Aden was close enough that she spat in his face. "Get the hell away from me you worthless excuse for a man."

"You will be singing a new tune soon, darling. You always

do. We've learned by now how to handle you. Every time we are too late, you have these episodes. Hence, the restraints." He looked down her body in such a way that made her uncomfortable. "Though, these may be useful in other ways."

His hand brushed from her ankle up her leg causing goose bumps to crawl along the skin he touched. Her eyes opened in panic as his hand stopped at her pelvis. Aden pushed his hand inside the top of her shorts and she screamed.

"No!" She tried to buck him away but the restraints stretched her out too far to move. "Get your filthy hands off of me." Aden didn't let up. His hands ventured further down and she screamed even louder as he pressed inside of her. "Help! Someone help me!"

With his other hand Aden covered her mouth. Tears poured out of the corner of her eyes wetting her hair and pillow while he moved his fingers within her. Her muffled screams against his other hand did her no good. No one came to her aid. Her body was at the mercy of a mad man.

"Aden, stop this." Jesse placed a hand on his shoulder. "The General won't approve."

"No shit," Aden laughed. "Nevertheless, here we are. Leave the tonic on the table and get out. I will meet with you soon."

The skinny man placed the tonic on her bedside table. His eyes looked worriedly at her and she felt like she was going to be sick. She screamed against Aden's hand but he gripped her cheeks tightly when she did so.

"Aden…"

"Jesse, get out before I lose my temper with you as well."

Before she realized it, she was left alone in her room with

Aden, tied to her bed and scared out of her mind about what was going to happen to her.

Aden produced a knife from his boot. Her body went still at the sight of the silver blade as it got closer to her skin. It moved up her leg and sliced through the thin cloth of her shorts like butter. He tugged them off her body and tied it around her mouth like a gag, only briefly letting her scream for help.

"That's better. This will be much more fun with free hands." Aden began to undress himself. "You are such a little whore, Julia."

Her eyebrows knit and she tried to say, 'Screw you' as clearly as she could through the material in her mouth.

Aden laughed at her, dropping his shirt to the ground. "I was wondering where you went off to. Judging by how lax you are below, it's quite obvious Ryan had some fun." She glared at him but it only seemed to fire up his enjoyment. "I will adore forcing this on you while you are still yourself. And when I am done with you, when I have used your body as roughly as I see fit, I will give you your tonic and you won't remember a thing."

CHAPTER XX

Damian

A CELEBRATION WAS IN FULL effect for them as they walked back down the streets of the city and to a portal that would lead them home. Rose petals were tossed in the air as the walked by and palm leaves were laid before them to walk on like a rug. Woman danced and men cheered in the crowd that gathered along the path. They were being treated like royalty.

This goodbye celebration felt a little over the top and unnecessary. He felt very uneasy about it actually. It was exactly the type of thing that happened in his old life and although he had very little regret about back then, he still felt remorseful.

Anna, however, seemed to be soaking up this experience. She was given a pack full of clothes that the local women insisted she take with her, along with jewels that would make any queen jealous. She deserved every bit of it too after the hell she had been through this past year.

Damian was just happy that their gear was returned to them in pristine condition.

King Aniruddha walked in front of them, waving at the public as they made their way through the crowd of people. Not a single face showed sign of displeasure. Everyone was smiling and wishing them well on their journey ahead.

Anna held his hand in hers, looking up at him, her face absolutely glowing. She made him excited for what the future held. It was something he'd been missing for so long.

"This is nuts!" Anna yelled at him over the cheers and the music that played.

Damian smiled. "If by nuts you mean insane and outrageous then yes." He squeezed her hand.

"I'm so excited I want to puke!" She beamed.

"Let's not have a repeat of last night," he laughed.

"I had too much wine. I'm not a wine kind of girl." She kissed his lips and his heart seemed to flutter. He was such a girl sometimes.

Once they made it to the edge of the island, King Aniruddha turned to face them with his arms held out wide.

"My new friends, I thank you for coming all this way. Your dedication to the preservation of life is what we all strive for in our existence. You truly are Warriors of the Gods."

"Thank you for your hospitality. We couldn't ask for better treatment, nor did we think we would receive it. Your city is marvelous beyond compare in every way imaginable."

King Aniruddha took out a semi-crescent shaped stick that was carved to mimic spinal bones out of his waistband. The air in Damian's lungs felt as if it were stuck. The last thing they needed in order to give themselves a fighting chance was right in front of him. Ryan would be so damn proud.

King Aniruddha handed it to him and smiled brightly.

"You should see your expression."

"I imagine it's quite comical." Damian closed his wide eyes feeling the groves of the spine in his hand. "You have no idea how thankful we are."

"When the time comes for our prophecy to be fulfilled, I imagine you would do the same for us." The king held out his hand towards the edge of the cliff.

Damian had no idea what he wanted him to do and his expression may have given that fact away. The king laughed a hearty and musical laugh and Damian felt his cheeks redden in embarrassment.

"I don't understand."

"You have to jump," King Aniruddha said casually once his amusement had calmed.

"That would be a big ol' no." Anna took a step back from the edge cautiously. Even Cato looked uncomfortable with the situation.

"You were brought here because you wished it so. Mortals have difficulties finding their way here since most are unworthy of it. Yet, it was simple for you three. An obvious testament to the outstanding charter you possess," King Aniruddha said. "Now you must prove yourself worthy again and take a leap of faith back into your world."

"Where would we end up?" Damian asked.

"Where you started of course."

"This is going to suck," Anna whimpered behind him and he had to agree.

The last thing he wanted to do was go plunging into the unknown abyss below and die miserably with no chance of getting the last piece of Brahma's Staff to Ryan. Thus, ending the world as they knew it. *No pressure here.*

"Go." King Aniruddha waved them on with a wink. The entire city was there smiling at them and urging them to jump. Peer pressure was at its peak right now.

"Ready?" Damian turned to Cato and Anna.

"Nope." Anna shook her head looking down over the edge.

"Let's do this." Cato smacked Damian on the ass before he leapt off of the island.

Before they could jump, Esha ran over to Anna. "One moment, Adrianna. I must tell you something before we part." She pulled Anna to the side, their voices were drowned out by they cheering crowd but he could tell by Anna's expression that she wasn't enjoying the conversation. Her face seemed to pale before his eyes.

"Is everything okay?" He wrapped an arm around her waist when she came back to him.

She nodded solemnly. "Yep."

"You don't look okay."

"I'm fine."

"Anna?"

"Drop it," Anna sighed.

Damian wanted to push her more on the subject but the king yelled at them to jump. He grudgingly turned towards the cliff and looked down into the nothing below. He gripped Anna's hand tight and she held on to his for dear life.

"Breath baby." He kissed her temple.

Together they jumped, the crowd roared behind them in celebration until the sound faded into silence as they fell deeper into the void. Darkness surrounded them and the fall felt like eternity. Damian was afraid they would be cascading into nothing forever but he knew better. The king wouldn't lead them astray.

Damian's heart started to involuntarily speed up and not just from falling. His body felt like it was beginning to freeze. Wind began to rush around him with drifts of snow whisking through the air. The wind was so intense he had to close his eyes from the sting of it.

Without knowing how it happened he felt his feet land on thickly packed snow and he opened his eyes. They were back on the Himalayas with Cato making a snow angel before him.

"It's about damn time." He held out his hand, Damian pulled him uneasily out of his snow art. "I thought you guys changed your minds or got lost or something."

"Sorry about that." Damian clapped him on the back.

"That was intense though, right?" Cato beamed. Damian couldn't believe how boyish he seemed after all they had been through. If anything Damian felt aged another thousand years.

"Now what?" Anna looked down at her feet. He knew instantly that something was wrong with her once she started plucking at her clothes. A nervous habit of hers he had come to recognize.

"Let's get back to the Domus. Hopefully Ryan is there now and we can figure out our next step." Damian refrained from questioning Anna for now. It was starting to eat at him slowly though. What had Esha said to her that changed her mood so greatly?

Despite Damian's internal conflicts, Cato had a huge grin on his face, which was somewhat contagious. "I can't believe we did it. We reached Shambhala and without Ryan!"

Pride swelled in his chest. It had been a very long time since he actually felt like he was out of Ryan's shadow and accomplished anything on his own. Hell, he was even praised for his attributes as a mortal in Shambhala. Now *that* was something he never thought possible.

Producing a small crystal he said, "Domus."

The familiar sight of the parlor room appeared out of thin air with its bookshelf-lined walls and plush, comfortable leather couches next to the fireplace. Never was he so excited to get back there as he was now.

"Let's go, I'm freezing my balls off." Cato nearly ran through the portal with Damian and Anna following behind.

Even though the feeling of warmth and comfort surrounded them now, Anna looked on the verge of tears. He desperately wanted to talk to her, but they had to get to Ryan before they did anything else. Who knew what Ryan would be doing right now waiting for their return?

Without a word between them, they made their way towards Ryan's room. Their wet boots squeaking against the marble floor was the only sound within the Domus, which set Damian's nerves on edge.

Once they stood in front of his doors, relief cascaded over his anxiety when he saw light protruding from gap under the door.

Damian knocked.

"Maybe he's sleeping?" Cato shrugged.

He knocked harder this time and heard a yell coming

from within, "Unless you have some helpful news, Emma, just fuck off!"

Damian cracked the door open enough to see Ryan perched on top of his dresser wearing nothing but black briefs and clutching a dagger in his hand. He followed Ryan's deranged eyes down to a map of the world painted on the floor.

"Ryan?" Damian braved walking into the room.

"Hmmm?" Ryan continued to look at his map, flipping the dagger back and forth between hilt and blade. Not even bothering to look at him as if they were never apart.

"It's Damian, what are you doing?"

As if reality sudden clicked on, Ryan jumped off of his dresser and embraced Damian so tightly he could barely breath. Ryan smelled awful and looked even worse. It was as if he had run a marathon for two weeks and didn't bother to shower once.

As soon as he let go of Damian he pulled Anna into his arms. A look of disgust came over her face but she didn't push him away.

Damian almost laughed at her reaction to Ryan's smell until he saw the marks left on Ryan's back as he let go of Anna. The wounds mirrored the ones they both received what seemed so long ago.

"What happened?"

Ryan turned to face him, cocking his head to the side. "What? The paint? I'm just trying to make a plan."

"Not the paint, Ryan. The fucking lashes on your back." Damian grit his teeth. "What happened?"

Ryan went into detail about their mission to save Grace and Colette and his heart went out to Ryan when he heard Zee was killed. It was obvious that it affected his sanity and created his current condition.

"Oh and apparently Aden is my bastard child and I am one-third god," Ryan said casually as he got back on his perch to study his map again.

"Hold the freaking phone." Anna closed her eyes and pushed on her temples. "Aden is your kid?"

"It would seem so," Ryan grumbled. The information rendered him speechless.

Cato placed a hand on Damian's shoulder and he realized he was just starring at Ryan with his fists clenched. He wasn't upset with Ryan in the least. What infuriated him was the hell his best friend was going through. No wonder he was going bat crap crazy right now.

"Aden is you son?" Damian asked the question again and Ryan confirmed with a nod. "How is it that we had no idea about him?"

Ryan told them what Aden had said while torturing him and then explained how Zeus had shown up at Zee's funeral.

"Don't look like someone just slapped your mother, Damian." Ryan continued to stare at the floor. "Zee is dead. Aden is my son. Zeus is partly my dad. Nothing we do can change any of that."

Standing in front of Ryan, he forced their eyes to meet his. The only thing that lay within Ryan's eyes was sorrow and beneath the surface he could tell Ryan was lost in his own thoughts. His mind wasn't fully present and any possible hint of happiness remained undiscovered.

"Talk to me."

Ryan shook his head, breaking their eye contact. "I am at

the point of breaking, Damian. After all that has happened, I still have to save the damn world."

"Do you want to talk alone?"

"No." Ryan sat down on the dresser. "So, how did you guys fair?" He was changing the subject.

Although annoyed with Ryan's reluctance to talk, he still handed him the piece of the staff. "It was not fun."

"I didn't think it would be but I knew you could handle it." Ryan forced a half smile as he jumped down off of the dresser. After retrieving the other two pieces of the staff from under the floor, Ryan held the last piece to them. Like a magnet, they pulled together, glowing brightly as they became one without any sign of being apart.

"Thank the gods," Ryan mumbled, as he looked it over in wonder. "We have a damn chance now."

"I'm going to go lay down for a bit," Anna blurted out, turning on her heel before anyone could say a word.

"Go." Ryan nudged him towards the door. At least his eyes shined a little brighter now. "She doesn't look too good."

"I can't. You obviously need me."

"I appreciate it, Damian. I really do, but she is your woman. We can talk later. If you want to remain on her good side I suggest you go after her."

"Speaking of crazy women," Cato started, "where is my sister?"

Chapter XXI

Anna

THE GUY WAS A wreck and she needed to get away.

She burst into her room and tossed her pack on her bed. Once she got out of her gear and into sweatpants and a tank top she felt a little better.

She briefly looked in her mirror only to find Damian in the reflection behind her, leaning against her doorway with his arms crossed just starring at her. She squeaked in shock and grabbed her pillow from the bed then chucked it at him.

"You scared me, you jerk!"

He gracefully dodged her pillow and it annoyed her for some reason but she didn't know why.

"Are you okay?" He made it across the room and sat on her plain white bed without any more pillows thrown at him. "Ever since Esha pulled you aside you have been acting strange. What did she tell you?"

Anna took a deep breath. "Nothing. She knows something about my future and I don't particularly like it."

"Tell me?" He kissed the middle of her palm. He was so sweet it was sickening, but she loved that about him. "Please?"

"I can't because who knows if it's even true," she started to ramble. "I mean she could be wrong, right? How can they know the future, right?"

Damian looked at her with those puppy dog eyes of his that always got him his way. "Baby, tell me."

Anna sat on her bed and crossed her legs. How could she possibly come out and say this without sounding stupid? "Well…" she paused.

"Anna if you are going to be my wife you need to be totally and completely honest with me about everything."

Damn him.

"She said that she thinks…" Anna paused again.

"You never have this much trouble talking. It's unsettling."

"She thinks I'm freaking knocked up, okay?" Anna covered her face in embarrassment briefly then forced herself not to act like a child. Never in her life had she ever said those words. Not even to Nathan.

Damian blinked at her. She couldn't see what was going on in that pretty little head of his but whatever it was he was mauling things over in it. He was frozen.

"Did I break you?" She waved her hand in front of his face.

Not a word.

His eyes were glazed over and his expression was empty. She slowly crawled off her bed and jogged towards the door. "I'll be right back." When she looked back at him he still hadn't moved.

She ran through the halls, bursting through Ryan's door startling him. Cato was no longer there and she was thankful there would be one less person to witness her embarrassment.

"What the hell?" Ryan whipped around to face her.

"I broke your friend. Come to my room."

Ryan was wearing gray sweatpants at this point and caught up to walk briskly beside her when she left his room. "What happened?"

"Oh you know, the usual." She shrugged.

"What exactly does that mean?"

"Well, this woman in Shambhala said I was knocked up, and it's probably not true." She tried to sound casual about it but Ryan grabbed her arm forcing her to stop.

The way he looked at her was a mixture of anger, disbelief, and somewhere along the line of happy. "You're with child?"

"The way you say that sounds stupid," she muttered. "I don't know. I don't think so."

"When was your last bleeding?"

"Jesus! Isn't that sort of personal?" She felt her cheeks redden.

"Anna, it's a natural part of life, don't be squeamish about it."

In her best attempt to avoid answering that question, she continued down to her room hastily. She honestly couldn't remember when her last period was. She never really kept track of it.

They made it to her room and to her surprise Damian was still starring off into space. They both just stood in the doorway looking at him and she whispered, "What's his deal?"

Ryan shrugged. "Damian has never had a child. This is a first."

Anna wanted to laugh just thinking about that. Damn, he must be good at playing it safe for over two thousand years. Now that was talent.

Ryan quietly padded his way to Anna's bed and sat in front of Damian.

"Hey," he muttered.

Damian's perfect posture gave out as he hunched over into Ryan's lap. His friend gently rubbed his back and leaned over him as they spoke quietly with one another. Was he that upset about her possibly being pregnant?

Ryan turned his head and grinned at her. That was a good sign. At least she hoped it was but then Damian's shoulders started to shake. She couldn't take it anymore. She walked over to them and was surprised to hear Damian chuckling.

"Damian?" she said his name cautiously.

His tear-filled eyes met hers. "Oh, Anna." He practically jumped off of the bed and pulled her into his arms.

She awkwardly pat his back not knowing what to do with herself. "Oh… Damian?"

He actually sounded thrilled when he said, "I cannot believe this!"

"Well you better hold on to those happy tears because we don't even know if it's true. Until we get at least twenty pregnancy tests, I won't believe it." *This has to be impossible.*

Damian lifted her up and spun her around forcing a squeal out of her. This was far from what she expected his reaction to be.

"Congratulations." Ryan looked genuinely happy. "It's about time you reproduced. I almost thought you were sterile!"

"I was beginning to think it would never happen." He

kissed her roughly on the lips and she yelped. "Oh no, did I hurt you? Do you need anything?"

"Look, we don't even know if this is a for sure thing and it's nothing to celebrate. The world is coming to an end and it isn't exactly the best time to be thinking about bringing a life into the world."

Damian exchanged looks with Ryan. She had no idea what they were communicating to one another with just looks. Quite frankly it was creepy they could do that.

"Everything will be fine," Damian assured her as he made her sit down on her bed. "I won't let anything happen to you two."

Anna couldn't help but roll her eyes. "Can we at least make sure there is anything to worry about before you two start acting like complete idiots?"

Ryan nodded. "Drink a bunch of water and I'll be right back." With one last hug to Damian he was gone.

Ryan

Despite the shit show he was going through, news of Damian becoming a father was making his depression begin to fade. Damian had always wanted a child and they both thought he was unable to do so until now. Even with the possible thoughts of it was exciting news.

With a shopping bag in hand, he swung open the door to Anna's room just in time to see Damian's hand stuck to Anna's belly.

He laughed, "It's not even able to know you are there."

Damian shrugged. "I don't care."

"If it's even there," Anna mumbled.

Ryan threw the sack of pregnancy tests on her bed and fell down right beside it. He leaned on his elbow and propped his head up as he pushed it towards her. "Your reassurance madam."

"Why are you so smug?" Anna growled.

Ryan grimaced when he looked at Damian. "I think the hormones are already kicking in."

Anna smacked him upside the head with a pillow and grabbed the sack off the bed. She made a beeline towards the bathroom with Damian at her heels. She shut the door before he could go in with her.

He knocked on the door. "Anna, let me in."

"You are not going to be in here while I pee on these things!" her muffled voice yelled through the door.

Damian returned to sitting on the edge of the bed. Ryan was glad to see a smile was permanently glued on his face.

"I can't believe it," Damian whispered. "We were already going to get married. Now a baby? It's amazing, Ryan."

"I'm happy for you." Ryan stared at his rough, calloused hands. "I really am."

"I'm sorry about the timing." Damian placed his hand within Ryan's and gripped it tight. "I can't even imagine how it's effecting you given the circumstances."

Ryan gripped Damian back and they let go. "I don't think I am meant for relationships with anyone, Damian. The women in my life always seem to find a terrible end and so do my children. However, I don't want you thinking I am the least bit sad about you becoming a father. I couldn't be happier for you."

"Really?"

"Truly." Ryan grinned. "I'm going to be an uncle."

"Uncle Ryan." Damian smirked. "This kid is going to be a trouble maker if it has you as an influence."

"At least you already accept it," Ryan said playfully.

He was trying his hardest to not be sullen for Damian's sake. There was little to no happiness in his heart right now. The possibility of a child brought a light within his soul he thought would remain in shadow. Yet, the demons within still remained.

Like all the women he had lost, Zee's death would eventually become easier to grieve. However, Aden was a whole different problem and he was still figuring that one out.

Then there was Julia. The woman he loved more than life itself had become an icy harlot, but when they slept together that persona seemed to melt away.

He got lost in the memory of wrinkled sheets and her bare flesh against his. Her innocence was there once again yet she was so intoxicating the second time around. What was he doing?

"Are you going to be okay, Ryan?" Damian asked again. "I know, I know, you'll be fine but really this is a lot of shit at once for you to deal with. After seeing you sit on your dresser in your underwear I've become a tad worried."

Ryan smiled half-heartedly. "Clothes are overrated and I was lost in thought about a plan of attack. After the Brahmastra is destroyed we still have to get rid of the Risen. They've taken over a good portion of the world. We have to unite our allies if we have any chance of defeating them for good."

"What about Zee?" Damian asked.

"What about her?"

"I know you liked her a great deal. Her death really seems to have gotten to you." Damian glanced back at the bathroom.

Could Damian really read him this well? Ryan barely even mentioned the event to him yet he knew Ryan was devastated about it. "It hurts like hell Damian, but I will be fine. People die everyday and I take comfort in the fact that she is with her family now." It was what Ryan kept telling himself. It still didn't make it any easier.

Thank the gods the bathroom door clicked open because Ryan didn't want to continue talking about Zee. Anna stood in the doorway with at least ten pregnancy tests clutched tightly in her hands. Part of him thought she was going to chuck them at him.

Damian hurriedly strode over to her. "Anna?" he sounded apprehensive. "What is it?"

Ryan could see she had paled even from across the room. "Every freaking one of them is positive. How is this even possible?" He could hear her begin to sniffle and he shifted uncomfortably on the bed.

He could tell she was less than thrilled about having a child. He really couldn't blame her. Her world had already been turned upside down as of recently and now to throw a child in the mix was a lot to take in.

"Well, when a mommy and daddy really love each other…" Ryan started when Anna actually did throw a pregnancy test at him. "Yeah, that's kind of gross."

Anna collapsed to her knees putting her head in her hands as she started to cry. "This can't be happening."

Damian sat on the ground, pulling her limp body against

his own and kissed the top of her head. "My love, I couldn't be any happier than I am right now. This is a blessing."

"I'm not ready for this," she groaned. "I have put my body through hell these past few weeks and that can't be good for the thing."

"For the baby," Damian corrected her.

"I can call it a 'thing' if I want to," she spat back.

With wide eyes Damian looked over at Ryan who had a smirk on his face. Hormones were hell.

"Well, I suppose this means we are down one Warrior," Ryan finally piped up after Anna got all her crying out of the way. "We should have someone look after her during the fight."

"No. No way am I sitting this out," Anna insisted. "You guys need everyone you can get."

"And right now you are not one of those people," Ryan said matter-of-factly. "You will not put that child's life in danger under any circumstances."

"I'll be fine." She grit her teeth, giving him a look that said he could go straight to hell.

"Anna, I consider you to be my future family, as is that baby inside of you. I am ordering you to keep your ass in this room during the battle. I will lock you in here or tie you to the bed if I have to. Don't think I wont." They stared at one another fiercely for quite some time.

Damian finally cleared his throat but neither of their eyes wavered. "I agree that you will be nowhere near the fight when it happens, Anna. Under other circumstance you would be at my side, but it's not just you in there anymore."

"This is stupid!" Her cheeks turned red. "You can't tell me what I can and cannot do. I'm not incapable of doing stuff just because of this thing. I can still function, dammit. I mean seriously, I just got back from Shambhala where I was almost eaten alive at least six times."

"By what?" Ryan looked at her curiously.

"Ugh!" She stomped back in the bathroom and slammed the door.

"It's like the hormones hit her all at once." Ryan smiled grimly.

"I think she's just stressed about it and she doesn't handle her emotions very well," Damian laughed to himself. "Now let me check your back and please explain everything that has happened to you while we've been away."

CHAPTER XXII

Ryan

THEY PATROLLED DOWN THE streets that evening, just the three of them and it felt good to get out of his room. He'd spent most of his time there since he'd been back. Non-stop planning was making him lose his grasp on reality while he locked himself away from his personal troubles. Fresh air was good.

"Tomorrow is New Year's Eve and at midnight is when all hell breaks loose. We need to figure out where they are going to perform the ritual." Ryan took in his surroundings. "Somewhere up high."

"Maybe on top of Nian hill?" Cato suggested. "It's the highest point besides the Domus and I doubt they would risk it there."

"Good thinking." Ryan pat him on the back and caught a small smile on his friend's lips. "We'll put three teams there and a few on Banshee Knoll just in case. The rest will monitor activity throughout the city to try and keep the peace."

"What about the teams Caleb sent out into the mortal world?" Damian asked.

Ryan grimaced but they had no other choice. "They will need to be recalled for the fight. We need everyone on this. The Risen's forces will be strong in numbers to prevent any disruptions, I guarantee it."

"Are you sure?" Cato seemed hesitant. "The mortals need whatever help they can get."

"If we don't stop the Brahmastra, the Immortals won't even be there to help at all," Ryan countered, putting an end to that particular discussion. "I need you guys to guard me while I recite the mantra. I know they aren't aware we have the Staff of Brahma, but just in case they figure it out I can't break my concentration. If they get to me I won't be able to stop the weapon."

"No problem." Damian nodded.

Ryan took a deep breath and gazed out towards Urbs. He'd spent most of his life in the Domus but coming back here was always a delight. He loved this place more than he ever thought possible. Now that it was being threatened he wanted to protect the sanctity of it and everyone he grew to love that was still here.

As soon as they were standing in the front of the Great Temple tears of anger began to form in the corners of his eyes. He could still see the blood from the members of the Council of Command stained on the white pillars.

Damian seemed to read his thoughts. "Such a terrible way to die in your own home. I can't believe they are all gone."

"I can't believe I barely found out about it," Ryan sighed. "What are we going to do without them?"

"Rebuild," Cato said simply.

He grew nervous as he made his way up the steps of the Great Temple. The possibility of there being more dead bodies of his friends was very real, yet he needed to know what else had happened here. He apprehensively pushed the doors wide open. Ryan's body stiffened at the sight before him.

Every statue of every god known to mankind was shattered into pieces littering the white marble floor. Ryan stared high above into each empty niche of the wall were the statues once stood. This was the ultimate betrayal to who the Immortals were and the gods that valued them.

Words escaped him. This was an unspeakable act beyond anything Ryan could imagine. He tried to walk into the temple but it was difficult with all the fragments of statues on the floor.

"They will never forgive this," Cato muttered.

"No, they wont," Ryan exhaled.

They could replace most of the statues. However, there were gods who were no longer remembered in here. Long ago forgotten by the people that believed in them and could never be replaced. So much history had been destroyed in just one act of violence.

Ryan squatted down and picked up remnants of a statue's arm.

"I'm nervous," he admitted.

The air between the three of them seemed to stiffen. Ryan for the most part kept his nerves at bay. Right now though, he was overpowered by worry. This was not just some war to be won for power or greed, it was bigger than him and his ambitions ever were. This was about saving humanity. The future rested on him alone.

"You need to stop thinking about the pressure and get your head in the game," Damian said gently. "If you are thinking about everything going on right now you won't be able to perform the mantra correctly."

"I know." Ryan picked up what was left of a snake-headed god. Damian couldn't be more right; he needed to clear his head. "Let's do something fun tonight."

"Like what?" Cato perked up instantly.

"I think we need to celebrate Damian's new addition to our family."

After leaving the Great Temple the three of them gathered in Ryan's room with bottles of alcohol and remedies to prevent a hangover for tomorrow. Tonight, they would forget all the stress and have a good time before their possible deaths in a little over twenty-four hours.

Ryan clinked a beer bottle against Damian's before saying, "I cannot believe you are going to be a father."

"Me either." Damian's grin was contagious.

"Can we order strippers?" Cato grit his teeth after taking a shot of whiskey.

"We are celebrating his baby not having his bachelor party." Ryan rolled his eyes, but then a brilliant idea popped in his head. "Wait. Can we do both? Let's get some action down here!"

Damian laughed out loud but to everyone else's disappointment said, "No strippers. The only woman I want on my lap is Anna."

"Well, she is going to be out of service for awhile now and why not get a little fun in before you practice eternal monogamy?" Ryan shuddered at the thought and so did Cato. "Could you imagine?"

"Nope." Cato took another shot. "I think the idea of marriage is somewhat ridiculous anyways. No offense."

"Coming from the man who never had a relationship lasting longer than a week," Damian teased. "No offense taken. Besides, when you find the right one it will all be different."

"And they call me the whore," Ryan laughed.

Cato shrugged pouring them all rounds. "I'm just a bit more tactful than you."

"Or maybe they just had nothing to brag about." Ryan winked and Cato flicked a bottle lid at him. "Calm down, little soldier."

Cato looked up at him with surprise. His tone was soft with a small smile on his lips when he said, "You haven't called me that since I was a kid."

Ryan pictured Cato as a young boy who was full of life and remembered how silly he was. He had become so used to the man standing in front of him that he had forgotten what he was like before he hardened.

"Your dad didn't like me calling you that," he admitted.

"Why not?" Cato's eyebrow rose.

"How much you admired me growing up made him jealous. He wanted to be your sole role model." Ryan remembered the conversation he'd with Cato's father very clearly. He'd said he only brought Ryan around to train Cato in the Greek style, not to bond with him. That Ryan needed to stop trying to raise his child. Not that he did much of it himself. Ryan wanted to be there for Cato because his father wasn't. He knew how it felt to be ignored and despised by your own father.

"He had more interest in Julia anyways." Cato shrugged. "She was his light."

"Men spoil their baby girls and teach their sons to be tough," Ryan countered. "I don't think it was anything other than that."

"Well it felt like it." Cato stretched his arm above his head. "All I know is, is that I'm glad they let me transfer over to Damian and your team after he died."

Ryan smirked. "We may have had something to do with that decision." He looked over at Damian who smiled wickedly into his whiskey glass.

Cato looked between them and a small chuckle escaped. "You two made them agree to let me transfer didn't you?"

Ryan finally took the shot Cato handed him. The burning sensation was a welcome relief after the hellish week he'd been through. "I promised your dad I would keep an eye on you. So sue me."

"Did you guys ever get along?" Cato asked. "Every time he came back from a mission with you two he seemed frustrated."

"Probably Ryan's loud mouth," Damian said cheerfully.

"Hey now, Marc loved me!" Ryan insisted. "I think he just hated being away from you and Julia. When we was killed he begged me to look after the both of you."

"Enough of the sad stories. Let's talk about something positive." Cato was well on his way to becoming drunk as he took another shot and propped his feet up on the coffee table. His father was always a touchy subject to discuss.

"Have you thought of any names?" Ryan asked.

"Actually no, though I am sure you are going to insist upon one name." Damian knew him too well.

Ryan dropped his shoulders. "I think Ryan is a good name. Or William. Or Henry. Or Spartacus!"

"I think you forgot a few." Cato lounged back against the couch.

"I wasn't very found of those other names." Ryan grabbed his beer and downed it quickly.

Cato asked, "Where did you get Ryan from? I forgot."

"Remember when Damian and I went to California on vacation during the eighties?" Cato nodded that he did. "Well, we were supposed to be on vacation but we found a temporary job being some rich girl's body guards for a few weeks."

"Who?" Cato leaned forward.

"I honestly can't remember her name. She was some sort of movie star or singer I think. Biggest breasts you've ever seen." Ryan imitated cupping massive breasts over his own chest. "Anyways. I was still using the name Herbert when-"

Cato burst out laughing. "Oh, I remember that name. Not good, man. Not good." He slapped his knee.

"Anyways." Ryan rolled his eyes. "I had to come up with a new name quick because little miss huge breasts laughed at it too. I told her I was kidding when someone walked by with a nametag on that said 'Ryan.'"

"That's it?"

"Not an enthralling tale is it?" Ryan smirked. "Needless to say the name change worked and we knocked boots a few times. The woman was good at what she did, I'll give her that."

"Yet you still don't remember her name?" Damian shook his head with a sly grin on his lips.

"Women are like gummy bears. Soft and delicious but do you care what the flavor is called? Nope, you just eat it."

"Anna is right. You are a pig," Damian chuckled.

"I am who I am."

Damian took a shot and chased it with a beer. Ryan was on the verge of telling him to slow it down. Damian and liquor could be dangerous. Sure, they had a remedy for a hangover but he really doubted Damian wanted to spend this night completely wasted.

After one more shot Ryan said, "Whoa, slow down chief."

Damian peeked at him over his glass. "What?"

"Do you really want to go back to Anna being piss drunk?"

"She hasn't talked to me much. I think she's still in shock," Damian admitted. From the look on his face Ryan knew he didn't want to talk about it. So instead of pushing him for answers he handed him a bottle of whiskey.

"She will come around. I imagine it's a lot for a woman to take in." Ryan was quite terrible at making someone feel better. That was Damian's job.

"Yeah. There are the hormones, not being able to eat certain things, not being able to do what you want." Cato shivered. "Could you imagine your stomach looking like it's on the verge of exploding?"

"I guess I didn't really think about those things," Damian muttered, he was mauling something over in his mind as he stared into space.

"I bet she is." Ryan patted him on the knee. "Give it time. She will get excited too. She's still very young, Damian. You need to remember that."

Damian nodded but his eyes gave away what he truly

felt. He was uncertain about what would happen to him and Anna. It was a look Ryan was all too familiar with as of late.

Moving away from another unhappy topic of discussion, they tossed back shots and made small talk about their past and what the future promised. They avoided talking about the coming day and the hardships they would face. They needed to enjoy one night away from the bullshit and just live in the moment.

CHAPTER XXIII

Julia

THERE WAS NO MORE time to change Ryan's mind before they ceremony was performed and she was determined to make him see the light before she left today. He was so stuck in his ways that it drove her insane. She hoped sleeping with him might help her cause.

If she had not promised the General she would try her hardest to change his mind she would have just said 'screw it' by now. She was done with his pathetic self. Alexander the Great? More like Alexander the whinny little boy that couldn't handle a stupid woman dying.

Julia smoothed out the white dress she'd decided to wear when she saw him. Right after she put it on she couldn't help but roll her eyes after seeing her reflection. She was more of a black dress kind of woman now. Not these pretty little girl things.

For now it would have to do. Ryan seemed to like them

and if she wanted to change his mind she would have to look like the old her.

She cracked her knuckles and knocked on his door quietly. Forcing a happy, lovey, carefree smile on her face before he opened the door.

When he finally answered he stood in front of her wearing his all black fatigues.

"Hey." He looked stunned.

"Hey." She smiled sheepishly. "Can I come in?"

Ryan opened the door wider for her to enter. Once inside, her eyes widened when she saw the map on his floor more clearly this time around. He was planning an attack but before she could study it further he cleared his throat.

"What are you doing here?" He rubbed the back of his neck.

She made mental notes about what she could before she scanned his weapons table full of cleaning supplies and gun parts that were spread out. He was obviously getting his weapons ready for tonight and she almost laughed at his vein attempt to stop them. He didn't have a chance.

"I just wanted to see you before," she paused for dramatic effect, "before all hell breaks loose."

"I didn't think you would." He closed the door quietly behind her and made his way back over to his weapons table. "You left pretty quickly the last time I saw you."

Julia mentally rolled her eyes at him. "I was afraid you regretted it." *Yeah, that was good.*

Ryan held out his hand to her and she slipped her hand into his. "I don't regret it at all, Julia." She found herself being pulled against his body. "I missed you. I actually felt like you were back."

"I never left," she mumbled.

"You did." Could he see right through her? "It felt like you were evil before. I even thought you were the enemy for awhile, but maybe you were just confused."

"I'm still confused." She was glad he was the one to bring this up. "I still wonder if what we are doing is right."

Ryan's hold on her became lax. "How could you think that? With so many people we know that have died? Not to mention all of the people they are about to kill if we can't stop them."

She reigned in her annoyance and asked, "Will you stop blowing up about it and just hear my concerns, Ryan?" The look on his face told her that he was willing to listen. "I just feel useless these days. Think of all the good we could do for the mortals if we were in command. I don't agree with all the killing, but maybe we could convince the General to do things differently."

"What?"

"I mean that I agree with what he is saying but not how he is going about it. Maybe he just needs someone like you to make him understand a different way of doing things? You are so smart and remarkable. I know he would listen. He would have to. I really think with your help we could stop this war and save so many lives if you just tried to find some common ground."

"I don't like this." He let go of her completely.

"I'm sorry." She looked down at her hands hoping she seemed ashamed of herself. "I'm just trying to think of a way to save lives I guess."

He tilted her chin up to look at him. "You've always had a big heart, Julia."

NICOLE CORINE DYER

"I know and it's my downfall," she sighed.

"Not at all." He kissed her cheek but his lips hovered against her skin sending chills up her spine. "But I think your faith in the Risen's sanity is misplaced."

"How is it?" She looked at him with the saddest eyes she could muster. "It would be worth a shot wouldn't it?"

"The plan you have still means the destruction of the Gods and that is not an option. I could almost see your point, but that is the flaw in your logic, my love." He froze after he called her that and so did she. "Sorry."

She shook her head at him. "It's fine." *It was most assuredly not fine.*

"You seem tense." He looked at her cautiously and she knew she was losing him. He was not as dumb as she thought. "What's going on with you?"

"What do you mean?" she asked.

"You would never even consider what you're saying before. Now I can tell you believe in it with all your heart. I don't like this Julia." He placed his hand against her cheek. "I can't lose you too. Not just physically but emotionally. It's why I fell in love with you in the first place. Your kind heart lit the darkness I was consumed by for so long."

Holy Jupiter he just said he loved me.

Her head instantly began to throb. "Please consider it, Ryan. It's New Years Eve and they only gave us until midnight. You have to try."

Ryan smiled weakly at her before tenderly kissing her forehead. "The Gods need us. We will not abandon them or make truces with such cruel people. You saw how they treated the mortals in Washington. It isn't right and their

276

behavior will not be forgiven. I will not work with anyone who kills the innocent so easily. Not ever."

She'd lost him.

Pulling away from him completely, she made her way towards his door without a second glance. There was no use pretending with him anymore and she had no reason to stay in his room. Ryan was far too loyal and he would never change. That much was obvious now. She needed to report back to the General at once.

Ryan caught her by the hand before she could open the door. "What did I do?" His eyes studied her face with a look of despair washing over him, figuring it out, piecing together what the truth was without her even having to say it.

"Wrong answer. We are done here." She pulled away from his grasp, leaving him broken and aged within a split second as she grabbed the door handle. That look would be her undoing if she weren't careful.

"Whoa, hold on. What the fuck are you doing, Julia?" his voice rose higher than she was used to. Quite frankly it made her nervous. "Don't think me a fool. I see what is going on with you. I have tried my hardest to look past it, hoping that I was wrong and that you are not apart of them but I see now I was mistaken."

"Are you sure about that?" She eyed him up and down. His fists were balled and she prepared herself for a fight. "You know what would happen to me if you accuse me of it, Ryan. Could you really condemn me to death?"

"I am perfectly aware but there is no doubt in my mind that you are part of the Risen. All this time I tried to trust what you told me, but now I see you for what you are. A traitor."

She smirked. "Get over yourself."

"You used me," he growled. "Why would you do that to me?"

She could hardly contain her amusement, laughing right in his ashen face. "Maybe you just needed a taste of your own medicine. You are the king of using women. It was about time one of us repaid the favor."

"Don't you dare try to make this seem like it was pay-back." His voice shook in either anger or despair, she couldn't tell. The look in his eyes gave her the answer as they welled with tears; it was both. "You used me to try and turn me."

"Look at how pathetic you are right now. I can't imagine why I even tried."

"Julia." Seeing a man looking as hurt as he did was un-imaginable. It was as if she could see his heart breaking be-fore her. Anguish filled his face, hopelessness reverberated throughout his entire body. He was breaking. "Please don't do this. I can't go into this fight feeling this small. I can't give up on you. I never will. I don't know what to do without you by my side."

"You never had me at your side."

She almost made it out the door before his arm wrapped around her waist pulling her into him. "Julia please don't do this. I love you."

"Well I don't love you. I despise you."

"I don't believe that," he whispered.

"Believe it." She got away from his wilting grasp and out of his bedroom. Before slamming the door behind her she called over her shoulder, "Enjoy what little life you have left."

Ryan

He was cleaning his guns when the most deceitful woman he had ever come to love walked in. Something was going on with her. There was no way possible she could be the woman he knew. There was no way she had always been this heartless. Could he be the cause? Had he pushed another woman to such malice just from being the way he was? Like Aden's mother, was he at fault for the demise of another good woman?

He stood in the middle of his room just staring at his door after Julia slammed it shut. "What the fuck?" he muttered to himself.

Should he inform someone? *No.* No matter how guilty he knew she was, he still couldn't bring himself to inform anyone of her treason. He couldn't be the cause of her death.

Ryan rubbed the back of his neck, feeling wary about what had just happened and went back to cleaning his guns for tonight in case he needed them. Once he was done with them he began sharpening his swords when a knock came on his door yet again. His pulse nearly stopped thinking it was Julia, but then Emma came waltzing into his room. *This woman does not let up.*

"Hey," She said quietly as she tucked a strand of blonde hair behind her ear. "Can we talk?"

"There is nothing to talk about," his voice was colder than he meant.

He went back to sharpening his sword when he felt her hands on his shoulders. His body tensed up. He tried to ignore her unwanted touch, continuing to work on the blade.

"Why do you hate me?" she asked softly. Ryan removed her hands from his shoulders as gently as he could muster in his current mood. He wouldn't look her in the eyes.

He gave up on the blade and got up to grab a bottle of water from the fridge. "I don't hate you. You're starting to annoy me, Emma."

"I don't know what I did," she complained. "We were fine until you got taken by the Risen and then everything went to hell. I don't know what I did."

Ryan almost felt bad for her. He was starting to realize just how much he used other people without a care. "Emma, we slept together on occasion and that is all it ever was. Nothing more and nothing less."

Like most women he gave this speech to, she was on the verge of tears. They grew feelings for him when he didn't feel the same. He really should have cut it off long ago. Looking at her, perhaps he strung her along because she reminded him of another certain blonde. One he couldn't have.

"Is something wrong with me?" she choked back sobs.

Ryan rubbed his hand along the stubble of his chin that was starting to become a beard. "Nothing is wrong with you, Emma. You are gorgeous and intelligent, but I just don't feel anything for you."

"So you just sleep with people you don't like?"

"Actually, yes." He was being honest but she looked like she wanted to shoot him. "Emma just leave me alone, okay? I don't want to be with you or anyone else for that matter. Not anymore. Not ever again."

As she got closer to him he felt an awkward tension run through his body. Her mixed emotions of rejection and desire were plainly written on her face. He knew what she was trying to do. How could he politely prevent this from happening?

"Sleep with me?" she cooed even with tears in her eyes.

Ryan growled in his throat from annoyance as she placed her hands on his chest. She was trying to be seductive. Given everything that had happened, sex was the farthest from his mind. It was a special occasion.

Stepping away from her touch, he made it to his door and opened it for her. "Leave."

She slammed the door shut by pushing him into it and pressed her body firmly against his. "We might die tonight and I want to have you at least once more."

"The feeling isn't mutual," he scowled. She was pushing him past his ability to be civil.

Emma stood on her toes to whisper in his ear. Her breath tickled his neck sending goose bumps down his arms. "Just once more, baby and I will leave you alone forever."

"Get off me."

Every dreadful feeling coursed through him as Emma ran her hands down his sides towards his belt buckle. Zee, Julia, his father, Ahmose, Aden, the world, it all wrapped around his mind in a whirlwind of anger. He slammed her back against the door, wrapping his hand around her throat.

"Is this what you want?" he hissed as he pressed his body against hers, keeping his hand firmly around her neck with a tight grip.

Her eyes widened in fright. "Ryan," she choked out.

He spread her legs apart with his own and pressed himself harder against her. "What Emma? This is what you want, right?" He kissed her roughly on the mouth but her inability to breathe prevented her from returning it.

She tried to push him off her but he was set hard against her. "I can't… breathe."

"I know you can't." He grinned maliciously against her mouth and pinned her arms above her head, releasing her throat. On rare occasions he had handled a woman this roughly. Some women had a preference towards this sort of thing. His actions right now were purely meant to teach her a lesson.

"What are you doing?" The fear in her eyes pleased him.

"You want me right?" He cocked his head to the side and she nodded. "Then deal with it."

"I don't like this. I want you sweet," she protested but it didn't make a difference. "This hurts."

She tried to pull her wrists down but he kept his grip on her firm. "Well, welcome to the new me," his hissed in her ear and felt her body tremble against his. "Now, make up you damn mind if you want it or not."

"Don't hurt me," she whispered. Tears flowed heavily down her cheeks leaving streaks in their wake.

"Is that a no?" He gripped her wrists harder.

She shook her head. "I don't like this. Let me go."

And he did.

Ryan pushed back from her and took in the sight of a woman trembling in fear. She looked at him like he was a monster and rightfully so. What he'd done had been a necessary evil. Emma needed to move past a man who didn't love her and would never let her into his life no matter how hard she tried.

"What happened to you?" She rubbed her reddened wrists.

"A lot of shit you don't get to know about. Now leave." He turned his back to her and felt relief when he heard the door closed quietly behind him. "Poor girl."

Everything was getting out of hand with his life and Emma had sent him over the edge. Looking down at his reddened hands he could only imagine how her frail skin must look and it chilled him to the bone.

Every bit of him wanted to apologize for handling her so roughly. She needed to move on and now she would because he was a monster. There was no denying that.

Chapter XXIV

Damian

H E WOKE UP TO the sounds of Anna's snoring. There was nothing he wanted to do but grin at her. She was so adorable when she snored with her hair messed around her head as if a tornado blew through the room during the night. She was the most beautiful thing he had ever seen.

He watched her for a few minutes just staring at her face. Those soft lips would occasionally pout in her sleep and her long dark eyelashes would occasionally flutter. Perfection.

Such simple thoughts were soon clouded by the realization of what today was. There was a lot to be done to prepare the other Warriors for battle. He dreaded the thought of leaving bed. He wanted to stare at Anna all day long and hold her in his arms. It was a sensation he never thought he would acquire in his lifetime.

Anna stirred in her sleep then stretched her arms and legs, making a squeak as she did so.

He beamed. "Morning, beautiful."

She forced her eyes open with obvious difficultly and smiled sleepily at him. "'Sup?"

Damian chuckled and kissed her forehead after he smoothed away her crazy hair. "Your mannerisms…" He trailed off as he kissed her neck.

She groggily asked, "What about them?"

"They're charming."

"Glad I can entertain you." She grinned as he kissed along her jawline.

Damian was in no mood to let this day go on without being close to Anna for what could possibly be the last time. "You do more than entertain me, love."

Her hands wrapped around his neck as she pulled him to her lips. Morning breath be damned. He was glad to see she was in a better mood. Damian felt as if she hated him since she found out she was pregnant, mostly due to her being un-believably cranky.

She broke away from his kiss and he nearly pouted from the absence of her lips. "I wish you would let me fight tonight."

Damian's eyes rolled. "Not this again, Anna." He grimaced.

"I can help."

"You would get in the way."

"What's that supposed to mean?" That irritable tone was back in full force.

"It means that I would be spending all my energy making sure you didn't get hurt instead of doing my job. You and our child are my main priority to keep safe." He rubbed her belly even though he knew she hated it. "I can't be distracted if we have any chance of winning this."

"This blows," she grumbled. Once again her words made him grin uncontrollably. "What?"

"Nothing." He leaned down to kiss her again.

To his surprise, she pushed him on his back and jumped on top of him. Her dark hair cascaded over her shoulders and her white top was somewhat askew. Knowing she must be feeling powerless he let her take control, even though he badly wanted to touch her.

Anna placed her hands on his bare chest. Not in a suggestive manner that he'd hoped for unfortunately. "I'm going to be so worried without you here."

Damian gripped her hips; he couldn't help it he had to touch her. "Love, I will come back to you two. Don't worry about that. Besides, we are going to be here at the Domus during the fight protecting Ryan."

"Here?"

"Yes. It's one of the highest points in Urbs and it is very unlikely the Risen would come here while they try to perform their mantra uninterrupted. So it's the safest place for Ryan to perform his mantra."

"So most of their forces will be wherever Ahmose is?" Anna looked down at him with sad eyes.

He was having a hard time focusing on their conversation instead of the beautiful woman straddling him. "Yes. Ryan doesn't believe they know about the Staff of Brahma so they have no reason to split up their forces. They will concentrate on just protecting Ahmose, waiting for us to attack them."

"Sounds good to me." She now was rubbing his chest suggestively and he grew beneath her. "Well, hello."

"Sorry love, you have that effect on me." He smirked and pulled her down against his chest.

They kissed hotly until she came up for breath. He tucked part of her wild hair behind her ear but kept his eyes on those swollen lips. "In like four months I bet you won't be saying that."

She was an expert at trying to kill moods. "Anna, I will always want you. Do you really think I would ever find you unattractive? Especially since you are growing our child within you? I love you even more for that."

She rolled her eyes. "Cornball."

"At your service." He kissed her again, this time rolling her on her back. "However, I need to take advantage of being able to be on top of you like this. You're going to get huge!" He laughed when she smacked his shoulder but her grin made him ecstatic.

A primal urge surged through his body when her smile turned to desire. Without hesitation he ripped her top down the middle and tossed the shredded cloth to the floor. With that action alone she seemed to catch fire as she quickly undressed herself as did he until there wasn't a bit of clothing between them. Both were breathing heavily in anticipation even before they'd even started.

Only a few moments passed with their bodies entwined before a knock on the door brought him momentarily out of his bliss. He continued to kiss her lips and neck while he rocked within her. There was another knock Damian ignored. He heard the doorknob turn and whipped around his head to see a red-faced Cato standing in the doorway.

"Shit, sorry!" He covered his eyes with his hands and

tried to walk out of the room but instead walked straight into the doorframe. "Shit."

"Dammit, Cato," Damian growled.

"Sorry!" He faced towards the outside of the room but remained within. "Ryan wants to see us."

Damian hastily picked his blanket off of the floor and covered Anna up with it. Her cheeks were flushed with embarrassment. "Now?"

"He wants to go over the plan." Cato bounced on his heels, clearly wanting to dart from the room as quickly as possible. "I'll tell him you will be there in twenty minutes."

"Make it forty!" Anna shouted at him.

Damian turned back to her and grinned. "Gods I love you."

Julia

After her encounter with Ryan she returned to her room to put on her gear for the nights battle. The dress she wore before was on the ground in a heap with the rest of those disgusting sundresses she owned. Never again would she have to degrade herself to wearing such childish things.

As soon as she was done lacing up her boots a knock came at the door.

"Shit," she muttered to herself. Had Ryan actually turned her in so quickly? With her hand on the hilt of her sword she called, "Come in."

Cato lightly pushed open her door and given his docility she knew Ryan hadn't told him anything yet. He crept into her room as if afraid she might throw something at him.

"Hey."

"What?" she growled in a very unladylike manner.

"Damn, Julia." He closed the door quietly and shuffled over to her. "What the hell did I do?"

"Nothing. What do you want?"

"To see my sister."

Tossing on her flak jacket she moved away from him. "Okay, you see me. Now go."

"What is with you?" He gave her a less than friendly look.

"I want to get out of here and you are stopping that from happening presently," she snapped back at him. She loved her brother, she would always love him, but she couldn't condone the mistake he was making opposing the Risen and so he had to pay the price. It was terrible and she hated it, but there was nothing she could do. Change required sacrifices.

"Look, I know what happened in Washington and I thought maybe you wanted to talk to someone about it." He took her hands in his. "I know how much it bothers you when our people get killed."

Looking him dead in the eyes she said, "I'm fine, believe me."

"Are you sure?" He seemed genuinely puzzled. Given her attitude as of lately, she had to wonder why. "Zee's death, the mortals being killed in front of you, seeing Grace and Colette like that, not to mention Aden torturing you. I will kill him for that."

"Don't bother." Turning her back to him she tried to leave

her room amidst his babbling but she found herself spinning around to look her brother face to face.

The look in his eyes would have made her cower in fear once upon a time but no longer. He gripped her arm tighter than he normally would and studied her with squinted eyes. "Why wouldn't I bother? You're my sister and that little disease hurt you."

Julia tried to break free of his grasp but that only made him squeeze tighter. "Right now you are the one hurting me."

"What is going on with you?" His lip arched up in disgust. "You are not my sister."

"Your sister is an adult now. Even if you don't agree with her." Julia pushed his chest hard away from her but it was barely enough to make him take a step back. Even so, he let her go. "Go run off to your master and leave me be."

"Ryan?" Cato laughed forcefully. "Now there's a problem with him too? What about Damian? Do you despise him as well?"

"That's the problem with all you men. You think everything is about you. You fail to look at the bigger picture." Julia slipped on her gloves. "You're all pathetic."

"Why are you getting ready so soon? It's only midday."

"What I do with my life is none of your business, Cato."

Cato held her face in his hands and pressed his forehead to hers like when they were younger. "Please tell me I haven't lost you too?"

"What?" she breathed.

"First mother, then father. I can't lose you too, Julia." The moment he embraced her, her heart felt as if it were sinking lower than it ever had before. He gripped her so tightly to him as if he needed her in order to survive. His breathing was un-even, almost panicked.

Her head started to throb. She needed to find Aden soon. The hurt in her brother's eyes was almost too much to endure. He needed to stop this. She had to get away from him other-wise losing him would be that much harder.

"Get off me." She shoved him away again.

His eyes were wounded beyond recognition. "Julia, don't do this."

"It's already done," she sighed. To make things perfectly clear she grabbed her long black cloak and fastened it on. Cato's eyes widened at the realization of her ultimate betrayal. "What? Don't seem so surprised."

"I have no words. Only disappointment that you are my blood." He turned from her and paused at her door. "Don't trust them, Julia. You are better than this."

Though his words stung, her purpose was still clear. "You don't know me anymore Cato," she hissed. She pushed him away from her as she walked out of her room. "See you on the battlefield."

Cato chased after her, stopping in front of her so she couldn't continue on. "Please don't do this. I know things have been somewhat tense with us given how I felt about Ryan and you, not to mention how I've been gone a lot lately. I haven't been there for you as much as I should have but please, Julia, I need you. You're my only family and we promised we would stick by each other for all eternity. I am begging you not to do this. I can't fight you, Julia. I could never hurt you."

"If I find you in our way I won't hesitate, Cato. Do you understand what I am saying? You either convert or you die.

Either way makes no difference to me." Her words felt like fire dripping out of her mouth even as she felt her belief in them waver. Did she really think she could kill Cato?

The look on his face broke every barrier of her heart but she had made her choice. She had to do this and get over the fact that he was now lost to her.

"I won't let you leave," he said with finality. "I am turning you in for the betrayal of the Immortals."

Leaning into his frame she stood on her toes to reach his ear as she whispered, "Try it."

He grabbed her wrist to maneuver it behind her back. She dropped to her knees and with her leg she swiped his feet out from under him. Cato got up almost as quickly as he went down.

"Stop!" He tried to take hold of her arms.

She didn't. Instead, she drove her fist up into his jaw and he stumbled away with his back to her. With him dazed she kicked the back of his knee and he dropped to the ground. Cato was much too fast and grabbed her ankle yanking it off the ground landing her on her back.

Julia couldn't remember actually ever fighting with her brother like this. It was always for training only. She could tell he was holding back but that would only work to her advantage.

Breathing heavily they both stood up to face each other. "Dammit Julia, don't make me hurt you."

"You won't get the chance to." She grinned. "Good bye, brother."

With every ounce of strength she had, she jumped in the air and kicked both feet into his chest as hard as she could.

His hips hit the railing and the momentum of her kick carried him over the side of the balcony and out of sight. She rushed to see if had fallen to the bottom but to her irrational relief he hung onto the edge with his feet dangling in the air.

Without a word or a second glance she left him to hang on for his life and departed for her true family.

CHAPTER XXV

Damian

AFTER CATO REVEALED JULIA'S true intentions to Ryan he became distraught. Nevertheless, they had to leave to give a pep talk to the rest of the Warriors before the battle began. Ryan gave them each a thorough explanation as to where he wanted their teams and what to expect. Everyone was determined for an end to the madness.

It was an hour before midnight when the teams of Warriors started to disperse to their positions, leaving Damian, Ryan, and Cato behind at the Domus. They were at the top of the steps looking down at all of Urbs. The city was eerily silent.

Damian brought Anna's hands to his lips and kissed them gently. He could only hope he would feel these hands upon him again. After wiping a tear off her cheek he pressed his hand to her stomach. "I'll be back in no time. I promise."

Anna tried to agree with a smile but her emotions gave way and she starting to cry even harder. "I don't want you to go but I know you have to. Please, just let me help."

"I'm sorry, but I need you both to stay safe." He kissed her lips tenderly and could feel her melt into his arms. "As soon as it's done I will come to you."

He held her tightly against his body with his arms wrapped protectively around her. If this was the last time he saw her he wanted every touch to count. He wanted to remember her smell of cinnamon spices and the feeling of her small body against his.

"I hate to interrupt, but she needs to get to safety," Ryan's voice came from behind.

Damian gazed into Anna's brown eyes and found himself kissing her roughly on the mouth. Unfortunately their passion was short lived when Ryan cleared his throat and they reluctantly let go of one another.

"I love you two. Stay safe."

"I love you too," she sniffled.

With one last quick kiss she turned and walked through the door into the Domus and out of sight. He felt an invisible string trying to pull him after her. Leaving Anna alone was one of the hardest things he'd had to do.

"It'll be okay." Ryan gave him a reassuring pat on the back and suddenly they embraced one another.

Damian felt a faint sense of relief come over him. "I hope so."

"Alright teams, is everyone in position?" Cato spoke through the headset they all wore.

A chorus of 'affirmatives' went through Damian's ear

and he released Ryan. He looked pale in the moonlight as it shone down brightly on them. Damian's nerves were on edge and he could only image how Ryan was feeling. Their fates were up to him and he could see the weight of it in his friend's eyes.

"You good?" he asked.

Ryan exhaled with his eyes closed. "I need to focus but I can't." Ryan took out his earpiece and tossed it on the ground.

"What can we do?" Cato tried to keep his tone calm but there was a hint of worry in it. Ryan didn't answer though.

They stood in silence until Damian realized the scene before them was changing. People were gathering on a hill dressed in black cloaks. Cato was right about their location.

"They are over there." Damian pointed towards Nian Hill. "I can see at least thirty of them but there are probably more hiding in the surrounding area."

Cato called into the headset. "Are any citizens outside?"

"No. The streets are clear."

"Everyone must be hiding."

"Saw movement. Going to follow."

"Be careful." Cato spoke into the set. "You better get in your Zen place Ryan or we're all dead. No pressure."

Ryan's demeanor seemed to change once he picked up the Staff of Brahma from the ground. The carved, wooden spine gleamed in the moonlight as if it knew it was about to face its foe.

"Do you think Olivia, Juniper, and Otis have made it to the hill yet?" Damian asked Cato. It was thirty minutes till midnight.

He heard Cato's voice come on the head set, "Olive, Juniper, Otis, have you reached your target?"

"We are directly below them. There are about thirty of them standing around with their swords drawn. I don't see guns but their cloaks might be hiding them," Juniper answered.

"Do you see Ahmose?" Damian asked.

"Affirmative. He is directly at the top. He looks like hell."

"If it's in your power, try to rescue him once the weapon is defeated," Damian said in his headset. "But don't risk yourselves for it."

Cato gave him a dirty look and put the headset on mute. "Don't risk it? We could just rescue him now."

Damian turned his on mute as well. "I won't risk more lives than we must. Ahmose has to summon the weapon in order for Ryan to defeat it. Once that happens they can't use it again for another lifetime, but if we stop it too soon then they could try again."

Cato rolled his head back with a growl. "Fantastic." He turned his headset on. "Don't engage until we tell you. I repeat, don't engage until we tell you."

"Understood."

"Now what?" Cato's mouth was set in a hard line.

"Now we let Ryan work his magic and keep our guard up in case they see what we are doing."

"It would be a lot easier if you guys would shut up," Ryan mumbled with his eyes closed.

"Shut up, Moses," Cato goaded.

Damian had to laugh. Ryan did look like he was trying to part the sea with his arms outstretched towards the sky holding a wooden stick.

Julia

She stood on top of Nian Hill among a fair amount of Risen's members with twenty minutes till midnight. She knew how the General liked to keep his word so they would wait until the appointed time.

She stood next to Aden and Jesse. Both men stared out over the city with a statuesque gaze. There was a nervousness rolling in her belly that she couldn't explain. No one could stop the weapon from being deployed according to the General so she knew the plan would go off without a hitch. Yet, something within her was clawing to the surface in an indescribable desire she couldn't place.

Ahmose sat cross-legged on the grass at the top of the hill with his eyes closed. His frame was so thin and frail. His skin was peppered with scabs that had started to heal over. He was not the dominating presence he had once been.

"Has he started yet?" Julia asked with impatience.

"I think he is getting himself in the mindset for it. I'm not sure how it works exactly," Jesse leaned over Aden to answer her quietly. The look in his eyes weren't determined, they were calculating with a sign of worry.

"Are you okay?" she asked but he didn't give an answer.

Ten minutes to go.

She turned her attention to the bottom of the hill and scanned along the tree line below. Their men were fanned out along the outer edge. If there were to be an attack, it would come from within the trees. She rubbed her temples as the waiting became exasperating.

"Are you well?" Aden asked gruffly.

She nodded. "Yeah."

"Here, take your tonic." He handed her a vile

"I'm fine," she lied.

"Now," he said more forcefully.

"Aden I don't have a headache I'm just thinking, okay?" she snapped at him. He looked like he was going to slap her but thought better of it. His eyes wondered in the direction of the General who stood next to Ahmose. Both of them had their attention out towards the city with their backs to Julia and Aden.

"General!" A man ran past Julia and up to him frantically.

Julia watched with interest as she listened to their conversation.

The General led the man away from Ahmose by the back of his neck, probably so he didn't break his concentration.

"What is it?" The man winced at the touch of the General's hand.

"I was monitoring the area like you told me and I caught sight of the Domus," the man squeaked out timidly holding up his binoculars.

The General snatched them out of the man's hand and peered through them over towards the Domus. Julia couldn't see anything from here, it was too far away. The General roared out in frustration and threw the binoculars.

He turned and pointed directly at Aden. "Gather men and head to the Domus. Stop them now and cut them down permanently." Aden opened his mouth to speak but the General shouted, "Now!"

"Yes, sir!" Aden pointed at four people from their ranks including Julia. "You all come with me."

Down the hill and across the city Julia wondered what

the General was so worried about. Whatever it was, it was a major threat to their cause and they only had ten minutes till midnight. Would they even have enough time to prevent what threatened their plan?

Once they reached the bottom steps to the Domus her group paused. Cato and Damian looked down at them with their swords drawn and at the ready while Ryan held some sort of t-shaped stick in his hand. She didn't have a clue what it was but it made Aden furious.

"What is that?" she asked.

"The one thing that can stop us." He dashed up the steps to engage.

They followed closely behind him with their swords in hand until Cato fired a shot off. It hit one of their men directly between his eyes and his lifeless body toppled down the stairs. One man she didn't know hid behind a statue that sat on the edge of the steps. *Coward.*

Julia was the first to reach the top and swung her sword down on Damian but in a flash he blocked it from slicing into his head. His eyes widened at the sight of her but his shock only made her grin.

"Hey there, sugar bear." She batted her eyes at him before punching him in the stomach with her left hand.

Damian took a step back from her, clutching his stomach with his free hand but Julia was on him before he could recover. She swung her sword at him again but even in his hesitation he blocked it. They did this dance for a few seconds until she finally slashed his arm.

Blood dripped down his black gear but he didn't seem to notice, as he blocked her continued advances.

"Julia, stop." He never swung his sword at her and stayed only on the defensive.

"Fight, you coward," she yelled at him.

Damian still wouldn't fight her and it frustrated her to no end. "Just stop and think," he breathed as he blocked her from slicing his leg.

"There's nothing to think about." She brought her sword down on him as hard as she could to no avail.

A throaty bellow filled the air drawing her focus to Jesse who was on his knees in front of Cato. He clutched his stomach as it bled out past his fingers while Aden raced from the bottom of the stairs. He must have tumbled down leaving Jesse to fight Cato alone.

"No," she breathed.

Without hesitation Cato placed his sword between Jesse's shoulder blades from behind and with one swift motion the sword disappeared into his back. Aden screamed as he ran towards Cato and tackled him to the ground. Both men's swords clattered against the stone steps as they began to wrestle for control.

Her distraction led to Damian wrapping his arms around her from behind and locking her wrists in his hands.

"Julia snap out of it." He struggled against her.

She twisted her body but he wouldn't let go. "Snap out of what?"

"What they did to you." He grunted when she pushed them back against one of the columns.

They were close to Ryan who was standing like a statue this entire time and she knew whatever he was doing was a threat to the Risen's plan. She managed to get one arm free and thrust her elbow into Damian's face. He instantly let go and fumbled back against the column. Julia made a mad dash towards Ryan with her sword in hand until the night sky lit up like and explosion.

With her attention drawn to the sky, she was caught off guard when Damian slammed her body to the ground and put his weight on top of her. Her sword fell out of her grasp and skidded on the steps. She struggled against him but he was overpowering her. She managed to snatch a dagger strapped to her side and thrust it deep into his shoulder.

Damian cried out from the pain and Julia could feel specks of his blood drip onto her cheek. Pushing him off her, he fell to his back. She quickly straddled him and thrust her knife towards his neck. Damian managed to catch her wrist before she could finish him. She put all her weight into pushing the knife down and with his injured shoulder he was barely managing to protect himself.

"Don't do this," he pleaded with widened eyes.

"Quit begging, it's pathetic." Her dagger neared his throat making her grin in triumph. He was weakening and she could feel the knife press against his skin. "Goodbye, Damian."

Chapter XXVI

Anna

S HE WAS ON THE balcony overlooking the city. Just below her were Damian, Cato, and Ryan. She wanted nothing more than to be down there with them but she made a promise and she intended to keep it. Regardless of how stupid she thought it was.

It was ten minutes until midnight when she spotted five people running towards the Domus. She remained silent, not wanting to distract Damian from the task at hand like he asked of her. It was difficult to remain so useless when she knew what she was capable of.

Anna's hands covered her mouth in horror as she watched as Julia run up to Damian and slashed her sword at him. Her stomach was in nervous knots just watching him block her savage thrusts with such remarkable speed. He never struck back though and that didn't help with Anna's anxiety.

The corner of her eye caught Cato fighting with Aden and

Jesse. With one swift kick to the abdomen, Aden went rolling down the steps leaving Cato evenly matched. She started to look back at Damian until a scream filled the air and Jesse fell to his knees. Watching Cato thrust his sword deep into his back made Anna's stomach turn.

The illness was soon overshadowed by the sky bursting open as if being engulfed by hell itself setting the night sky ablaze. The clouds that filled the sky begun to swirl around in a maddening vortex as if ready to plunge deep into the earth like a tornado.

Anna's skin was quickly becoming moist from the heat that radiated in the air and it was becoming hard to breath. She jumped when thunder-like sounds cracked so loudly it shook the Domus and threw her into the railing of the balcony.

Despite the alarming scene above, Anna's attention was instantly drawn to the scene below when another scream filled the air. She could barely see the end of a blade sticking out of Damian's shoulder. Suddenly he was thrown to his back with Julia straddling him. Her knife was inches from his throat.

Without a second thought to herself or her promise, she was running towards the entrance of the Domus. Her feet brought her faster than she thought possible and she found herself tackling Julia off Damian before her mind could catch up.

His body was limp when she crawled over to him. Before she thought her worst fear had came true she realized he was just exhausted. She helped him stand up before Julia swung her fist at her. Anna saw the punch coming and managed to duck out of the way.

"Get out of here!" Damian yelled at her and she could see the fury in his eyes.

"I'm sorry." Her eyes filled with tears.

She tried to make a run for it until someone came up behind her and wrapped their arms around her tight. Damian had became preoccupied with Julia and wasn't aware what was happening to her. Anna managed to elbow her assailant in the stomach.

There was a sword on the ground near her and she picked it up, swinging it pathetically at her hooded attacker. He blocked her with a swipe of his blade and continued towards her. She swung again. The man was so close that he grabbed her wrist and twisted it enough for her grip to give out.

"Let me go!" Her eyes pricked with tears as he twisted her wrist harder.

The man laughed at her from under his hood. She pulled it down with her good hand revealing a young man she had never seen before. His smirk disappeared when she yanked the hood down hard making him stagger off balance.

"You little trollop," he hissed. Ripping his hood from her grasp he pushed her to the ground.

She tried to stand but he struck her across the cheek making her fall on her back. He stood above her with his sword raised high. There was no way she was going to die like this, not with a new life inside of her. So she kicked the man's balls with every bit power she had.

He roared out in pain, his sword clanging to the ground. "You little bitch."

Anna scrambled to retrieve the blade but the man was too quick even in his pain. She crawled away from him as he came at her. "Help!"

"Anna!" She heard Cato yell from behind the man as he tried to reach her.

Quick as a flash, Cato had run up behind her injured pursuer and stabbed him through the back. She could see the blades point sticking through his chest and he looked down at it in shock. With a grunt her attacker fell to the ground on his side, his eyes still open but the life faded from them.

"Anna are you okay?" Cato pulled her up to standing and she wrapped her arms around his neck. "Whoa, don't give Damian the wrong idea." He laughed when she punched his arm.

"Thank you." Tears ran down her cheeks but she wasn't sure why. Cato put a reassuring hand on her shoulder but before he could say anything Anna yelled "Behind you!"

Barely in time, he held up his sword to block Aden's advance on him. The man was bloody as hell and Anna almost screamed from how terrifying he looked.

"I see your latest recruit cannot handle herself." Aden laughed at her. Cato swept his feet out from under him but it didn't stop him from talking. "I could tell from the first moment I saw you that you would be worthless. Damian always chose poorly in a mate."

Anna felt fury build inside of her and she lunged towards him. Cato stuck out his arm and held her back. "You little bastard." She pushed Cato's arm away.

"True. I am a bastard," Aden said thoughtfully as he stood. "Cato, get rid of this pathetic excuse of a Warrior so the real men can fight."

"Oh do shut up, Aden." Cato grit his teeth.

"Dammit Cato, get her out of here!" Damian interrupted them as he continued his fight with Julia.

"Yes, Cato. Follow your orders." Aden grinned.

Before Cato could say a word she ran towards the entrance of the Domus. The clouds whirled faster and lighting went off in every direction within the deep red sky. She would not allow Damian's distraction of her to be his downfall. She didn't stop running until she was safely within the Domus.

Even though he was upset she put herself at risk, Damian was grateful Anna came to save him. Julia had nearly pierced him with her dagger. His right arm had grown weaker from where she'd stabbed him. Right now earthly limitations needed to be set aside and he had to push through the pain.

Ryan remained statuesque through all the commotion. He never flinched, not once. His mind was far away from the dangers around him. The thought brought both worry and comfort to Damian. He was on task yet vulnerable to attack.

Julia elbowed him in the stomach once again and he was getting sick of the abuse. As much as she was trying to force him to fight back he wouldn't, although it was becoming awfully tempting.

"Julia, will you fucking stop!" He never cursed at women, but he couldn't help it when one was constantly hitting him.

"Why would I?" she laughed at him with malice.

"This isn't you," he grunted when he blocked another hit from her.

Julia ignored him and continued to fight against him. "Aden, get Ryan!"

"I can't get to him!" Aden yelled at her.

The sky was already thrust into hellfire and from across the way on Nian Hill he saw where Ahmose must be as the surrounding area began to glow. It had to be past midnight but he figured Ahmose might be having trouble pulling the trigger on the weapon. Soon though, very soon it was about to happen.

"Damian! We're about to have company!" Cato yelled at him as the clash of steel rang through the thundering air. Damian looked to the steps below and Damian's heart dropped significantly.

More members of the Risen had come to join the fight with the General in the lead. Damian and Cato couldn't possibly stop ten people on their own. Especially trained ones.

With a jab to the cheek he turned to face Julia who had a smug look on her face. "Looks like your time is up, Damian." She seized a dagger strapped to her thigh and swung it at him.

How many more weapons does this woman have on her?

Damian ducked and rolled out of the way, grasping a sword from the ground on his way up. He was suddenly back-to-back with Cato as he parried with Aden.

"We're fucked."

"Yep," Cato heaved heavy breaths. "We should have had more people stay with us."

Damian blocked a swing from Julia as he spoke into the headset. "We are getting overrun here at the Domus. So if any of you aren't busy it would be lovely if you got your asses back to the Domus before we get killed! Thanks guys."

Multiple teams confirmed they were on their way. Damian could only hope it wouldn't be too late. Ryan stretched them out too thin. He put too much faith in Cato and Damian to protect him on their own.

The sky burst open like an explosion. Flaming rocks plummeted to the ground leaving trails of smoke in their wake. Fires burst into the city as stores and homes began to burn. Damian's head snapped toward Ryan who started to radiate a golden aura around his body. A feeling of serenity briefly washed over Damian. Ryan thrust the staff further into the air as he continued to concentrate.

All fighting had ceased as those around him watched in awe the scene before them. Damian's eyes dodged back and forth between Ryan and Ahmose trying to depict who was winning and who was losing. Ahmose had a bow and arrow shaped weapon in his hands that shone as bright as the sun. The Brahmastra was fully summoned.

In the corner of his eye he saw Julia making a quick dash for Ryan but he grabbed her arm and slammed her into the ground. It was as forceful as he would dare be with her and he put all his strength into keeping her still. The only person that seemed to be moving besides them was the General as he dodged the flaming rocks shooting down upon him as he raced up the steps.

Before Damian could try and come up with a defense against the General, a loud whistle resonated from Nian Hill. An arrow as bright as the sun itself was launched up into the sky. Ahmose had done it. He set the Brahmastra out into the city of Urbs.

Ryan held the staff as high as he could as if sensing what

was taking place. He glowed just as bright as the Brahmastra, almost blindingly so. Yet Damian could see his face was controlled, set in stone and lacking any trace of desperation. As if the entire world was a calm and peaceful place.

"No!" he heard the General yell from down below. He was still too far to interfere.

The Staff of Brahma begun to pull at the air like a vacuum. The arrow Ahmose had shot into the sky hurdled towards them, then straight into the Staff of Brahma and disappeared into it's light. Soon, the inferno in the sky appeared to be drawn into the staff itself with such speed that Damian was nearly picked up off of the ground by the force of the wind.

Lights flashed through his closed eyes and thunder roared like a train from hell. They were in the belly of the beast as it was struck from this world. He anchored himself to the steps as well as he could until all of the Brahmastra's magic was pulled into the staff leaving a calm clear night sky in its demise.

Damian dared to open his eyes as Ryan collapsed to his knees with his shoulders hunched over. He had won.

Chapter XXVIII

Ryan

R YAN LOOKED DOWN THE steps to find that the Risen was in battle with the Warriors. There were a few causalities yet the Warriors numbers were not in their favor. The Risen outnumbered them two to one but the lack of training in the Risen was obvious. Their ranks were filled with those unworthy to call themselves a Warrior.

"No!" Julia yelled to the sky, drawing his attention to her. She was marching up the steps towards him, her anger was completely fixated on him as he lay on the ground with the staff next to him. "You bastard."

Ryan pulled himself unsteadily to his feet. His eyes were coming into focus as if waking from a deep sleep. His body was in such a state of relaxation that he barely had time to block the sword that slashed towards his neck. He blocked another blow to his gut and his legs wiggled in protest from his quick movements.

"You ruined everything!" Julia swung her sword and missed but was able to land a left hook to his chin. "That's what you do best though, isn't it? Ruin everything?"

Ryan shook off the hit. It actually helped him focus more on reality instead of the peaceful state he was just in.

"Julia, stop this." He continued to block her with the minimal energy he had until Damian came up behind her, wrapping his arms around her waist.

"Enough of this. Let us help you," Damian grunted against her wriggling body.

She elbowed him in the nose and Damian fell backwards clutching his face. Without missing a beat she was back on Ryan. "I am going to enjoy killing you."

She moved with precision, hacking at him with more force than he thought her possible of until she finally landed a deep cut to his arm and he grit his teeth. As he looked at his wound for a split second he quickly found himself landing on his back when she took out his feet from under him.

Her head tilt back, laughter escaping her lips. "Alexander that Great, defeated by a woman." Her sword hovered above his throat. "How embarrassing for you."

"Actually, I think it's fitting," Ryan admitted. His body was draining of energy. "Whatever I have done, especially to you, Julia… I hope this makes up for your pain."

"What pain?" she laughed hotly. "Ignoring me for years? For being with other women non-stop right in front of me and never once thinking how it made me feel? For not trying to save me?"

"Yes."

He could see an internal struggle brewing in her eyes.

Something was at war in her mind as her hand began to quiver.

"Why would I want to kill him because of that?" she whispered more to herself, but Ryan could hear her. "Because he deserves it. That's why. Don't forget who he is."

He squinted his eyes at her. She was deliberating with herself as if another person was there. It was a sign that her mind wasn't fully her own.

"Yes." She nodded. "Okay."

With her sword pressed tightly against his skin he could see the finality of her choice in her eyes yet her attack never came. Instead, her attention was hooked on the Domus' doors as Grace and Colette limped out past them and began to descend down the steps towards the fight below.

Grace's head was bandaged, blood visible through the wrapping. Colette had a cast on her leg. They both looked near collapse yet determination remained in their eyes.

"What are you doing? Get out of here!" Julia yelled at them. When both women looked at her they had the appearance of a mother's disappointment in their child.

Ryan rolled to his side and watched as they headed down the steps towards the General. He could hear Julia from where he was.

"Go back inside now. You both will die."

"We are already dead, traitor," Grace spat at her. Ryan had never heard Grace speak like that to anyone, especially not Julia. "I know what you have done. You have disappointed us more than you could ever imagine."

"Out of our way." Colette pushed Julia away, leaving her standing frozen from the harshness of their words.

Damian ran down the steps before the two women were able to reach the General. He was trying to prevent an inevitable slaughter yet when he swung his sword at the General he was blocked with a swift motion. He had to admit the man had extraordinary talent with a sword as he watched Damian and him continue their dance of death.

Grace and Colette slowly came to his aid when Damian yelled, "No, get back inside." Neither woman listened as they poorly attacked the man with their blades. Their injuries wore heavily on their strength.

The General didn't have to defend himself from three attacks for long. Grace moaned loudly when his sword struck deep in her belly and out through her back. He pulled the blade out of her before she dropped to her knees.

Ryan tried to crawl down to them. To do anything he could to help even if that meant using himself as a distraction, but he couldn't. His energy was gone. His eyes fluttered closed as he tried to stay awake. Inevitably he gave into the darkness.

Julia

Julia snapped out of her immobile state, screaming as she ran down to Grace's fallen body.

Grace. The woman was everything her name represented and now she lay in a heap on the ground, her blood staining the pure white steps as her life came to an end.

Dropping to her knees, she pulled the woman into her lap and clutched Grace's limp body. There was no sign of life in her eyes as they looked off, frozen and unblinking. The woman who had been like a mother to her was dead.

Colette suddenly fell down beside them and her heart strained within her chest. Thank the gods though, she was still breathing. She must have been knocked out because her chest steadily rose and fell with each intake.

Julia cradled Grace's head in her hands and kissed her forehead. "I'm so sorry," she mumbled through her tears. Her head pounded and her insides began to churn from the revulsion of her decisions. "Please forgive me."

It seemed like hours had passed while she looked into Grace's lifeless face but it was merely minutes. Julia snapped back into the world around her after a loud yell came from above. Aden was lying unconscious a few steps up while Cato and Damian battled with the General. She knew their desperate attempt to keep him away from an unconscious Ryan wouldn't work. They didn't stand a chance.

Damian fell to the ground. He seemed dazed and barely able to stand. The General slashed across Cato's chest and blood instantly drenched the front of his body. Cato fell to his knees, dropping his sword as another blow of the General's blade slit open his back making Cato scream out in pain.

The sight of her dying brother cleared her head for the first time in quite awhile. The General was wrong about everything. She hated him. Hated the Risen. Most of all she hated herself for acting as she did.

There was no explanation as to why she was on their

side. Not one bit of her soul believed in their cause. Her eyes were open to the extremist genocide they believed in. They needed to be stopped.

Julia let go of Grace's body and ran towards the General as he brought his sword up in the air to strike Cato one last time. Without a second thought she slammed her body into the General's sending them both tumbling down the steps until they landed hard in the middle landing of the long stairway. She scurried to stand with a dagger in hand but her entire body froze at the sight before her. The General's hood had fallen down and had finally revealed the man behind it.

His dark hair was cut close to this head and he had a thick, shortly trimmed beard. His skin had an olive tone to it and there were three scars stretching diagonally across his face. Her insides screamed to run but her feet stood planted in front of him.

"Father?" she croaked out.

The General did nothing but smirk as he moved past her and back up to Cato with his sword still clutched tightly in his hand. Julia ran after him and tugged on his arm to stop him but he merely laughed at her attempt.

"Move, little girl."

"You cannot kill your own son." Her father had died so many years ago that she could hardly believe what her eyes were seeing. How could he be standing right before her alive and well?

Her words made no difference as her father made it to Cato, who was sitting on his legs now gripping his sword weakly. He grabbed Cato by his vest and held him up high enough that his feet dangled above the ground.

Realization hit Cato's face like a ton of bricks as he stared into their father's eyes. "Father?"

"Hello, Cato." Tears started to roll down her face once she realized their own father was about to kill one of them with a smile on his face.

"You were killed," Cato spat and winced in pain from his injuries.

"Immortals are experts at faking their deaths. Use your brain for once Cato, it isn't difficult," their father's voice dripped with annoyance. "You were always a disappointment."

"Let him go!"

He turned around to glare at her. "Girl, as soon as this is over with you will forget who you are. I don't care about the loss of your memory. I will mold you into whoever I want you to be. This little tonic seems to be failing quicker and quicker each time you take it. It's time for a more permanent solution."

"You drugged me?" She wanted to slap him but due to years of obedience to her father she didn't.

"Of course." His smile had no warmth in it. It was almost mocking. "You wouldn't join me and I had plans for you. I still do and your brother is just excess baggage. He is too much of a slave to Alexander."

Cato huffed, "You were just a shitty role model." He spit in their father's face. "Mother would despise you."

"I imagine so, but it is because of the gods that I lost her." The General released Cato's vest and dropped him to the ground without any thought to his safety. "Enough of this reunion. I'm going to put an end to the source of both my children's issues. That man right up there."

"No." She swung her fist at her father but he caught it quicker than a person should be able.

"Little girl, you better show your father some respect." The look he gave her made her cower like a child again.

"Our father is dead," Cato was painfully forcing the words from his mouth. "Our father would never do something like this. He was loyal. Good. Loving."

"Things change, Cato," he said. "I would love to explain why but I need to kill Alexander. Or Ryan, seeing as that makes you all feel better about hiding your identities. Either way, that man will die for taking my son's respect from me and my daughter's heart."

"That was your own fault." Cato grimaced as he clutched the front of his chest.

"Enough. You are still as much of a child as you ever were." He left them behind as he walked up to Ryan's limp form on the ground.

At some point Damian and Aden had regained consciousness and were fighting each other near Ryan's body. They were both tired but both refusing to back down. She felt torn about where to go but decided to hold her brother in her arms as he lay bleeding on the ground.

"I'm so sorry." She seemed to be saying this a lot lately.

"I knew that wasn't you." He grinned and brushed his fingers against her cheek. "No need to be sorry."

"Tell me what to do," she begged.

"Go help Ryan."

She shook her head. "I can't leave you to die."

Cato laughed halfheartedly. "Julia, I'm not going to die. I just need to get stitched up. He didn't cut open anything I need. Go."

"You're lying."

"So. I'd rather you lose one of us than both of us. He needs you." Cato closed his eyes with a small grin on his lips. "Just hurry up so you don't lose either of us and get me to a damn healer."

Julia couldn't waste time arguing so she kissed his forehead and ran off towards Damian and Aden. She gathered her sword that had clattered down the steps and swung it at Aden as soon as she reached him. She sliced open his arm and he looked at her in shock. Julia stood next to Damian as a sign to whose side she was really on.

"Are you back?" Damian whispered.

"Hell yeah," she answered. "Help Ryan."

"Are you sure?" Damian seemed hesitant.

"Yeah." She glared at Aden. "This bastard drugged me and made me do things I would never dream of. I plan on killing him."

"You weren't complaining when you were shouting out my name." Aden's jaw clenched tight.

At that she couldn't help but laugh. "You aren't the only one who can fake things."

Damian's body was beyond drained and thanks to evil Julia he was bleeding everywhere. When the General lifted Ryan's limp body up enough to be face-to-face, he mustered up all his strength to tackle him to the ground before his sword could pierce Ryan's skin. Ryan's body fell down hard, a groan escaping him. Both men scurried to stand with swords in hand. Damian stopped in his tracks as he looked at the man in front of him.

"Marc?" Damian wondered out loud.

"Good to see you survived this far, Hephaestion." Marc grinned.

"It's Damian."

"Whatever." Marc rolled his eyes. "I would think this would be a momentous occasion. Meeting your old teammate once again, yet here you are stuck on which name you prefer."

Damian was indeed in complete disbelief over the fact Marc was alive and well. He saw him die with his own eyes while Ryan was trying everything that he could to keep him alive. His heart stopped beating. Damian had felt that himself yet here he was in front of him, alive and well.

"I don't understand this." Damian shook his head. *This can't be real.*

"I wouldn't imagine this isn't easy for any of you to grasp but here I stand." He held out his arms. "How's my son doing as my replacement? He seems rather incompetent for his age. Maybe another thousand years would do him good. Though I highly doubt he will have the opportunity given his current condition."

Damian followed Marc's eyes down the steps to where Cato lay. His chest rose up and down heavily, his blood starting to pool around him. He needed a healer quickly.

"You did that to your own son?"

"Don't act so appalled. It's a waste of time and energy." Marc, the General as he called himself, nodded towards were Julia and Aden were sword fighting. "She, however, is the epitome of what I expect from my children. Strong, independent, and always respectful of her father."

"I haven't realized until now but you are all kinds of messed up, Marc." Damian held up his fists. "Let's go."

Marc readied his stance with his fists bawled in front of his chest. "My pleasure."

"General!" Aden yelled at Marc. "We must go."

Both Marc and Damian looked over to where Julia and Aden still fought. Aden managed to point at the bottom steps between blows. Damian was stunned to see that the Risen were retreating and the remaining Warriors were marching up the stairs towards them. Marc looked around for any sign of his followers but they were already gone.

"Pathetic." The vain on his neck pulsed and his faced reddened. "Another time then old friend."

"I'm counting on it," Damian spat.

With a smug look, Marc and Aden took off running down the stairs. They managed to push past the Warriors after a few fists were thrown and ran out of sight.

Julia had already made it to Cato when Aden left and Damian ran down to them. Cato was in bad shape and he needed attention quickly. With some difficulty he picked Cato up and trudged painfully up the steps. His arm hurt like hell from when Julia stabbed him and he was somewhat nervous about dropping Cato.

"You lard ass."

Cato wrapped his arms around Damian's neck. "My hero," he said weakly but the small smirk on his lips gave Damian hope he would be fine.

Caleb caught up with them on the steps with the rest of the Warriors when they made it to Ryan's limp body. "Is he dead?"

Winded, he answered, "Just ridiculously exhausted I think. At least I hope."

Damian wanted to laugh when Caleb threw Ryan over his shoulder to carry him inside while Ryan's arms dangled down past his knees. Ryan was much bigger than Caleb but that didn't seem to bother him.

Julia picked up the Staff of Brahma from the ground, twisting it in her hand as she studied it. "What's this?" she asked.

"I'll explain later," Damian grunted.

They barely led the Warriors back into the safety of the Domus when Julia started barking out orders. She pointed at a Warrior named Nadya. "Tell those who are able to gather the dead and wounded and bring them to the healers quarters."

Nadya's face was drenched with sweat and visibly exhausted but she listened without question as she gathered men and women for the task. Damian didn't want to stay and see who was dead and who wasn't. From what he could tell, there were at least twenty casualties on their side if not more.

A light breeze blew through the open doors and his drenched hair welcomed the feeling. The sky outside was perfectly clear from the blazing inferno that was just above them and a sense of peace washed over him.

"Quit grinning like a weirdo and get my ass up to the healers quarters," Cato groaned.

"Oh shit, sorry."

Chapter XXVIII

Ryan

H IS MIND WAS A *haze as he woke up in his bedchambers. Pushing the linen sheets off him as he sat up Ryan rubbed his hands over his face in exhaustion. Once he was finally able to focus on his surroundings he nearly jumped out of his bed.*

He wasn't in the Domus, he was in his room in Babylon from his mortals days. The bed he slept in was wooden with intricately carved designs overlaid with gold and silver. The mattress was stuffed with wool and when he reached his hand under his pillow he tensed.

The dagger he kept under his pillow every night was there. It was a curved blade with a hook-like hilt, a small version of his kopis sword. His eyes wandered to his beside where a thick scroll he knew to be a section of his copy of the Iliad lay rolled neatly on the dark wood.

He needed to wake up from this nightmare. A rush of heat washed over his body as his anxiety peaked and he began to hyperventilate. In his dreams he sometimes relived the past, but this one felt real.

"Hello, love."

Ryan's eyes widened hearing her sweet voice behind him. He didn't dare move. He felt paralyzed. When her hand gently caressed his shoulder he shivered from her touch. With her chest pressed against his bare back she hung her head over his shoulder enough that he could see her face. Her long curly black hair tickled his chest as she kissed his neck.

"Roxane?" his voice trembled just saying her name.

"Don't be afraid." She smiled weakly at him as she turned his body to face her. "I needed to see you, Alexander."

"Am I dreaming?" He studied her dark eyes, the ones he gazed into for hours after making love.

Placing her soft hand against his cheek she shook her head. "I can't explain where you are, but you are not dreaming. For many years I wanted to come to you and now I have finally been granted the chance but only for a moment."

"Please forgive me," Ryan blurted out. "I shouldn't have left you and our son alone. If I were there you both would have lived. I was selfish and cru-"

Pressing her finger to his mouth she silenced him. "Alexander, I forgive you. Your son forgives you. Time and time again we have watched you save the lives of others. You put the innocent before your own life. We couldn't be prouder of you."

"How can you possibly think that about me? After what I was when I was mortal. The way I treated you both like you didn't matter. It's not okay. It will never be okay."

"Quit living with guilt of the past, my love. It was long ago and something we cannot change. Live for the future. Don't live

to avoid the past. Forgive yourself because we have forgiven you. I love you, Alexander. You are the hero you were always meant to be."

Ryan woke with a jerk. Taking in his surrounding he was at least glad he was in his room and not in the healer's quarters for once. That must mean his body was well and no one stabbed him when he passed out.

The sun peaked through the curtains and stretched towards his bed. Once his eyes cleared fully he could make out Damian sleeping on his couch still in his fatigues. How Ryan was so lucky to have someone so loyal to him, he would never know.

For a moment he just studied his sleeping friend until the blood staining his gear caught Ryan's eye.

"Damian!" Ryan yelled.

Damian jumped up off the couch in haste and looked around ready to attack. His eyes were wild and his hair stuck up in odd places. Ryan wanted to laugh but the sticky blood on his gear kept his mind on Damian's wellbeing rather than his tattered appearance.

"What the…" Damian looked around.

"Are you okay?" Ryan tried to sit up more in his bed but his body felt stiff. "Are you hurt?"

Damian looked down at his chest and removed his shirt revealing stitches on his shoulder and arms. Other than that Damian's body was plagued with only bruises. It was a relief, he could only imagine what happened while he was in the realm of peace.

"Julia did a number on me," Damian complained. "Aden too."

"She fought with me too." Ryan wished it were a dream but he knew it wasn't.

"Don't worry about it too much. She was drugged by Aden and the General this entire time. Who by the way is Marc." Damian nodded when Ryan's jaw dropped. "Yeah, Cato and Julia's dad. Apparently he didn't die."

Ryan was having a hard time processing all this but Damian said it so casually as if he'd already accepted it.

"Marc is alive?"

"Yeah. I just said that. Don't ask me how because I don't know. All I know is what I saw and it was Marc. He seemed so cold. It was odd. He was always a free spirit like you." Damian ended up sitting on Ryan's bed. "He isn't the man we once called brother, that's for sure."

Ryan sat in silence trying to process the complicated revelations before him. Julia had been drugged. Thank the Gods for that, because he didn't know how he could handle her actually being evil. Would the rest of the Immortals see her as a traitor given the circumstances? And Marc? *How could he do this? Why would he do this?*

Ryan finally managed to sit up but his sore body gave him the indication he had a massive bruise on his hip. He groaned and looked down at his black and blue covered side.

"What the hell? I don't remember this happening."

"You might have fallen a few times after you passed out," Damian answered him. "Oh and Jesse is dead."

"What?" Ryan felt like an overwhelming amount of information was being thrown at him but Damian didn't stop there either. He went on to describe in detail what happened.

"So Anna came and saved you from Julia?" Ryan tried to

get all of this straight and when Damian nodded he continued, "But when Marc was about to kill Cato, Julia was herself again."

"Yes."

"This is all really fucked up, my friend."

"Agreed, but now we need to concentrate on getting our forces put together to completely wipe out the Risen." It was an obvious statement but Ryan just wanted to relish in the fact that he was able to stop such a powerful weapon. Not to mention so many questions were finally answered.

"I have already begun planning for that. Right now everyone needs to rest and regain their strength." Damian looked as if he were going to ask what his plans were but Ryan stopped him. "I need to see Julia before we discuss anything further."

Damian's mouth opened and closed then opened again. "Are you sure about that? She tried to kill us both."

"Positive."

"Well she's with Cato right now. Their father did a number on him and he is in the healers quarters." Ryan's eyes widened. Damian failed to mention his injuries were that severe. "Don't worry, he'll be fine. He's getting a blood transfusion and has been stitched up. Mentally though, he isn't well."

"I can't imagine he would be," Ryan mumbled. He knew all too well what it felt like for your father to attack you. Even try to kill you.

Damian lifted Ryan's blanket from his bruised side and studied his hip. "Does it hurt?"

"It's nothing. I got off easier than you all," Ryan answered.

"Yes, because leaving yourself open to get killed and hoping your friends save your hide was so easy." Damian rolled his eyes. "I don't know how you were able to concentrate with all the commotion. I really don't."

"That's all a part of it, Damian. You have to be a master at it and even though it seems like I have a terrible attention span I can harness the calm if I really want."

Damian shrugged. "Whatever, you kicked ass."

"You are sounding more and more like Anna when you talk. Have you noticed?" Ryan laughed.

"It's terrible. I feel as if my dialect is becoming less colorful and dumbed down." He frowned but Ryan could see the humor in his eyes. "I will make a mental note not to sound like a twenty year old from the twenty-first century."

"I gave up on that." Ryan swung his legs over the bed and stood up, then swayed from getting up too quickly.

"Easy, sparky."

Ryan closed his eyes with a smile on his face. "Go read a book and gain your intellect back."

"I think that ship sailed a long time ago when education became obsolete to the masses. We've gradually joined the club." Damian pushed Ryan's chest lightly making him fall back on his bed. "I'll go get Julia. You keep your world-saving-ass in bed."

"Yes, Mom."

Julia

Julia made her way back to her room from the healer's quarters. Her flat white shoes padded down the hallway and her blue dress flowed in the light breeze. From the sound of it the people in Urbs were actually becoming brave enough to stroll their way back into the world. After the show last night they had to have assumed the threat was over and they could go about their lives.

Cato was looking a lot better, but she still couldn't shake the guilt in her heart. She had been a traitor. Even though it was against her will, it didn't change what she did. She murdered her own and tried to kill those closest to her.

Her father was the master of evil and her ex-fiancé was a psychopath. She was good and she knew it. Her past actions shouldn't and couldn't be forgiven. The only thing that would balance the scales would be her life ended in execution.

With her mind submerged into dark thoughts, she didn't realize she had made it back to her room so quickly. When she pushed her door open her breath caught in her chest. A small leather box filled with the tonic she was made to drink sat on her bedside table. Aden had brought it to her last night. As it just sat there harmlessly staring at her she felt irrationally afraid of it.

A heavy hand weighed down on her shoulder compelling her to face Damian who looked at her apprehensively. She was just standing in the doorway staring at the box realizing she never bothered to walk into her room. Meeting his eyes she could tell he was still being cautious of her and it devastated her.

She cleared her throat. "Hey."

"Hey." He ran his hand through his hair then placed them in his pockets. "Ryan wants to see you."

"Oh, okay." She didn't know if she wanted to see him just

yet. After everything she had done she could only imagine how much he hated her. Damian undoubtedly did too right now. "How are you?"

Damian shrugged then winced. "Shoulder hurts, but I'll live." He took a step back. "How are you?"

"I feel like I want to break down in tears and be punished for everything I did," Julia admitted. "I don't deserve to step foot in this castle."

"As much as you hurt a lot of us, we understand that it wasn't you." Even though he said it she could feel that he didn't fully believe it. "I'm going to check on Cato. Ryan is in his room."

Without another word Damian left her standing in her doorway. She wanted to disappear and never be seen by anyone again. Everyone she held dear was treating her like a disease they were afraid to catch.

After a few moments she took a deep breath and gained the courage to make her way to Ryan's room. It felt like the shortest walk of her life. She had no desire to go see him. But once she stood in front of that familiar wooden door she felt a longing to throw herself into his arms.

Forgetting to knock she made her way into his room in time to see him pull a black shirt on over his bruised body. Without thinking she ran to him and once he turned to face her, jumped into his arms wrapping her legs around his waist. She expected him to push her away but his arms wrapped around her body in a tight embrace with his head nestled into her neck.

"I thought I lost you," his voice was low and soft.

"You almost did." Hot tears ran down her cheeks as she held onto him as if her life depended on it.

He walked over to his bed and sat on the edge with her legs still wrapped around his waist. Ryan pulled back from her so he could wipe the tears from her cheek with his thumb. It was then that she started to cry even more but he merely smiled at her in amusement.

"Don't cry, Julia. We're all fine." Ryan rubbed her back in small circles. "I'm fine."

She shook her head as her sobs made her almost incoherent. "I d-did t-terrible things. Things I s-shouldn't be forgiven f-for."

"It wasn't you. It was someone else they twisted and molded inside your body." He tried to reassure her but she felt the complete opposite.

"I n-need to tell you something." She was able to calm herself down when she didn't meet his eyes.

"What is it?"

She tried to shift away from his lap but his hands remained firmly around her. He wasn't letting her go so she just came out and said it, "I killed Zee."

Her eyes darted to the blank expression on his face. It sent chills down her spine yet he didn't say anything. He sat there looking into her eyes, his grip on her never faltered or even tightened. They sat there for what seemed hours just looking at one another before either spoke.

"I see," he managed to force himself to speak.

"Ryan?" He remained a statue until she said, "I want you to turn me in. I need to pay for what I did."

At her statement his distant eyes turned into a fierce glare. "I don't think so."

"But what I did is-"

"Unforgivable, I agree," he finished for her. "As I said before, that wasn't you. So if I am going to blame anyone it will be Marc and Aden. Without their influence you would never even think about doing something like that."

"It was my hand that thrust the blade into her, Ryan," she argued. "It was *me*."

Ryan pulled her tighter against him and she felt his heart beating through his chest. "I mean it, Julia. It wasn't you. I will admit, I am furious right now and the anger I feel is aimed at you partly but I also realize you are a victim as well."

"How could you possibly see it that way? I killed her, Ryan. Her blood is on my hands," she insisted.

"Stop it now. You are not to blame and I won't hear anymore about it."

"I stabbed Damian. I tried to kill him." She placed her head on his shoulder. "I tried to kill you."

"Stop." Ryan let go of her body and laid her down gently on his bed. His body hovered over hers and she finally felt she was in the right place for the first time in a long time. The memory of Grace unexpectedly came to mind. Ryan was leaning down to kiss her when the tears started to flow again. Alarmed, Ryan asked, "What? What did I do?"

"Grace." She began to weep uncontrollably again. He pulled her on top of him, before his arms wrapped around her. His very existence calmed her down to mild tears.

She hated feeling weak like this but Grace was always there for her. She knew Julia's mother the best out of anyone and had taken her under her wing when she died. Julia would have grown up to be nothing more than a shop keeper had it not been for Grace's recommendation to join her mother's team when she died.

"I'm so sorry about Grace," Ryan spoke softly in her ear. "She was a rare beauty, inside and out."

Sniffing back the tears she muttered, "All of this is my fault."

"Actually if you're going to blame anyone, blame me. We had a mission to do and they offered to go into the mortal world to keep you at bay. Had I not agreed, they wouldn't have gotten caught."

"This is too much to handle." Julia ran her hand along his soft sheets. "I can't do this."

"All of this is one big disaster. We need to quit blaming ourselves and realize that this is just the way things are." Ryan kissed her on the forehead and she couldn't help smiling from the warmth radiating between them.

"When did you become so mature?"

"If you haven't noticed, I've grown up a lot since you broke my heart." He tried to smile playfully but she still felt shameful. "I love you, Julia. Now let's work together to bring the bastards down, okay?"

"Okay."

If you loved
INDEFINITE,
Don't miss out on book four of
THE INFINITE SERIES,
ETERNAL.

Ryan

Six months later.

TIME GOES BY FAST when you are in a constant battle with the world.

Ryan sat in the C-17 aircraft with Damian, Cato, and a group of United States Army personnel.

During the past six months, the Immortals had been doing nothing but leading, commanding, and recruiting mortals that opposed the Risen. It wasn't hard to convince the American's given most of them were hell-bent religious believers to their very core.

Some people just would not change their minds no matter what so-called proof you give them. He had to admire that.

The entire world was a battleground now. Nowhere was safe from the religious war. Children were spared, their innocence their only savior but some would become orphans. It was a fact that infuriated Ryan.

There was no clear winning side as of now. Both seemed equally matched in their forces. How the Risen gained such a following so quickly was beyond him.

Every Immortal alive that remained on their side was now spread across the world in command of their troupes.

They now called this World War III. It was in fact a literal world war. Nowhere was unaffected. Some have even called is the War of the Followers. It was fitting for both sides of the equation.

"We are nearly there, sir," a young army man yelled across the aircraft. He was hunched over from the weight of his rucksack hanging in front of him. "I just wanted to say it's an honor to be in your presence, Sir."

Ryan, Damian, and Cato stood out from the rest of the men. Their gear was all black as opposed to the dark camouflage the army personnel wore. There was no mistake for the leadership.

Ryan nodded to the man and faced his friends.

"Ready?" Ryan adjusted the straps on his parachute. The harness of his chute was crushing his balls.

Cato tapped his feet anxiously. Ryan remembered he loved jumping out of planes. "Yep."

He had healed surprisingly well since his fight with his father. The General was merciless with his son, nearly killing him for his own ambition.

Ryan stoop up, the rucksack between his legs was heavy. "Alright boys." The cargo grew as silent as it could be with the humming from the engine. "As soon as we reach the target head to the base. Do you all remember where that is?"

Everyone nodded so he continued on, "We might come down with some fire but more than likely the area is secured by our guys. Once we get to the base you will be assigned your different duties."

All the men, and a few women, prepared themselves for the leap out of the aircraft.

"You fuckers ready?" Ryan looked at Cato and Damian.

Damian shook his head. "You've been around the American's too much."

"I like it," Cato said. "They have colorful language."

"No, they curse. Hardly colorful," Damian countered.

"Back to my original question, are you fuckers ready?" Ryan asked.

The two side doors of the C-17 opened and Ryan's ears were consumed with the fury of the wind. Their men stood in lines ready to jump.

They watched the red light on the plane to turn green, signaling for them to jump. Ryan placed the first man in front of the door until the light turned green. He smacked the man's ass letting him know to jump. He continued this until everyone was off the aircraft.

"Don't even think about smacking my ass," Damian yelled at him over the near deafening wind.

"Come on, baby, for old times sake?" Ryan grinned.

With a roll of the eyes, Damian, Cato and then Ryan leaped out of the door. Ryan kept his body tight as he was sucked out of the aircraft. His shoot opened and he plummeted down to earth. The city of Rome glistened in the night sky as he soared through the air.

He was glad everyone seemed to be untangled and a decent way from one another. Last thing he wanted was for someone to get tangled up in a chute and crash down to earth.

Just as the Vatican came in view, Ryan guided his shoot to St. Peter's Square. Some of their crew had already landed safely. Ryan dropped his rucksack once he neared the ground and bent his knees slightly. His feet hit the ground hard and he rolled his body over. As soon as he landed he ripped off the parachute pack, tossed his rucksack on his back and ran towards the entrance of the Vatican.

Ryan could hear gunfire off in the distance and thundering sounds of larger ammunition being used.

They climbed up the steps when bullets collided with the buildings walls.

"Get in!" Ryan yelled to the crew as they piled inside. Damian, Cato, and Ryan covered them while they squeezed into the entrance, shooting at the men propped on the columned walls the curved around the St. Peter's Square.

He fired his gun in their direction, hopefully killing them but ultimately wanted them to cease fire long enough for them to get in. His plan worked and once the doors were closed Ryan let his M4 Carbine hang from its strap.

They made their way to the rest of the group who stood around anxiously waiting for instructions.

"Everyone good?" Ryan asked. They nodded. "Okay."

"I'll go get Fredrick." Damian made his way to a tall thin man with dark hair and bags under his eyes.

"Ladies and gents', this is Frederick. He will be your commanding officer here," Ryan started. The group nodded and Ryan shook hands with the man. "Good to finally meet you in person."

Frederick nodded. "You look smaller on TV." The both starred at each other and laughed after a beat. "A pleasure, Ryan. It is nice to finally meet the leader of the resistance."

Acknowledgements

To put it simple, I want to thank everyone that has helped me along my journey as an author. It has been humbling and difficult to put myself out there and I cannot thank everyone enough for their support.

To my editor, Jennifer, thank you for being so patient and understanding of everything. You are seriously an amazing human being and I will never take you for granted. You helped me do so much, not only in my writing but in life as well. So thank you, my friend.

To my Granny, my number one fan, I love you and you have pushed me to my dreams. You are pretty much the one person I can count on to love my books.

About the Author

Nicole Corine Dyer is an author from Kansas with a Degree in Liberal Arts. After work and being a single mother she finally was able to publish the third installment of the Infinite Series and is now writing the fourth.

Reading has always been a passion and to be able to become an author was a lifelong dream, finally taking form. Never give up on your passions, a belief Nicole plans to pass on to her children.

Contact Nicole

Website: www.nicolecorinedyer.com
Facebook: Author Nicole Corine Dyer
Email: nicolecorinedyer@gmail.com
Goodreads Author Nicole Corine Dyer

OTHER BOOKS

The Infinite Series

Infinite, Book 1
Obscure, Book 2